W9-BPK-014

NOV   2012

DISCARDED

Silver

COLLECTION MANAGEMENT

7/1/5 13-1 529M		

THOUSAND OAKS LIBRARY
1401 E. Janss Road
Thousand Oaks, California

NOV 2012

DISCARDED

Silver

THOUSAND OAKS LIBRARY
1401 E. Janss Road
Thousand Oaks, California

Silver

Rhiannon Held

A TOM DOHERTY ASSOCIATES BOOK
NEW YORK

This is a work of fiction. All of the characters, organizations, and events portrayed in this novel are either products of the author's imagination or are used fictitiously.

SILVER

Copyright © 2012 by Rhiannon Held

All rights reserved.

A Tor Book
Published by Tom Doherty Associates, LLC
175 Fifth Avenue
New York, NY 10010

www.tor-forge.com

Tor® is a registered trademark of Tom Doherty Associates, LLC.

ISBN 978-0-7653-3037-6 (trade paperback)
ISBN 978-1-4299-9109-4 (e-book)

First Edition: June 2012

Printed in the United States of America

0 9 8 7 6 5 4 3 2 1

Fiction

To Dad, because when I said if I could be anything in the world, I'd be an author . . .
He said, "Why not?"

ACKNOWLEDGMENTS

Many people have helped shape this book, and I owe a great debt to all of them. My parents began it by telling their children they were hardworking instead of telling them they were smart. Yes, Mum and Dad, it worked. I'm also indebted to my sister for the last-minute emergency brainstorming sessions.

I attended the invaluable Odyssey Writing Workshop before this novel was even a twinkle in my eye, but Jeanne Cavelos and the attendees of TNEO '09 critiqued a first draft. My local group, the Fairwood Writers, tirelessly worked to help me improve it. Renee Stern, David Silas, Erin Tidwell, Kim Ritchie, Christopher Bodan, Corry Lee, and Paul Dixon, this novel would not have been nearly so good without your efforts.

John Pitts has been my author mentor, and kindly answers all my silly, panicked questions, as does my wonderful agent, Cameron McClure. I'm indebted to my editor, Beth Meacham, and the whole team at Tor. And to all my supportive coworkers and friends, including my fellow role-players, thank you.

Silver

1

The lone werewolf smelled like silver and pain. Or maybe it wasn't pain, maybe it was fear. In human form, Andrew Dare's nose had missed that undertone altogether, and even in wolf it was elusive. Her trail wove beneath one of the power line towers straddling this strip of grassy, undeveloped land, and the metal bar clipped the top of Andrew's ears as he padded under. He twitched his ears, checking again for any nearby humans, but he remained alone for the moment.

Pain and fear or not, she was a Were carrying silver, and that could mean only one thing: she was a European. Only European Were used silver on each other and would therefore have reason to carry it, and damned if Andrew was going to let any of them cause trouble in his alpha's territory.

The lone's trail had followed the power lines for several miles but now it diverged into a suburban development probably close enough to be considered part of Nashua, New Hampshire. Andrew stopped where the tangled unmown grass met a path into a cul-de-sac and considered, panting. The summer sun was low now, the heat was easing, and the scents he got from the development were fogged with car exhaust as everyone returned home for the evening.

Risky, to follow any farther in wolf form. The human scents Andrew found on the wind were few and far between, suggesting an upper-middle-class neighborhood with big lots. People in those neighborhoods didn't ignore strays, they called animal control. And animal control knew the difference between a dog and a wolf, and a wolf and a creature that massed much larger than any natural wolf.

Andrew sniffed again and allowed himself a growl when he smelled no humans close enough to hear it. Damn that European. It was one of the oldest tricks in the book to stick to heavily populated areas so cars would drive away one's scent and pursuers would have to sacrifice their wolf form's superior nose, but knowing it didn't make it any easier to counter. He'd have to push himself running back to his clothes and his car to not lose any more time. He was already—Andrew put his nose to the trail again—half a day behind as it was. But standing here debating would waste as much time. He started back.

It was good to run. Andrew had spent too much time stuck in traffic driving up here from Virginia. His muscles protested the pace at first, an aching commentary on how much time he'd been spending in human lately. Why bother shifting when he had no real pack to hunt with?

His nose caught a rusty tang and he jumped a few wires remaining from an old fence as he turned his thoughts instead to what the European Were might hope to accomplish here. Was she scouting the territory for the rest of her pack to follow, or did she plan to challenge and replace one of the sub-alphas in the larger Roanoke pack herself? He'd chased another silver-smelling lone last year, but that man had disappeared over the Mississippi into the Western packs' territories long ago. Much as Andrew had hated to let the lone go, he trusted the Western packs to deal with him.

Andrew doubted this lone was after him personally, either. If so, she was long overdue. He'd escaped back to North America a decade ago. Still, the fact that she had brought silver suggested she was looking to punish someone. Andrew didn't intend to allow that. Once he caught her, he'd drag her back to explain herself to his alpha. If she didn't have a good enough reason for her failure to ask permission to cross Roanoke territory he'd have the pleasure of shoving her on a plane and out of Roanoke for good.

When he reached the bush where he'd hidden his clothes, Andrew crouched low and drew in a deep breath. Shifting at this moon phase was an effort, though at least the moon was waxing rather than waning. Andrew concentrated, eyes closed, pushing, pushing, until he felt the blessed tipping point. Everything fell into the new configuration: sight and scent and arrangement of muscles. He stretched his arms to settle his mind into it, and then pulled on his clothes.

It took a frustratingly long time to find the right cul-de-sac by car from the other side, but when Andrew finally returned to the spot he'd left off, traces of the Were's trail still remained. He jogged a little to make up time as he followed the scent on foot in human form. At least the Were hadn't been running. Her scent was thick, suggesting she'd wandered.

Andrew grew more cautious as the trail turned into a yard. He couldn't say for sure with his human nose that no one was home, but the windows were dark and no car was in the driveway, so he strode up for a quick look. The sun's angle made the window reflective against a faint background of blinds. A complete handprint stood stark against it. The placement—Andrew matched his hand to it—suggested someone trying to look through. He peered, but the blinds had no crack big enough to see anything beyond.

But the air held no hint of Were other than the lone anywhere in this neighborhood. A werewolf in human form eating garlic would have been able to tell that.

The trail wound away from the window through front yards until it reached some trash cans beside a garage. The lone's scent was on them as if she had poked through after knocking them over. Looking for something?

Two women approached, pushing strollers, so he righted the cans to look like a good Samaritan. This house was blocks away from the first one where she'd been looking in. That made no sense, even if the Were had a grudge against some particular humans. What was this woman after?

———

Silver had been running for a long time. It began with the monster. The monster poured fire into her blood and smiled as she screamed and her wild self fled. He'd thought her so far gone in burning, he'd not watched her closely, and she'd escaped. She sensed him distantly behind her now. Following her trail. She couldn't let him catch her, or it would begin all over again.

The monster chased distantly, but Death followed close behind. He stalked her with endless patience, waiting to claim her when the monster's snakes of fire finished their task. She glimpsed him behind her when she could no longer run and had to walk. Her ears strained to hear the forest's voices beneath the padding of his feet. They had something of an unspoken accord, she and Death—she did not run too fast and he did not catch her just yet. Instead, he padded in her footsteps, tongue lolling out in canine laughter as she tried to ignore him and strained for the scent of her wild self. If only she could find her wild self, then perhaps she would be whole again. But the fire made her head pound so much it was hard to think.

At night, sometimes Silver would invite Death to sit with her. He hulked there opposite her, smug and black. He was blacker than night or a raven's wing or anything Silver could remember when words and memories wiggled and twisted from her grasp. But then, he was Death. That was description enough.

Sometimes at night the wind tossed the branches of the stately columns of trees around Silver, and the small monsters at the light's edge shrieked and warbled, making the forest's voices whisper in concern. Then Death would howl to the Lady's round, shimmering disc and make the fire burn in Silver's veins. Your death is in you, his howls told her. In your blood. You cannot fight what is in you.

Silver screamed and begged the Lady to make it stop when the fire burned bright. She curled around her useless arm as the fire pulsed. Each time Death called to the fire, the snakes engraved on her skin grew longer and twined their hissing, traitorous way from the cup of her elbow ever closer to her heart. Silver begged the Lady to protect her from Death, begged the Lady to help Silver find her wild self.

Sometimes the forest crooned a comforting counterpoint to her screams, and sometimes it drew back in shocked silence. Death panted and laughed. The Lady did nothing, as she had done nothing when the monster poured the fire into Silver's arm.

This day, as Silver trudged through the forest, calling her wild self and searching the trees for a gray flicker of muzzle or flank, she wondered if the Lady still loved her. The Lady had given Silver her wild self from love—perhaps She had taken that wild self back when love waned. Maybe Silver had lost that love by taking the Lady's gift for granted.

But the Lady had not waned. She was full and luminous above Silver, as always. And surely it was a sign of the Lady's favor that the monster had not caught her yet?

Coming upon a stream, Silver found a still place with few ripples and looked into her eyes, searching for her wild self inside as well as out. Her wild self could as easily have hidden deeper rather than running outward from the fire, but Silver saw no sign of her. Dimness made it hard to see, since though the Lady's light fell all around her, it did not touch Silver except indirectly.

Even in dim light, Silver's hair showed nearly all white now, brown chased away. She blinked in surprise. The fire had burned the color from it, of course, but only the new growth. New growth was old now, and she wondered at Death's patience. She pressed her hand flat against the stream's cold surface, printing it before Death shattered everything into ripples as he lapped at the water.

At her midday meal, Silver did not invite Death to sit with her. Alone, she forced down the foul-tasting carrion she had found. She drew off her shirt to trace the snakes' path on her dead arm, tickling their diamond-scaled backs with her fingertip. They writhed in pleasure and hissed to her. Silver frowned, trying to understand Snake. If she could speak their language, perhaps she could persuade them to leave her.

Surely this could be solved by cleverness. Perhaps it was even a test for her to prove herself worthy of the Lady's gift. Silver considered this. Death must be outwitted somehow. She frowned at him. Invitation or no invitation, he sat on his haunches nearby, nose tipped to test the air. When he felt her gaze on him, Death turned to face Silver.

"Let go," he said in her brother's voice. Her brother was dead, so Death had his voice. He had all the voices of Silver's pack. "Please. We miss you, Silver. Come back to us." Silver knew that it was not her brother speaking, and Death knew she knew, but he liked to taunt her.

Silver sat up and threw a rock at Death, missing him by a

wide margin. She needed to keep moving, and not let him distract her, or the monster would catch up. Thorns curled up to bind her feet and hands, trying to hold her there until the monster arrived. She tore free before they could take proper hold, though they rustled triumphantly at the blood they had captured from her. Time to run faster again. Always running.

2

Blood. Andrew smelled blood, werewolf blood, sharp as a shout on the wind. Fresh blood. He pounded into a run, sacrificing discretion for speed. The smell came from a triangle of protected wetland surrounded by a chain-link fence. The cut metal ends glistened red where someone had squeezed between links and post, hard to see but immediately obvious even to Andrew's human nose.

He strode to the fence and hid his hands with his body in case of observers, then bent the links back far enough to squeeze through. The land sloped too much for Andrew to see the water below, but he could smell it as a tang of freshness that meant it was running. The Were's silver-tainted scent was clear on top, mingling with the blood and pain again. She must have hurt herself badly.

But that made no sense. Her werewolf strength should

have let her bend the fence back as easily as his had. Why expose herself to scratches when she had to know she was being followed? He could smell fresh blood still, up ahead. A healthy werewolf would have healed mere scratches by now.

He followed the path worn down to the stream, past beer bottles and crumpled chip bags. He kept his hand out to stop the hanging blackberry tendrils menacing him at face level from scoring any hits.

He saw a flash of white as the Were straightened from a crouch. She was scrawny, her scuffed and dirty jeans caught on her hipbones. By human standards, she looked around twenty-five, but werewolves aged slower as well as lived longer, so she was more likely in her thirties to forties. One sleeve of her plain gray, zippered sweatshirt hung free, the arm a lump held against her chest. The sweatshirt's bagginess hid anything else about her figure. Blood still seeped from cuts on her hand and cheek.

Up close, the stink of silver was muddier, not like a carried object but mixed in with everything else. The scent of her pain reminded him powerfully of injured humans he'd smelled. A hint of infection, under the blood. But werewolf wounds didn't last long enough to get infected. Under the poison lurked the more normal stink of someone who hadn't bathed in far too long.

After her scent, the strangest thing was her hair. Even dirty, the locks straggling to below her ears were recognizable as white. Werewolves didn't go white before their first century, if ever.

"You're in Roanoke territory," he said, voice low so as not to carry to any humans on the relatively still air, but still plenty loud for a werewolf. "Who are you?" The Were just stared at him. Did she not understand English? He repeated it in Spanish, since he'd been fluent once upon a time, though she didn't have the look of any of the Spanish packs. Her face showed no more response.

The woman dropped to a crouching stance, one hand on the ground, as if ready to run on four legs. She stared intently at his face for a moment, and then stared just as intently at a point in the air beside his feet. Andrew knew it was empty, but he instinctively checked again to be sure. Nothing.

"I lost my name. The Lady has turned Her back on me, and my wild self is gone. I walk only with Death." The woman's voice was soft and breathy, probably with pain, but it didn't waver. Her eyes swung back to a point somewhere in the matted grass covering the small stream, empty but for a snagged plastic bag.

Something about the reverence with which she invoked the Lady made Andrew's arm jerk reflexively, ready to bow his head and press his thumb to his forehead. Childhood training ran deep, but he caught himself. Bullshit, like all religions. "What pack do you belong to?"

Blankness again, like she hadn't understood and used English a second before. Either she was playing a deep game, or she was brain-damaged. Andrew didn't see how any werewolf could be, but it was hard to argue with the evidence before him. She smelled so wrong—silver and blood and infection—his instincts screamed at him not to touch her. No European or other troublemaker would be able to fake that, or her apparent insanity. He needed to find her help.

"Why don't you come with me?" he said, keeping his words simple, like speaking to a child. For every step forward he took, she took a matching one back. He was no good at this. As Roanoke's enforcer, it was his job to drag people back to their punishments, not to coax them.

She bolted past him. Andrew grabbed at her, but she still had a werewolf's speed. She dodged and escaped through the hole he'd made in the fence. She took off down the street, running flat out, head down.

Andrew growled under his breath and followed, jogging more than running. He didn't want anyone passing to see a grown man chasing a scrawny and pathetic-looking girl. He could outrun her if it came down to it, but he'd rather try letting her slow down naturally. She smelled too hurt to keep up the pace for long.

She started panting within a minute and slowed to a jog as shadows from the maples lining the sidewalk slid up and over her hair in rhythm. The rushing sound of traffic on a main road oozed up with its choking exhaust to blanket them both.

Andrew's breath caught as the woman didn't turn aside on the last residential cross street as he had expected, but kept going right for the traffic. "No!" he called after her. "Wait, that's a good girl. It's all right."

That made her pause, at least. A concrete wall shielded the houses along the road from the noise, and the woman caught its end to hold her up as she snarled silently at him. "I won't let you hold me here. The monster will find me while you're still deciding whether to listen to me."

Andrew didn't know what monster she meant, but who knew what she thought she saw, acting as she was. He strode forward and she jerked away from the wall, toward the cars. He couldn't reach her before she reached the road, so he stopped again. Stalemate. "It's all right—"

The woman's expression grew harder. "Stop insulting my intelligence. It's not all right. Death says I'm supposed to trust you, but Lady knows why." She took a backward step toward the road. "Just let me go. I'm no threat to you. The monster chases me, and I run. Death follows to take *me*, not you or your pack." She cocked her head, listening to something that couldn't be heard. "But you have no fear of him, he says." She snorted, and spoke to the air. "That's a dubious recommendation, at best."

Andrew let silence fall as he chose his words carefully. Something told him these would be the last words he'd have time for before she was gone, crushed by one of the SUVs barreling past. If religious metaphors were so important to her delusions, he'd use them too. "Fair enough, but I'd recommend you run somewhere else." He nodded to the street behind her. "Death hunts those lands."

The woman twisted her head over her shoulder to frown at the cars. "I can swim," she objected, but her stance changed, no longer braced to run in that direction.

Andrew didn't allow himself a sigh of relief yet, but he held out his hand to the woman. "Come on. If the monster comes, he can deal with the wrath of Roanoke's enforcer, and by extension, Roanoke's alpha."

The woman ignored the hand, but she did join him. "I would not dismiss the monster so easily if I were you."

Andrew put a hand behind her back, not quite touching, to guide her back to the car. "So what's your name?"

The twist of the woman's lips made her abruptly look much older. "I told you, I lost my name. Death calls me Silver."

Andrew choked. She didn't seem like she was trying to shock him, but if it was a joke, it was in poor taste. Who in their right mind would name themselves after a torture method? Though he supposed that was the operative phrase here—the woman clearly wasn't in her right mind. "But what do you call yourself?"

The woman smiled without humor. "Who am I to argue with Death?"

The man was some kind of warrior, Silver decided. He was the first she'd seen since she started walking in the Lady's realm who seemed quite real, besides Death and the monster. He didn't shine with Her light from within like one of Her champions, but Silver didn't mind. She would have hated to be reminded of the Lady's true favor forever denied her. It was bad enough that the Lady's light caressed his skin from above.

The warrior's wild self was scarred, rough patches scattered in the steely gray fur. Silver watched the wild self pace beside the man and saw the play of muscles catch and hold in places, where more scar tissue lay hidden below the surface. His tame self did not show the injuries, as was the way of tame selves, but had the same confidence. His short hair was dark, and his features and muscles had a fineness to them that suggested his power came from training, not sheer strength. No brute, he. No wonder Death approved.

Death exchanged sniffs with the warrior's wild self, two old alphas too confident to bother with the ritual of challenge. The warrior's wild self had more muscle, but Death had no injuries and moved with the quickness of night swallowing the sky when a cloud passed over the Lady's light.

"He brings you voices?" Silver asked Death. "Is that why you like him?" Death returned to stalk her rather than answer. Silver braced herself for his howl to come, but she could never brace enough for the burning, hissing pain that consumed her. The snakes paralyzed her muscles, forcing her to fight to break free before she could even writhe with the pain.

"Is he going to cut my voice loose for you?" she asked, when she had the breath for words again. "Is that why you wanted me to go with him?"

Receiving no answer, Silver ignored Death in turn and curled over her arm to sing the snakes a lullaby. *Sleep, sleep, don't hiss, don't bite.* They ignored her and her mind gnawed at the problem of this warrior, keeping her from her own sleep. He seemed kind, kind enough she had no wish for the monster to catch him too. He probably thought he could defend himself, but the monster had weapons he couldn't counter. She should leave to protect him, but she was tired, so tired, of running.

3

Andrew led Silver back to the car without fuss, but she started making soft, distressed sounds when he guided her into the passenger seat. He cursed the compact's limited head room that prevented him from examining her. He couldn't see any injury he might have disturbed. She babbled something about voices, and then convulsed when he pulled the seat belt across her. He let it go and watched helplessly as her back arched with an apparent seizure.

They'd have to chance the ticket for an unbuckled belt. When Silver finally relaxed and curled into a little ball, he straightened from leaning over the open door and returned to the driver's side.

Andrew had planned to drive at least half the distance between New Hampshire and the Roanoke pack house outside of D.C. in Manassas before stopping, but that didn't seem like such a good idea anymore. Traffic on the Beltway would probably still be bad whether he hit D.C. later the next day or not. Unlike other packs, Roanoke was named after the original colony, not their city of residence, but Andrew often wished they did live in the backwater for easier access.

Andrew turned off at the first chain hotel he found, and checked them into a ground-floor room at the back. Silver was still dozing, babbling to herself again, when he returned to coax her in through a side door.

The room stank of cleaning products layered over strange humans, but that was true of any hotel. He got her onto the closest bed, where her clothing looked even more dingy against the overly cheerful shades of the bedspread. When she was settled, he reached for her sweatshirt's zipper to examine her arm, but she lashed out. Andrew avoided the blow, but he suspected her whole strength had been behind it. He retreated to the other side of the room to allow her to relax again.

When she subsided into a doze, Andrew flopped down on the room's armchair and got out his phone. Time to figure out what to do with this poor mystery woman. He paused with his address book open. Technically, he should go over the local alpha's head. He was under Roanoke's authority, and this was strange enough Roanoke should get involved. But it was the Boston alpha's territory, so it would be at least polite to inform him of what had happened.

Besides, Boston was Andrew's favorite of the sub-alphas united in the Roanoke pack. They'd clashed since Andrew had taken the job of enforcer, but Boston was gentlemanly even when working against Roanoke's orders. More than once, Andrew had privately agreed with the older man.

But then, Benjamin was over a century old. While were-wolves could see two centuries if they were lucky, few from earlier generations had made it that far, not in an era when wolf slaughter was practically institutionalized. Benjamin's age gave him the politeness of another era and a wisdom it was hard for younger men to match.

"Ah." Benjamin's voice was warm and satisfied when he answered, like he'd seen a good friend's name on the caller ID. "Dare. Did you manage to find our lone?"

"Yes, but she's a lot more than I bargained for." Andrew scrubbed a hand along his jaw. "She smells like silver, sure, but she's been hurt. I'm starting to wonder if she's the victim of a European, rather than one herself. She's definitely crazy."

Andrew wished he could smell Benjamin's reaction in the pause. The silence didn't tell him anything. Finally Boston asked, "Anyone you knew in your time there? Someone they might use as a message?"

Andrew growled. He supposed when Benjamin had taken him in and helped him through the worst of his darkness after he'd returned from Spain, he'd earned the right to bring up the subject. "I did think about it, when I thought she was a European herself, but I can't see why they'd come after me after all this time. I haven't tried to contact my daughter lately." Andrew had to clench his free hand to keep his voice steady.

"I'm sorry." Benjamin blew out a breath. "It had to be asked, Dare. Are you taking the poor lone to Roanoke, then?"

"Unless you have some other suggestion." Andrew almost wished Benjamin did. Rory was a decent alpha, but he sometimes had trouble with bigger-picture stuff. Europeans were good at subtle backstabbing and manipulation, difficult to catch unless you watched the big picture.

"I trust your judgment."

Andrew could almost hear Benjamin's flickered smile at the pronoun—Andrew's, not Rory's. But Rory was the alpha, and Andrew liked it better that way. "At very least, the Roanoke doctor should be able to help her. Then maybe we'll get some sense out of her." Even beyond what his duty required for dealing with a lone, he found she roused in him the instinct many high-ranked werewolves had to protect those of lower rank.

"Mm." Benjamin paused again. "Where are you staying the night? You could come here."

The concern in his voice could have been just for the hurt lone, but Andrew had heard variations on this tune often before. Benjamin thought his life as enforcer wasn't healthy, exercising Rory's authority over Roanoke's sub-packs but belonging to none.

It was tempting to spend some time with a pack. But he'd set himself outside the local pack structure for a reason. He wasn't going to be responsible for anyone's life again anytime soon. "I don't want to try moving her again until she's had time to rest. We'll make the run to Virginia tomorrow."

"Fair enough." Benjamin sounded disappointed, but not surprised. "Take care of yourself, Dare. And her."

They said their good-byes and Andrew rose to check on

Silver. Still sleeping, if fitfully, whimpering to herself every so often. He wondered if she was deep enough under he could chance leaving to get dinner. His stomach was starting to growl. With his earlier shifting, his metabolism wasn't very tolerant of missed meals.

He'd have to risk it. Andrew drove to a fast-food restaurant a few blocks down and took the drive-through to pick up two burgers, stacked with multiple patties and cheese and bacon. He'd never been sure how humans managed them, but they hit the spot after shifting.

He left one in the bag for Silver and munched on his as he approached the room. He folded the paper back over the burger and moved the bag to the same hand to free up a hand for the key when he reached the door.

Silver slammed into him the moment the door opened. Andrew dropped the food and snatched a handful of her sweatshirt as she bolted down the hall toward freedom. He wrestled her into his arms and lifted her feet from the floor, hoping she wouldn't scream. A story about a teen runaway dragged home for her own good or some such would only hold up so well when he was healthy and male and she was female and pathetic. Fortunately she only panted harshly as she struggled. Andrew kicked the burgers into the room and slammed the door behind them the moment he set Silver down.

"The monster is *coming*," Silver hissed, crouching. "I can't stay here. Can't lead him to you. Let me go." She gasped and curled around her arm again.

"I am trying to get you to help," Andrew snapped. He

stayed blocking the door until he was sure her gasping was not an act to get him out of the way. "I'm taking you to people who can protect you from monsters." Whatever those monsters were. Hallucinations, most likely. Hopefully the doctor could take care of those.

Instead of answering, Silver subsided into silence and lay in a curl on the floor, eyes closed. Andrew waited a few minutes and then knelt beside her and rolled her shoulder back so she lay in a more open position. She kept her eyes closed, but Andrew could smell she was conscious. It was awkward, but he needed to know what he was dealing with. He eased down the zipper on her sweatshirt to reveal an equally grimy tank top underneath, though no bra.

He drew out her arm and she fought him, straining her shoulder muscles against his pull. The rest of her arm muscles seemed unable to respond. Another moment and she sighed and gave up. He laid her arm flat on the carpet, exposing angry red welts running from the inside of her elbow toward her heart. His fingers brushed one of the welts as he tried to angle her arm for better light and pain shot up his arm like he'd touched something red hot.

Or something silver.

Andrew's breath caught and he recoiled. What had been done to her? He knew European use of silver as punishment well enough from when he'd lived there. But that created burns in obvious places. Around wrists or ankles from binding. On the face or lower arms that had been raised against blows. Across the back from whipping.

The human world was also filled with silver, but those

wounds were accidental and thus on extremities, like a burn on the palm from shaking hands with someone who wore a ring. In the past, the Catholic Church had used it on purpose to defeat or torture what they thought were monsters, but no one had believed in the Were for over a century. None of those things fit with the welts Andrew saw here.

Andrew leaned over the arm again, careful not to touch this time. If he made himself think in human terms the welts looked less like burns and more like blood poisoning. Had silver remained against her skin for a long time? Andrew traced the welts back to their source in the cup of her elbow with his eyes, and drew in a breath.

That looked like a needle mark.

Had she been injected with silver in a liquid form, like silver nitrate? Was there still silver in her blood? That would explain why touching the welts had burned him. His stomach clenched as nausea rose. There were stories—myths, really— that the Catholic Church had tried injecting silver into the Were they had picked up along with the vampires that were the Inquisition's real target. All kinds of impossible stories existed about the Inquisition, however, most easily disproved.

More important was to figure out what he could do about it if she had been injected. She should have the silver removed as soon as possible, but if it was in her blood—should he cut her? Hope the silver drained before she bled out?

The silver did look like it might be fairly contained in the welts, especially since touching the rest of her skin hadn't burned him. But what if cutting into them released it into the rest of her bloodstream instead of bleeding it out? Did it work that way in humans? Andrew had no idea. He would have immediately forgotten the information if he'd come across it before.

Better he let the doctor the Roanoke sub-packs shared look at her before he did anything stupid. Andrew left her injured arm where it was and checked her wrists and ankles for other signs of silver, but found nothing.

After watching her a little longer, Andrew scooped the woman up, laid her on the bed, and returned to his now much squashed burgers. He needed the time to settle before he presented this to Rory. Injected silver. He could barely believe it himself.

When he could put it off no longer, he got out his phone and called his alpha.

"You find her?" Rory sounded distracted.

Andrew checked his watch. He'd probably caught the pack getting ready to go out for an evening run. "Yes. She's brain-damaged from silver exposure."

Shocked silence. Then, "Did a European dump her after her punishment?"

"It's injected silver, Rory. That died with the Inquisition, if it ever happened at all."

"I wouldn't put it past some of the European packs. Though I suppose you'd know." Rory tossed off the comment as if he didn't realize how insulting it sounded.

"I just married a European. I'm as North American as you are." Andrew stopped to ungrit his teeth enough to continue speaking. Rory was just rattled by the European politics ending up on his doorstep. "You're the one who resorted to silver when things went wrong in Memphis." And given his reputation, it was Andrew who had taken the blame for that incident. Of course.

"Don't forget Sacramento's son, down in Florida. That was all you. I never told you to kill the boy."

"A clean death, without silver. You agreed with me at the time, Rory. It was necessary." Andrew flexed his free hand into a fist. This old argument was beside the point. "Trust me. I've never heard of a Were doing something like this before."

Rory growled. "Humans, then. It has to be."

"Humans don't believe anymore, not in this century." Silver jerked in her dream and Andrew paced over to look down at her. "If a werewolf can't exist, you don't bother using silver on it." But. But it did sound exactly like the stories about the Catholic Church.

"Whoever it was, we have to find them. Is she going to be able to tell us?"

Silver gave a soft cry and covered her face with her good arm. "I doubt it." Andrew pulled the blankets free and laid them over her.

"Well." Robbed of the clearest path to action, Rory sounded a little lost.

Andrew rubbed his temple. "Warn the doctor we're coming. We'll leave in the morning. Maybe she'll get more lucid once she's been treated."

"Right." Rory sounded annoyed as he hung up, and Andrew suppressed a sigh. Normally he would have worked to make it sound more like the other man's idea, but it had been a long day.

He checked the windows to make sure they didn't open wide enough to allow an adult woman through, then returned to the door. He would hear if she got up, but he didn't know if he would be able to catch her before she reached the door if he slept in the other bed. There seemed to be nothing else for it but to sleep in front of the door.

Andrew grabbed a towel from the bathroom and dropped it on the floor. Even more shifting with the moon not yet full would tire him out, but it would save him a crick in his human back. He could feel the day's efforts building to exhaustion in the time it took to push into wolf, but he made it, and curled up on the towel after scuffling it up around him.

4

Silver woke before the snakes and she lay still for a long while, reluctant to disturb them. She heard the warrior's sleeping breaths on the other side of the den. Death was nowhere to be seen. That gave Silver hope, and she eased her arm back to its place against her chest. The snakes hissed in their sleep, but did not wake, so she sat up.

The warrior's wild self was ascendant now, so he must have switched it with his tame during the night. Both selves dozed, curled against each other.

Death sauntered into the den. He didn't even acknowledge the warrior this morning. Instead, he sat on his haunches, watching Silver. The grace of his movements was arrogance today, the Lady's full light glinting on his fur as it ruffled up with his strides.

Silver looked down at her hand to find it bathed in familiar dimness and waited for Death to speak, but he was clearly enjoying her anticipation and discomfort. She gave in and spoke first. "You seem pleased with yourself."

"He's going to take you away, Silver."

Silver shivered. Death had never used her mother's voice before. She wanted to wince and promise to obey like the cub she had been when she heard it last. "He doesn't have the monster's smell on him. Maybe he'll protect me as he promises. I'm tired of running. Maybe the Lady is telling me I should look for help instead." She lifted her chin, defiant.

"Leave him. He doesn't care for you like we do. Why won't you come to us? We'll help you. Your brother and his mate, we'll all help you find your wild self."

The guilt pulled as strongly as if her mother really had spoken, even when Silver focused on Death's tongue-lolling smirk. Why didn't she join her family? If Death hadn't taken them, she would have run to them first. She had to remember that these were not her family's words, they were Death's. Her family would never want her to surrender to the fire. And if Death didn't want her to go with the warrior, perhaps that was just what she should do.

Andrew woke to Silver's voice, but it was quiet enough he didn't register specific words for several moments. Probably just rambling again. He shoved himself back to human during a pause.

When he was done, he found Silver watching him. "Where

will you take me? To your pack? The monster follows me. You might be leading danger to them." She looked at his face, rather than off into empty space like before.

"What danger?" Before, he'd assumed the monster was a hallucination, but *someone* had injected her. Was that who she feared? But she folded in on herself, whimpering again. Andrew blew out a frustrated breath. One moment the woman seemed lucid—he'd had no idea she'd processed enough of his conversation last night to understand he was taking her somewhere—and the next he asked a simple question and she was lost to the poison again.

"Yes, I'm taking you to the Roanoke pack. You're in Roanoke territory now, remember?" If she even knew what Roanoke was. It might be better if she didn't. The Western packs believed it was only a matter of time before Roanoke started pushing its territory past the Mississippi. If she came from a Western pack, that mistrust might have survived subconsciously.

Silver straightened. "Will they help me? Help me find my wild self?" She tipped her chin to her arm. "If any of them speak Snake, they could ask. I think the snakes know where she went."

"Uh. Sure . . ." Andrew said. Snakes? Rory's mate was a patient woman. Maybe she could find some sense in the hallucinations if the doctor couldn't stop them.

Silver stayed still while he dressed and packed but followed willingly enough when he shouldered his bag and took her arm. "You never said they were your pack," she commented as he guided her across the parking lot to the car. "Where's your pack?"

"Rory is my alpha, but I'm not part of his pack. Since the Roanoke pack unites a number of alphas, it's a huge territory and Roanoke himself can't be everywhere." Andrew had heard Rory's father managed to make it seem like he could by sheer charisma, back when he built the pack before Andrew's time, but that was neither here nor there. "That's why he has me as his enforcer. I can't really belong to a particular pack when I have to keep them all in line."

Andrew nudged Silver to sit in the passenger seat. He didn't try to buckle the seat belt this time, and she sat calmly. "It must be nice to be lone, then," she said.

Andrew eyed her for a second before he shut the door on her. Something about her tone was disconcerting. She sounded like she knew too much even while she spouted nonsense. He wasn't lone by nature. He felt the itch to have Were around to talk and run with, sure, but circumstances had intervened. He left her in the car and stomped to the lobby to check out.

He hit the same drive-through again on the way to the highway. The half-dozen breakfast sandwiches smelled greasy and tasted worse, but they provided a fast way to replace the calories he'd burned. He pulled across two parking spaces to unwrap them and tossed three to Silver. She almost choked herself trying to eat the first one-handed and too quickly, but she growled at him when he put a hand out to try to slow her down. He let her be. Who knew how long she'd been on the run, half starving.

"Where did you come from?" he asked when they were on the road again and she'd had time for the food to settle.

Silver stared out the window. "All I can remember is fire. Ask Death. He remembers the path I took escaping." She paused a beat. "Why does it matter to you so much? I'm not in your pack."

Andrew scrubbed a hand along his jaw, feeling the bristles. He hadn't bothered to shave this morning. He was just doing his job, that was all. He'd have been taking the woman to speak to his alpha as a normal lone anyway, just less gently. "I'm taking you to my alpha, so you'll be somewhere safe. Then I'll catch whoever did this to you because I'm the enforcer. If someone's doing that to Were, they have to be stopped before they do it to someone else. So anything you can tell me about where you came from or who did this . . ."

"Death will love your voice if you chase that trail," Silver snapped. She maintained a stubborn silence after that and Andrew let her be. He snorted to himself. He'd dealt with worse in his time than an imaginary Death. He'd drop her with the pack and then he'd get on with doing his job, dealing punishment.

5

Silver and the warrior ran through flat fields all day without trees to shield them, sometimes flushing prey from the taller grass. He gave her the first part of his kills like an alpha making sure the old or the ill got their share. It burned, to be forced to acknowledge that she was so weak and unable to catch her own prey with her wild shape fled. She would find it soon enough, but until then, fresh meat made a change from carrion.

But she didn't understand him. He smelled like a pack wolf too long alone. She had thought that ache was the emptiest feeling in the world in the before times, but it was nothing like the emptiness of half yourself ripped away. And yet he implied he was a lone. Perhaps he was running from something too. It was a comforting thought until she remembered that soon it wouldn't matter. He'd leave her with his not-pack and be gone again.

"You don't need this warrior. If you come with me, the monster won't be able to find you," Death said in the voice of her brother's mate. Always sensible. Sensible advice.

"If I go with you, he will have won." Silver gritted her teeth. "I won't let him win. You can't have me."

Death laughed. "Better I don't have you yet. Better you lead him to others, and then I'll have many voices." It was the same voice, but sounded nothing like Silver remembered her brother's mate. Too smug. Silver hugged her knees closer to her chest. She'd never thought she might be selfish, until now. The warrior could at least give the monster a good fight. This not-pack of his would have cubs and those couldn't fight, and the monster would take them all when he found Silver with them.

What voices would Death take, because of her?

As twilight fell, Silver looked forlorn, a scrawny thing with her knees pressed to her chest and white hair catching glancing flashes from streetlights. Andrew was counting his exits, but she kept muttering to the air, catching his attention. Her words seemed to revolve around people not being able to have her, but they didn't seem to be addressed to him.

"Silver. We're almost there."

She jerked her head up to look at him, a little white around the eyes, then subsided with a nod. He had to watch that he didn't miss any turns for the last few miles as trees tended to obscure the street signs and opening the windows gave him only the scent of exhaust, nothing trackable.

Andrew's headlights showed several cars in the long driveway loop as his crunched over the gravel. The house had the raw newness and huge floor plan of one of the backwoods mansions that had sprung up across the country. Andrew thought it was ugly, but he supposed one didn't have much choice in designs for a place with five or six guest rooms. Besides, it wasn't his money that had been sunk into it.

The front door opened to show Rory waiting, bulky shoulders filling the frame. He was built on football player lines, hulking muscles under his deep tan. He might have actually played football back in human high school for all Andrew knew, though young Were were discouraged from participating in activities where their enhanced strength could be noticed.

Silver's head came up, her attention fixing on the alpha. She pushed at the car door, unable to figure out the mechanism on her own. She tumbled out the moment Andrew came around to open it for her. She sniffed the air.

"Roanoke. Is Sarah there?" Andrew dipped his head and then guided Silver to the front steps with a hand on her shoulder. He could have made his greeting less abrupt to avoid any appearance of disrespect, but Rory had never required much ceremony of him. He was especially glad of it at times like this. Tonight he was not in the mood for groveling when everyone already knew his status.

Rory frowned, but stepped aside so Andrew could see his

wife. She stood inside on the staircase's bottom step so she could see over the heads of Rory's beta, Laurence, and another woman who loomed behind him. The scent of their hostility drifted to meet him. Laurence had his arms crossed over his chest like a cheap rent-a-thug, trying to make up for his slight stature with bravado. The golden-haired woman beside him wore her strength with more loose-limbed confidence. She'd joined the pack recently and Andrew still couldn't remember her name.

"This is her? The one they injected?" Rory came forward, and though Andrew motioned Sarah to follow, the woman stayed where she was, head bowed. She was pretty enough, in a long-legged, willowy way, but Andrew hated when Were wouldn't look him in the eyes. They made him feel like he would hurt them if he wasn't constantly on his guard.

"Yeah. In her arm. If Sarah wants to take her, we could talk—"

Rory ignored Andrew and came over to unzip Silver's jacket.

Silver bristled and slapped his hand away with enough force to make a sharp crack. Rory stared, apparently unable to immediately process the insubordination. The rest of his Were seemed similarly frozen.

"I'm sorry, have we been introduced?" Silver speared him with a glare. "Death says he does not know you, and you don't seem particularly blessed by the Lady's light to lord it over all."

Andrew suppressed an impolitic bubble of laughter. Good for her. Rory had deserved that for treating a strange Were like she was automatically low-ranked. "Rory, this is—" He hesitated over her name. But if they couldn't tell something was off about her even before the name, they needed their eyes and noses checked. "Silver. She's been talking about Death the whole time. It seems part of her delusion."

Sarah gasped and pressed her thumb to her forehead at the name. Rory only looked disgusted. At his gesture, his beta and the golden-haired woman settled. There was no point in trying to teach a lesson about insubordination to a mad-woman.

Andrew took hold of Silver's zipper himself, giving her time to object if she wanted to. She stood quietly. He drew her arm out, angled so his fingers would be well away from the welts. "You have to look closely to see the needle mark, but it's there."

"After the monster killed all the others trying to burn away their wild selves, he did the same to me. But mine ran too fast for him, and now she's lost. I can't find her." Silver's eyes settled on Rory's face with tight intensity. "Have you smelled her? Did she precede me here? The Lady's light is blinding, and all I can see is Death."

Andrew ignored the part about Death and the Lady and frowned down at Silver. Others? What others?

"You poor thing." Obvious concern made Sarah push past Laurence. Andrew shook himself out of his thoughts, folded Silver's arm back against her chest, and stepped aside. Sarah brushed Silver's hair from her face. "Don't worry. The Lady still watches over you."

Andrew frowned. "Are you sure you want to encourage her delusions? She thinks she sees the Lady. Literally."

Sarah turned away from finger-combing Silver's hair into some kind of order. "If the Lady can help her to keep calm—"

"Yes, but—" Andrew cut himself off even before Rory's expression warned him that arguing with the man's mate was a bad idea. As the only atheist in the room, or at least the only one who admitted it, it wasn't an argument he was going to win.

"Come to my office. We'll talk." Rory jerked his head at the office door. Laurence started to fall in behind Rory, but the alpha gestured him away with a flick of his hand. "Help Sarah and the doctor with the girl," he told the beta.

Laurence's shoulders snapped taut and his scent soured with anger as Andrew passed him. Andrew gritted his teeth. The beta and other high-ranked Were hated his position above them in the hierarchy enough without Rory emphasizing it.

Rory's office was decent sized, but shelves on every wall stuffed with a staggering DVD collection made it feel small and dark. A messy snowdrift of work from Rory's telecommuting surrounded the computer and a spreadsheet was open on the screen.

Andrew waited until the door shut behind them to describe the circumstances in which he'd found Silver. Not that it clarified much. It was clear she'd been running for some time, so who knew where her injury had occurred.

Rory stood frowning out the window as Andrew spoke. When he finished the alpha flopped down in his leather computer chair and propped his feet up on the secondary desk with his printer. "Well, she's not Roanoke."

"Your powers of observation astound me," Andrew said. Why did the man have to be so short-sighted? The point wasn't that they didn't technically have responsibility for her, the point was they had a responsibility to deal with what she represented.

"Pardon?" Rory stretched his knuckles against his opposite palm, not quite popping them. Andrew should possibly have apologized, but Rory allowed his enforcer a fair amount of leeway in private. When Andrew remained silent, Rory continued. "I doubt she's from one of the Western packs, either. We would have gotten an inquiry before now, however much they hate us. She looks like she's been living rough for months. She'll have been a lone. Or one of the splinter pairs. Someone no one would miss."

After he killed all the others, she had said. "I'm not so sure." Andrew pressed his lips together for a moment, thinking. Rory wouldn't like what he was about to suggest, but she acted like a pack Were, not a lone. "I think it's time the Western packs sounded off."

"What?" Rory swung his feet back to the floor. "They'll never stand for us poking into their business like that."

Andrew drew in a breath. How important was this? How sure was he based on some ramblings and vague instinct that she was pack? He couldn't explain it, but that instinct was very strong. "What if she is pack? How would we even know one of the Western packs was missing? Discounting Alaska, since I don't think she could have survived coming cross-country from there even in this season, I don't even know how many there are at the moment. Seven? Eight? They're always splitting, combining, or moving and not bothering to tell us. And if a whole pack is gone, it's serious. Really serious."

Rory rubbed a thumb across his opposite palm. "I'm not sure it's a good use of Roanoke resources to deal with this, though. Her injuries must have happened in the West, so it's the West's responsibility to take her in and kill the humans that did it."

Andrew's lip curled on a snarl he didn't voice. No one could know for sure the injuries had happened in the West. He took a deep breath and tried to stand relaxed so frustration wouldn't leak into his scent. The more you pushed Rory, the more he dug in his feet on the path he'd chosen, no matter how stupid. "No harm in calling to see if someone doesn't answer, is there?"

"I'm not going to threaten what little reputation I have scraped together with them these past decades just to ask after some girl." Rory pushed himself to his feet.

"The reputation your father built and you've been steadily pissing away," Andrew snapped before he could stop himself. Once he started the swing, better not to pull the blow, though. "Don't be a coward. If something's coming after packs, we need to stop it before it leaves the West." Andrew clenched his muscles so hard he could feel them shake to keep himself from moving and distracting Rory from his words with a physical challenge.

"She's fucking crazy. And you're out of line." Rory came to stand before Andrew, letting the other man feel viscerally how much he was outmuscled, then casually smashed a fist into his jaw. "Call them to convince one to take her. She's not staying here."

Andrew took the blow like a good underling, and stayed with his head bowed until Rory had left the office. Then he kicked savagely at the desk's leg. Purchased for a Were household, it was of sturdy construction and hardly wobbled.

Even knowing he could twist the order to accomplish what he wanted didn't ease the sting. Rory needed to get his nose out of the sand. His difficulty in dealing with threats outside Roanoke's immediate sphere had never been so starkly illustrated before.

Since Rory had left his computer on, Andrew sat down and browsed until he found the man's address book. Permission to poke around in the personal data could be considered implicit, if one stretched. Andrew certainly didn't have numbers for all the Western packs. The ache in his jaw faded with healing as he worked.

He checked his watch—earlier over there, but not outside polite hours to call—and used the house phone beside the computer. He suspected the packs would be more likely to answer a call from Roanoke than one from the Roanoke enforcer's cell. For some reason people got jumpy when Andrew contacted them.

Still, four of the eight numbers Rory had went to voice mail. Andrew somehow doubted that so many of the alphas had forgotten to charge their cells or had left them in their other pants. After the first two without answers, he realized he'd have to ask the Western alphas he did reach if they knew of suspiciously silent packs or odd disappearances. He'd never figure anything out by process of elimination.

The first to actually answer was Billings. Andrew could only read so much from his tone, but he suspected the man thought Andrew was overreacting, and had only found a lone with normal silver burns and a flair for the dramatic. But he was polite enough, once he'd determined that Andrew wasn't calling in his capacity as Roanoke's enforcer. Why the Western packs thought Rory would ever sink to such depths of stupidity as to send Andrew as a single Were to violate their sovereignty and take them over for Roanoke, Andrew didn't know. They all seemed varying degrees of convinced that it was only a matter of time.

Billings said he'd spoken recently to most of the other Western alphas, and his pack wasn't missing any members. He was just as polite in refusing to take Silver, but Andrew shouldn't hesitate to call again if he had any other questions.

Alberta answered, but hung up the moment he'd finished his explanation. He hadn't really expected to get much information from them about other packs. The packs were more influenced by human countries than they liked to admit, since Were usually had human birth certificates and passports. A Canadian pack wouldn't know much about the doings of the American ones, and the only other Canadian packs were out in the wilds above the Arctic Circle, or east and strong allies with Roanoke. Ottawa or Halifax would have called immediately about someone missing.

Salt Lake gave much the same answers—no one he could

think of was missing, why was Andrew asking, again? But the alpha seemed to be playing the game where he asserted his dominance by pretending that he was so busy, every word he spoke to someone else was an imposition. Andrew wasn't fooled, but it was still a pain to wade through the constant repetition of "Is that all?" And of course Salt Lake had enough on his plate taking care of his pack as it was without taking on someone else. His pack was really too big, but the alpha didn't want to kick anyone out—Andrew didn't pursue the question.

Next came Reno. Andrew wanted to growl in frustration when he finally hung up on the man. He had to assume that if Reno had a missing Were, the alpha would have said something, but the man seemed determined not to give any information. The conversation had been all rapid-fire questions: Where had Andrew found her, again? Why was he asking about missing Were? What made him think someone had done it to her? What made him think she was from the West? Why was he asking about missing Were? Andrew didn't bother asking if they'd take her.

He couldn't figure out what Reno thought Andrew was trying to get away with. Did he think Andrew had manufactured Silver from whole cloth in order to—what? Get information about missing Were? That made no sense.

That left Seattle, Portland, Sacramento, and Denver. Andrew considered trying them again on his personal phone, but that could wait until morning.

The hall sounded clear, so Andrew let himself out, pausing at the bottom of the stairs to try to untangle scents to determine Silver's location. He rarely went upstairs, so he couldn't tell which were guest rooms and which were private except by the smell.

A cry of pain from one room settled the question. Andrew took the stairs two at a time and jerked open the door. Laurence's back blocked his way. The beta whirled to face him, jumpy from the tension in the room. Andrew put a firm hand on the man's shoulder and moved him aside. Sarah skittered aside without him having to do anything.

Silver was scrunched up against the bed's headboard with a pillow brandished like a weapon. Across the room the brisk-looking Were who served as Roanoke's doctor waited with strained patience. Most packs had one member with bits of nursing or medical training, but Were had so little need for a real doctor this woman was on call to all Roanoke. It wasn't a perfect system, having her so far away when a real emergency came up, but it had worked well enough so far. Mostly her job involved rebreaking bones or digging out embedded bullets when quick healing hadn't proved such a blessing.

The doctor sighed and picked up a second pillow from her feet. "Are you the one who brought her in?" she asked Andrew. "I've been trying forever to get her to let me examine her, never mind do anything about it. How did you get her to show you her arm?"

Andrew frowned. "There's no trick to it. Just be gentle." He sat down on the side of the bed. Silver's brows drew down and she smacked the pillow against his shoulder. Andrew caught and held it so she couldn't pull it back. She calmed down a little, like she'd gotten something out of her system.

"Stop treating me like I'm not here." Silver glared at him.

Andrew tossed the pillow aside and scooted closer. "I don't think anyone has any doubt you're here."

"If you pull out the snakes they dig their teeth in deeper. Deeper and deeper—" Silver's voice changed to a whine, and Andrew lifted her bad arm away from her chest while she rambled. He held it out with one hand under her wrist, the other supporting her upper arm, and jerked his head for the doctor to look.

She was good at controlling her expression, but from this close Andrew could smell her shock. She rolled up her sleeves and reached out, but pulled back when Andrew made a strangled noise. "Enough silver left to burn you." He opened his hand to show the fingertips, still angry red from his first encounter with Silver's wound.

The doctor nodded and remained silent through her examination, directing Andrew to angle Silver's arm by flicking her fingers. "Well, your conclusion seems as good as mine would be. I've never seen something like this before, but the needle mark is there, and if the skin burns you . . ."

"Should we bleed her?" Andrew set Silver's arm down. "I wondered that the first time I saw it, but I didn't know—"

"No," the doctor said, smoothing a light wisp of hair back into her French braid. "I've seen enough silver to know the wounds don't heal right. We may get rid of the silver, but she'll just keep bleeding afterward. I don't think we should risk it, not when she's otherwise stable."

Andrew nodded and stood up as the doctor gathered her bag. Silver watched them both suspiciously, but the longer they left her alone, the more her eyelids drooped. He paused in the doorway to watch her after shoving Laurence out after the doctor and Sarah. She pulled all the bedding onto the floor, and curled up like she was in wolf, back pressed against the footboard.

"Watch her, she's run before," Andrew told Laurence after shutting the door. The other man's lip curled at Andrew ordering him, but he nodded acknowledgment and stationed himself in front of the door.

Sarah fell in with him as he headed back downstairs. Or perhaps followed was more accurate, as she automatically positioned herself so that she was beyond Andrew's reach.

"How long is Rory going to let her stay with us?" she asked, matter-of-fact.

Andrew stopped in the front hall and focused on the front door as a distraction from Sarah's huge fear-fueled personal space. She made him feel guilty when he'd never done anything. "Who knows. Might be a while until I can find one of the Western packs to take her, though. They're helpful, on balance, but not helpful enough to want to take on the entire responsibility for a madwoman any more than your husband is."

Sarah made an apologetic little noise. "It's not that he doesn't want to, it's just—"

"It's just that he doesn't want to." Andrew rubbed his healed jaw. He shouldn't snap, but it had been a long day, and he didn't want to listen to Rory's justifications delivered by someone he couldn't argue with.

Sarah preserved a worried silence for a few moments, and then cautiously offered, "You'll be traveling with her, though. You can make sure she gets to the right people."

Andrew frowned. He supposed he would be. In Silver's current state, one couldn't just put her on a bus or plane unescorted. Another long job he didn't want. He'd have to consider it as a vacation. He'd only gotten permission to visit Western pack lands a few times in his tenure as Rory's enforcer—and that was only to attend the annual alphas' convocation the years it was held out West, no sightseeing allowed. The land was beautiful out there.

"I have to get home," he said at length. "Nothing's getting settled tonight."

Sarah took a step after him as he moved to the door. "It's late. Why don't you stay? We have plenty of space. There's the futon in the TV room." Andrew stifled a yawn just at the thought of the two-hour drive down to his place in Richmond. Sarah took that as agreement and brightened a little. "Since you'd just be coming back in the morning."

She did have a point. Andrew didn't want even more driving, but neither did he want to have to sleep with one eye open to make sure the more aggressive among Rory's pack didn't try something. Ritual combat was only for the alphaship, but they could gain points among their fellows for being the one to kick his ass.

As if summoned by the thought, Laurence came down the stairs. Andrew braced himself. Maybe he wouldn't even have to wait until he was half asleep. He'd been counting on guard duty keeping Laurence busy for a few hours yet, dammit.

Laurence stopped on the bottom step, however, body language neutral. He shook his head at Andrew's pointed frown. "Alpha had me relieved. He says you'll need a plane."

Sarah slipped past Laurence without any apparent qualms about how close it brought her to him. He was properly pack and thus not a threat, Andrew assumed. Lucky him. "I'll make up the futon," she said, and to Andrew's surprise, Laurence didn't object. The man really was staying on his best behavior. Sarah disappeared back into the house toward the basement stairs.

"Well, I'm not going to be able to take her commercial, that's for sure." Andrew eyed Laurence, but allowed the man to enjoy the height advantage being on the bottom step gave him. He needed it.

"Guy I know who does charter needs a little warning, or it's pretty fucking expensive." Laurence crossed his arms over his chest again, but for him his voice was neutral. "Where are you going?"

"Damned if I know." Andrew shrugged. "Whichever pack'll take her. Most likely all the way out to the West Coast, it's looking like."

Laurence looked up the stairs in the vague direction of Silver's room. "That's a long way for her to go just to end up with strangers." A muscle jumped in his jaw, but having come that close to commenting on his alpha's orders, he swerved away again. "Not just going to dump her, are you?"

Andrew blinked. Was that something that might even be a second or third cousin of concern in the man's voice? "Not without checking who it is that I'm dumping her on, if that's what you mean. Even non-pack, she deserves better than that."

Laurence nodded once. "Good." The golden-haired woman crossed the hall to get from living room to kitchen, and Laurence's manner changed immediately. "You would know, wouldn't you? Being as good as non-pack." His mouth curled into a sneer. Laurence jostled Andrew as he moved off into the house. Andrew smoothed his expression so his lip didn't curl in contempt. That man was a beta, and yet he didn't have the confidence to stand up for his opinions in front of the pack? Pathetic.

Why shouldn't Andrew stay the night, anyway? As enforcer, he had a right to be here. They could remember that for once. He headed out to the car to get his overnight bag.

6

Silver couldn't remember being so warm in a long time. The den glowed with a soft version of the Lady's light that showed a healthy pack lived here, and Silver could smell cubs somewhere around, though they were being kept away from her. She knew it was probably foolish, probably dangerous, but she let herself sleep anyway. Really sleep, casting herself into the mist of dreams until nothing around her felt the Lady's light either.

When she woke, the disrespectful alpha's mate was still sitting nearby, watching over her. She bustled about, bringing Silver morsels picked from the bones of their earlier kill, and crisp water from the stream. Silver set it on the floor nearby for Death to drink too. After he'd had his fill, he brought his muzzle up too fast and droplets scattered, glittering crystalline on black for a moment before they soaked into his fur.

Silver let the alpha's mate show her where to bathe and then groom her, because it kept the woman calm. Silver didn't blame her for being on edge, not with Death prowling around like he owned the place. Silver had lost her fear of him only because he refused to leave her, and she knew his ways intimately by now.

The alpha strutted in and frowned down at her. His mate smoothed her hair a last time, glow from her simple, pure kindness lingering on the white strands for a moment. "Don't get too attached. We're looking for her last pack, if she was a lone, so we can send her to them." The alpha looked at his mate as he spoke, as if Silver wasn't even there.

Silver watched the snakes twine on her arm. She'd find no protection here, then, despite what the warrior had promised. It surprised her how much that hurt.

Death came up beside the alpha's wild self, which was heavyset and muddy gray. He bit down into the fur around the alpha's neck, a play nip that didn't reach the skin. The wild self didn't even notice. "Wouldn't use his voice even if I had it." Death whuffed and then lolled out his tongue as if to rid his mouth of the taste. "Has to shout to carry his authority."

He spoke using the voice Silver thought of as his, though of course it wasn't. It was simply the voice of a dead man she'd never known.

The alpha looked at her straight. "This would be so much easier if you'd stop babbling nonsense and tell us where you came from."

That wasn't a direct question, so Silver ignored it. Not for this man would she brave the fierce agony of the fire that threaded through her thoughts and memories of everything before. She closed her eyes, letting his voice wash over her as she came to a decision.

If this alpha did not wish her here, she would leave. The others guarding her had watched closely. Their alpha did not. Silver ignored his questions and waited for her moment.

Despite his worries, Andrew slept unmolested until around eight when Rory's nine-year-old daughter Ginnie peeked in at him. Her light brown hair was mostly caught back in a ponytail, but plenty had sprung free around her forehead. He could have sworn she was inches taller than the last time he'd seen her. That had only been a few weeks ago. He remembered her birth, and she couldn't be more than three or four years from her first shift now. Where did the time go?

Her mother followed close behind her and they argued, low-voiced on one side, much less so on the other. Ginnie tried to convince her mother that Andrew would be delighted at the chance to watch her morning cartoons with her.

He resolved matters by pushing the door open between them to carry his overnight bag to the bathroom. He arrived back showered and dressed to find Ginnie ensconced in a nest she'd made from his blankets, bright cartoons warbling at her.

Ginnie muted the TV when she saw him. "Mr. Dare? I had a question for you."

Andrew huffed in amusement, and Ginnie must have taken it for agreement, because she launched into her question. "I wanted to ask if you were related to the Virginia Dare we're learning about in school. Like, I know Daddy's descended from one of the original Roanoke colonists, 'cause I'm Virginia Howe. They said in school the colony got lost, only I know it was because they found out a whole pack came over with them. Because everyone else was starving and we could hunt for food, and they noticed, you know. And they tried to kill us, only we killed *them,* and went off into the forest when people came back to find them later. And there was a story about Virginia Dare being a white deer, only that's stupid, and I'm named after her, and I'm gonna be white too, after my Lady ceremony, and I wanted to know if you were like, her great-grandson or something." Ginnie hardly paused for breath.

Andrew had to smile. He remembered the first time history class in human school had intersected with the Were history he'd learned at home. He'd been just as surprised at how wrong the humans had gotten it. That was probably something every Were child wondered, why they had to go to school when the humans just got it wrong, but people asked questions about children running around who weren't in school. Besides, it was better to socialize the children into human culture early, since with a few exceptions they'd have to survive in it for the rest of their lives.

"I'm her grandnephew. With a few greats."

Ginnie grinned at getting her answer, and something about the expression of young triumph recalled Andrew's daughter powerfully to his mind. When she opened her mouth to ask something else he made his expression forbidding enough that her words dried up. She turned back to the TV and punched the volume back up.

"You can watch with me, if you want?" Ginnie offered when Andrew made no move to leave yet. Going upstairs now meant dealing with the pack half awake, which would make them feel more vulnerable and irritable. Better to wait a little. He half sat on the couch arm, well away from Ginnie, and watched. The show seemed to be something about superheroes, what little he saw between the commercials.

Silver's angry scream jerked him to his feet in the middle of the climactic battle against evil. He pounded up the stairs two at a time only to be stopped by the clot of people on the first floor, watching something.

"What in the Lady's name is going on?" Those at the back parted for him at his tight question. Silver struggled against Rory's grip on her good wrist, pulling for the door. Rory had dried lines of blood from bites all over his arm. The underlying wounds had healed, but the initial blood remained. Andrew scrubbed fingers over his lips to avoid a smile. No wonder Rory now held her at such a remove.

"She tried to run again," Rory growled. He gathered himself, yanked Silver right off her feet, and pinned her arms when he caught her. He growled more deeply when she scored several good kicks, but those trailed off when she realized they weren't making him let her go.

"Because you don't know how to watch," Silver snapped. She hung in Rory's hold, panting. "All your questions! Stupid, useless questions! I don't have answers, and if I did, why should I give them to you?"

"Should have just let her go, if she wants to so badly. Let her run right into Western territory to no longer nip our flanks." Rory turned and thrust Silver at his wife, who enfolded the woman in a protective hug.

"She'll be gone the moment I find someplace to take her. You know she's in no state to be on her own." Andrew came forward to stand between Rory and the two women. "Since you can't get her to tell you anything about her pack, you need to let me track them down. No Western pack is going to take her in because you tell them to, unless we find the one with some connection to her." He hesitated a beat. Rory might want to just dump the mystery of her attacker on someone else, with Silver herself, but Andrew knew better than that. He hated to work against Rory's wishes in front of the pack, but this was important. "And then once I take her back to a pack that knows her, I can start tracking down her attacker."

Rory opened his mouth to object and stopped. Andrew sensed an undercurrent of support for him from the other Were in the room. They probably didn't want to have to worry about meeting Silver's monster either. "Don't take too long about it," Rory finally said.

Sarah lifted her nose, sniffing. "Her breakfast smells ready."

Rory snorted and turned away. The Were parted to let him out and he disappeared into his office, closing the door behind him more firmly than necessary. Everyone else filed out and Andrew left Sarah to coaxing Silver to the kitchen. Time to start playing phone tag again. Hopefully none were late risers, given the time difference.

He let himself out the front door to crunch around the

gravel drive as he dialed. Someone could probably still eavesdrop if they really tried, but at least this way they'd have to make the effort. None of the remaining packs answered this time either, but he left voice mails. He kept it simple, describing Silver and what had been done to her, and then asking if they knew of anyone missing or quiet lately.

Occam's razor would suggest those packs hadn't answered because they'd checked their caller ID. Especially Sacramento, who would have every reason to bear a grudge for what Andrew had done to his son. But Andrew's mind kept circling back to the possibility the silence was because one pack no longer existed, except for Silver. Wouldn't the others have noticed? The Western packs didn't cooperate with each other, but they always knew what their neighbors were up to, if only to make sure it wasn't mischief. He hated to rely on badgering information out of Silver, but there didn't seem to be any other choice.

He returned first to the kitchen, where he walked into yet more yelling. Sarah stood by the kitchen table, frozen with her hands on the back of a chair she had been pulling out. Silver had her good fist balled up as she shouted, "No! Leave me alone!" She jerked the chair from Sarah's hands and tossed it aside. The back caught the plate sitting on the table in front of it and sent that crashing to the floor too. Silver backed up, muscles rigid. Andrew blocked her way into the rest of the house, so she darted into the living room and crouched in front of the couch. The room had no other exits, so Andrew let her be.

Sarah bent to pick up plate shards mixed with scrambled eggs. "I'm sorry," she said, voice breathy with upset. "I don't know what set her off. I wasn't asking any questions, like Rory was. She seemed interested in the food."

Andrew motioned for Sarah to get up. "Why don't you take her some food in there. Leave the plate on the floor or something. I'll get this." He scooped up the bigger shards and accepted a dustpan and brush from Sarah for the rest. He waited in the kitchen when he was done, letting Sarah approach Silver without the pressure of another Were. It seemed to work. Silver didn't shout, and he could hear her eating when Sarah returned.

Andrew gave her a little longer to get the food into her, then padded into the living room, curving around the couch. Silver had climbed up onto the cushions, and now ate scrambled egg chunks from her plate with her fingers. She dropped one or two to the carpet every so often. She made a *hsst* sound when she heard Andrew come in, shooing away whatever delusion crouched there.

Now that he had a chance to examine her properly, the difference after a bath this morning startled him. Her white hair reflected the light softly when clean. Someone had taken her sweatshirt away from her, and while the lack of dirt made her thinness clearer, a new navy-colored long-sleeved top clung to what would be curves when she was well fed.

"Silver." He waited until she met his eyes. He knew his timing was bad, but when would the timing ever be good with Silver? "I'm waiting to talk to the alphas in Denver, Seattle,

Portland, and Sacramento." She showed no reaction. "Nothing?" She shook her head before going back to her food. He seated himself in a love seat facing her. "I need something. Anything you can give me."

"No one is forcing you to concern yourself with me." Silver brought up her plate to give it a broad-tongued lick, like a child needing more lessons on passing for human. She stood to leave, but he caught her upper arm.

"Anything, Silver. Anything you can give me. Tell me about your pack." He kept his voice low and gentle even as frustration crowded in at the words' edges. To have someone sitting right in front of him who knew the answers he needed but couldn't tell him was almost worse than having nothing to go on at all.

Silver caught his eyes again, hers intensely blue. "The others are all dead. You cannot speak to them. Death uses their voices, but it is not truly them speaking."

Lost for any other way to jolt her out of the rambling, Andrew shook her. She braced against the motion rather than go rag-doll. "A place, then. Tell me about your home, Silver."

"The monster—"

Another shake. "Where, Silver?"

"Why don't you ask Death, since he likes you so much?"

Andrew took a deep breath so he didn't accidentally clench his fingers tighter. Patience. It wasn't her fault the silver had left her mad and unable to help him. "Where, Silver?"

Silver whined. "Not on the water, but close enough for salt on the wind. Not quite close enough to hear it. Crash on the rocks, gulls in the air. Mocking gulls. The wind was off the water, when the monster did it. The Lady pulls the sea. I called to her into the wind, but it blew the wrong direction. She didn't hear me." She shivered so hard Andrew let her go, and she scooted along the couch away from him. "Don't go there. He'll find you too."

Andrew sat back. That took him down to three packs that bordered the ocean somewhere in their territory. Some progress, he supposed. Seattle, Portland, or Sacramento. No closer to what might have happened or who might have done it, of course. Had Silver been in one of those packs, or a lone suffered to live on the edge of their territory?

As for who had done it, all he had were the usual stories that could be traced to rumors that could be traced to threats to keep the children quiet and in hiding. A vampire that had somehow escaped extinction at the hands of the Inquisition. Secret government programs, designed to study and then warp Were to their own ends. Bullshit, all of it. In this century, humans didn't believe. The Catholic Church had believed longer than most, but even they had given up their persecution of supernatural creatures long ago.

His phone chimed. PORTLAND, the screen said. "Dare," Andrew said as he slipped into the kitchen and out through the sliding door. He thumped over the back deck and into the scrubby woods beyond. Again, it was no guarantee of privacy, but better than nothing.

"I suppose you plan to keep leaving voice mails until I answer." The woman's voice was resigned and quiet in her authority. Even though Andrew knew Portland had a female alpha, it was still strange to hear her voice. Fewer women than men had the strength to hold a pack, and even those who did frequently preferred more subtle forms of power.

"That was the idea." Andrew pushed through some sassafras and found a sapling strong enough to take his weight when he leaned his shoulder against it.

"And you're not speaking for Roanoke?" She could mean the Roanoke pack as a whole, but more likely she meant Rory's formal title.

Andrew grimaced. He'd been hoping to slide past the politics, but he couldn't really claim Rory's voice in this matter. For any other official business, he would have. Portland knew that. "Did I say that?"

The woman—Michelle, Andrew dragged from his memory—laughed. "That you never once mentioned his name in your message was more noticeable. So he's loosened your leash enough now to allow you side projects? I can't imagine the other Western alphas are pleased about that." Never mind the other packs—her voice was plenty sharp.

Andrew pinched the bridge of his nose, deciding which of the implications there he wanted to answer. Maybe it would be better to have his reputation out in the open so he could address it. Pretending it didn't exist certainly hadn't gotten him very far with the other alphas. "And what exactly is everyone worried I'm going to do when out of Rory's control?" That came out sounding too angry, but he couldn't take it back.

"I seem to recall certain rumors about 'the Butcher of Barcelona,' Dare." Michelle's humor turned on edge to slash him. "Killing other Were is bad enough, but the stories say you didn't exactly stop there in Spain."

Andrew clenched his jaw until his teeth ached. He hadn't encountered that nickname before. Anger's familiar burn tightened his muscles. He had to keep his cool. If Portland said no to taking Silver, he didn't have many other Western packs left to try. Better to put up with the barbs long enough to get a chance to convince her. "I can't say anyone's ever been stupid enough to repeat the stories to my face, but exaggeration is guaranteed."

"Mm." Michelle's voice was flat. Andrew couldn't read anything from it. "Sacramento's still sore about his boy."

Andrew let out a breath and forced his muscles to relax a little. He was on firmer ground here. "He was raping human women. Sacramento's welcome to be sore, but he would have had to do something about it himself eventually."

"So say the other rumors." Something in Michelle's voice made Andrew think either she or her source had personal experience with the boy. He'd been an oily little shit. "But it still means you're not afraid to kill. Or use silver, like you did in Memphis. It's all very European of you."

"Memphis was—not my idea." The growled words slipped out before Andrew could stop them. Revealing he had disagreed with Rory was borderline insubordinate, but if he didn't do something to convince Portland, he would never be able to track down Silver's attacker. "Trust me. You'll notice that never happened again."

Michelle snorted. "Your reputation aside, your mystery woman isn't one of ours. I have no idea who she could be."

"Wait." Andrew spoke quickly into the pause that probably came from her getting ready to end the call. "Like I said in the message, she needs somewhere to go. She can't stay here."

Andrew took his phone away from his ear to check the call was still open as the silence stretched. Finally, Michelle sighed. "Say we take her. What do *you* want out of this? Information about missing Were isn't going to do you much good on that coast. You want permission to cross territory out here to do your own search?"

Andrew winced. He'd planned to wait to ask for permission to cross territory when he was already there, having escorted Silver out. He'd hoped it would be harder to throw him out than it would be to deny him permission over the phone.

"I want to be able to track the one who did this, yes. But that's secondary. The priority is finding Silver somewhere to go."

"She goes by Silver, does she?" Michelle let out an incredulous breath, then lapsed into another long silence.

Andrew clenched and unclenched his hand to try to release tension from other muscles too. He wished she'd just say no and get it over with, as the others had. What alpha would want to let "the Butcher" onto their territory, knowing he'd want to stick around?

"I want to meet her. Maybe one of my pack will recognize her. And if I do let her stay, it wouldn't be such a bad thing to be able to say I did Roanoke's duty for him." Her sarcasm was no less acidic for not being directed at Andrew. "And we'll see about your permission to cross when you get here."

Andrew released a breath, ragged with unexpected relief. "Thank you. We're chartering. I'll text you the flight details once I have them."

7

Silver didn't like it when they flew. They went so high up into the sky she felt like she should be able to touch the Lady, but Her presence was still veiled from Silver. It made her ache inside. Not as badly as the ache left by the absence of her wild self, but bad enough. Why had the Lady left her? Why couldn't Silver feel Her light on her skin?

The wind stung her face after too long, and Silver curled into a little ball, letting the warrior carry her against his chest. "At least the monster can't track our scent," she told Death, trying to sound optimistic.

"Why would he need to, when you're going toward him?" Death said. Death didn't mind flying, and not a hair ruffled out of place as he ran along the air beside them. "It would be better to give in now."

Silver avoided Death's gaze by looking at the ground below. That was almost worse. The rivers and paths looked like snakes. "I can't run forever. I have to trust someone. Maybe I can only find my wild self if I go back to where she first ran, and follow her trail properly. I've been looking inside all this time. Maybe I need to look outside."

Silver heard how little it sounded like she believed that. Death's contempt for her self-delusion was clear. "He's not helping you search. He's hunting the monster."

Silver's stomach clenched. No, the monster was too strong. You had to run, run as far and as fast as you could, to stay safe. She'd known in abstract that the monster might catch the warrior, following her. Might catch him in fire and burn him down to ash. But hunting would take the warrior to the monster even faster.

"And when the monster defeats him, you will be handy." Death dropped his jaw in a grin, adding a flash of teeth to the humor. "Think of the trouble the warrior will have saved him."

Silver didn't deign to answer, but Death's words twisted in her mind. This was why she should have kept running alone. Of course a warrior would think first and only of his prey. She would search for her wild self, alone, and after that she would run again, alone.

The only people around to see Silver were the pilot and a few people at the small airports where they stopped to refuel. The pilot, either the guy Laurence knew, or a guy that guy knew, made no comment. Andrew tried to encourage him in his disinterest by playing the reluctant caretaker to a mentally disabled relative. Silver bristled at the patronization at first, but once they got airborne, she seemed too far gone to register anything he was saying.

She didn't seem to notice him buckling her in each time, just allowed it before curling into a tiny ball with her knees against her chest. On the first leg, she talked monsters and running, but the ramblings got progressively more indistinct as time went on, until on the last leg she was silent.

Her arm also seemed to pain her more. Frustration at sitting beside her doing nothing made his jaw ache. He wanted to help, but he had no idea what he could do. Would aspirin work for her? He couldn't remember hearing about a Were bothering to try it. Even if it would work, he hadn't thought to bring any. How the hell had he ended up with this job? Better they had sent Sarah or someone to take care of Silver on the trip, and he had gone separately to track her monster. Tracking and dishing out punishment was what he was good at.

He took her good hand, for lack of anything better. That seemed like it might be the right thing to do, as her fingers closed around his with a werewolf's strength. He let her keep the hand for the rest of the flight.

It was dark when they reached the Hillsboro airport, chosen since the charter company didn't fly into Portland International. Andrew was unclear as to how Hillsboro related to Portland, but Michelle hadn't had any questions when he sent her the information, so he'd let the locals worry about that.

For the walk across the tarmac to the terminal building,

Andrew shouldered his overnight bag and the bag Sarah had packed with clothes and toiletries scavenged from the female pack members. With luck he could hand both it and Silver off to Portland to care for. Andrew hoped that once they met Silver, they'd want to protect her.

Keeping Silver close when he had a bag on either side proved a challenge, but he kept a hand on her back. She started to resist as they entered the tiny terminal building. The signage suggested that other businesses leased the second floor, and companies had carved up much of the rest for their specific traffic.

Silver bit her lip. "Why do I have to go to this pack?"

"Because they might know who you are. Or know who would know. And you should stay put with them until I figure it out."

"So you can hunt the monster. What makes you think they'll agree to let me stay even if I wanted to?" The look she gave him was so dry it took him aback for a moment. He might have liked this woman when she wasn't crazy.

Then he shook his head and laughed. He flicked her chin with a thumb. "Just make your eyes real big. Maybe tear up a little. They'll be eating out of your hand."

Silver batted his hand away, no real strength behind it. "You should try that sometime. Catch them off guard." She was away and heading for the front door, laughing, before he could reply. He chuckled.

Her burst of strength waned in the outside air. She slowed and hunched over her arm. "Shut up," she hissed to nothing. "Shut up!"

Andrew wondered if the scents reminded her of home. The Pacific Northwest air was unmistakable, sharp with the tang of rain still locked in the overcast skies. The lack of humid summer heat was a blessed relief, too.

"Come on." Andrew took a gentle grip on her upper arm, supporting a good deal of her weight when she didn't quite straighten her legs and walk properly. "I was suggesting you *act* helpless. No need to be so convincing."

A female Were waited a little way into the parking lot by her BMW. She held herself like an alpha secure in her power, lounging with her ass hitched up on the trunk, one foot on the bumper, while the Were with her paced. Andrew assessed the woman, undoubtedly Michelle, first. Unless Andrew did something overtly threatening, the man wouldn't move on him without his alpha giving the word.

She was an interesting one, at first glance. She was short, but rather than wearing ridiculous heels to compensate, she dressed to fit her small frame. It gave her a look of compact, concentrated power. She had her arms crossed over a medium-sized chest, and dark hair in loose waves to her shoulders. Her cheekbones spoke of Latina blood.

"You didn't say it was the Butcher coming with the girl," the man with her said sullenly, drawing Andrew's attention back to him. It was hard to tell if he was beta or not—the fact that he was the only one there suggested it, but Michelle's manner toward him was slightly cold. Perhaps he was standing in for the beta for some reason. The man looked weather-beaten, and his angular block of a jaw carried a load of stubble that roughed the planes of his face even further.

"You wouldn't have gotten a veto even if I had," Michelle said, and dropped to her feet. She extended a hand to Andrew. He shook it, keeping his grip light. Not a good idea to go flaunting your strength when you were on a strange alpha's territory. Especially a woman's. She seemed confident enough so far, but he wouldn't have blamed her for feeling a little hunted as the only female alpha in North America.

The man with her didn't offer his hand. "What if the girl's just an excuse for him to get out here?" He moved closer to his alpha, protective.

Michelle made an annoyed gesture to cut off the man so she could concentrate her attention on Silver. "I've made my decision. This is not the time to argue, Craig." She returned to stand in front of Silver. "What's your name, sweetie?"

"I lost it," Silver said, pain washing back over her face.

Andrew pushed her to the side of the car before she could get too far gone. "We should get her back to your house before she gets bad again."

Michelle nodded, and opened the back door for Silver. Andrew nudged her in and then went to the other side. He discovered he'd missed more silent argument. Craig held the front passenger door open for him, rather than getting in himself.

It might be better to stay near Silver, but Andrew needed this alpha's favor, and she'd maneuvered him into the higher status position in the car for her own reasons. Probably to remind Craig of his place. It seemed counterproductive to maneuver himself out again.

Once in his seat, he turned to watch Craig's face as he

climbed in next to Silver. The man looked worried, like he expected Silver to start sobbing or ranting at him any moment. Andrew couldn't resist tweaking him. "Don't worry. If Death likes you, you're in."

Craig's expression turned acid. "What?"

"Don't ask me. Ask her." Andrew enjoyed confusing people as inflexible as Craig seemed.

"Death got tired of all the flying. He's hunting." Silver's lips quirked at Andrew. "I'll ask him when he gets back."

Michelle pointed out a few local sights on the way to the pack house, but otherwise they didn't really talk. Andrew liked her manner. The confidence she projected was restful. Even in suburbia, the scenery wasn't bad, either. Everywhere was so green. Huge evergreens loomed up in the empty land between light industrial parks or in the yards of older neighborhoods.

The house surprised him, when they arrived. All the other packs he'd encountered favored houses large enough to hold the whole pack, and huge yards filled with trees to prevent prying neighbors. This was just one house among many in a development, with a postage-stamp yard. It must have been built in the last decade, as the squeeze for space in the city was felt. One car was pulled along the sidewalk, and two in front of the three-car garage. Someone had put a kennel in the side yard in some vague effort to be discreet, at least.

Michelle drove into the third open spot on the driveway. No one was so crass as to peek from the pack house windows, but when Michelle opened the door an awful lot of Were had tasks that seemed to require them to either be in the foyer or pass through it slowly. Their attention went first to Silver, with her striking white hair, but it wasn't long before Andrew felt the weight of their stares. Roanoke's enforcer and the Butcher of Barcelona right on their doorstep was the end of the world, obviously.

One young man straightening the tangled mess of people's shoes and boots in a cubby smelled of surprise, not fear. He set the sandal he was holding down on the cubby, away from its mate, and grinned at Andrew. "Dare!"

Andrew frowned at the Were. His dirty blond hair was shaggy over his forehead, and he was taller than he should have been. Or taller than Andrew remembered him, Andrew realized. The boy's scent rang a bell, and he was lanky like he'd finished his last growth spurt before hitting his twenties.

"Ah, come on." The boy pulled a face of mock disappointment. "Don't tell me anyone broke my record for being the most colossal pain in your ass since I left." He came forward and offered his hand. "Tom. Formerly of Boston."

Andrew left Silver looking amused in the doorway, and took the hand before slapping Tom on the back. The boy tried to throw him off balance with a jerk to their joined hands. Andrew grinned and kicked Tom's feet out from under him. He kept Tom from falling by holding on. "Jackass."

"Dick." Tom got his feet back under him and released Andrew's hand with a smirk. "You still have that squeaky toy I sent you as a thank-you for posting my bail at the pound?"

Andrew snorted. He'd forgotten that. He couldn't recall any cub he'd busted more times after his Lady ceremony for stupid hijinks, but you could say this about Tom: he never endangered any Were secrets by shifting once he'd gotten himself into trouble. He just hunkered down and waited for someone to come fish him out. Even the times Andrew had beaten his ass to teach him a lesson, he'd absorbed it with good humor.

"I thought you were on the road loning it for the foreseeable future," he said, eyeing the boy. He'd grown into himself a lot, and looked more graceful in his size now.

"Fell in love," Tom mumbled, tipping his head until hair fell forward into his eyes. "So I got permission to join."

Michelle coughed, and Tom seemed to realize that he was keeping a guest in the doorway. "C'mon in," he offered, gesturing through a side archway into one of the living areas.

It looked much more lived in than any such room in the Roanoke house, where Sarah's decorating scheme had added coordinated paint and window treatments. This room had two battered couches with matching slipcovers but different profiles beneath, and books and magazines and bills scattered over most flat surfaces. Michelle escorted Silver to a couch and gave Tom and another girl a pointed look—it was probably their responsibility to keep the place tidy. They hurried to corral the clutter into the next room where the guests wouldn't be invited.

"Well, that's one endorsement for you anyway," Michelle told Andrew sardonically, returning to lean her shoulder against the side of the archway into the room. Craig gave a grumpy half-growl from behind her.

Tom stopped with a bundle of newspaper in his arms. "What? No, he's cool. I was such a punk-ass kid, I deserved everything I got. I used to do things like go out to the dog park to lick the cute chicks' faces. Ended up in the pound several times."

"So not everything was a killing offense?" Craig shouldered into the room and flicked a glance to his alpha, but she didn't stop him. Wanted to see how the argument played out, Andrew assumed. Lovely.

"What in the Lady's name are you talking about?" Tom put the newspapers back down on the end table they'd come from.

"Oh, you know Dare. Practically European himself, with his Spanish wife. Didn't you guys in Roanoke hear about what he did to the Madrid pack?" A muscle in Craig's jaw clenched.

"Barcelona." Andrew squared off with Craig but kept his gaze on a point just over Craig's shoulder. If he met Craig's eyes now, it would turn into a straight dominance contest. He didn't want to have to deal with the consequences of walking into a strange pack's house and challenging their beta. He was secure enough in his masculinity not to have to challenge every new Were he met. "I was part of Madrid." It was so hard to keep himself to those few polite words when he wanted to scream at the man. Would the rumors never die?

"So? They probably deserved it." Tom's staunch tone bolstered Andrew's shredding control. Oh, youthful idealism. He hadn't earned the approval, but he appreciated it nonetheless.

Craig growled outright. "Deserved to be beaten, maybe. Not killed. Not killed like that." He jabbed a finger into Andrew's chest. "What did happen, Dare? I heard they surrendered, and you just ignored it."

Andrew pressed one hand into the other, popping his knuckles. Control. He had to keep control. But he couldn't help thinking the beta would have trouble throwing insults if Andrew was beating him.

"Craig." Michelle's tone carried the snap of command. "He has permission to be here." Craig looked back at her, weighed his possible punishment visibly, and then ignored her.

"I heard you mutilated them. Burned the bodies to try to hide it." Craig pushed forward into Andrew's personal space. "How could you?"

Andrew gave in, let the pounding of his blood swell up, and smashed his fist into Craig's jaw. Craig rocked a step back and waited as the bruise on his jaw bloomed through a rainbow of healing colors. Then he smirked and raised his fist for a return blow, what he'd clearly wanted an excuse for all along. The expression drained away as he encountered the resistance of his alpha's hand on his wrist, however.

"Enough," Michelle said to Craig, though her eyes went to Andrew's immediately after. He could read the message clearly enough. She'd let the blow go as Craig's punishment for disobeying his alpha, but nothing further.

Andrew throttled the anger he'd just released back down. He needed space to breathe if he was going to manage this. He pushed past Craig and Michelle toward the door. "Why don't you stay here for a bit, Silver. The rest of you will want to be careful, she runs sometimes when she gets a fit."

Tom skidded on the entryway's hardwood floor in his

stocking feet as he hurried to get in front of Andrew. "Did you want to go hunting, maybe? I mean, after a long flight, and it's close to the full, so . . . We have a really sweet spot I can show you—"

"Permission to hunt?" Andrew kept his voice flat and his eyes just over Michelle's shoulder. He especially didn't want a dominance contest with her.

"Permission granted. We can discuss Silver when you get back." Her tone remained even.

When Andrew looked back to check on her, Silver was dozing, not even the tension in the room able to keep her eyes from slipping half shut. Tom pulled on his boots, ignoring the laces for the moment.

Tom let out a sigh of relief as they got outside. He gestured to a crappy pickup parked along the curb. The body was blue, but one door panel was black. "Lady. Sorry about Craig. I think he wants to justify his place in the pack by protecting Michelle, but when there's nothing to protect her against, he makes shit up."

Tom opened the door with his key and hit the electronic lock button inside the driver's door a couple times before giving up and climbing across the seat to unlock Andrew's door. Andrew knew he was supposed to answer, but if he did, he'd probably say something cutting to the boy since he couldn't say anything to Craig. Tom didn't deserve that.

They drove in silence, Tom taking them to a place closer than Andrew had expected. The small highway took them from suburbia straight into farmland, and then it wasn't long before Andrew spotted a sign for a recreation area. It didn't look big enough to be completely safe, but being closer to the city gave security in another form. People wouldn't be surprised to see a stray dog or two, especially when darkness disguised details.

Andrew stopped to draw in the scents when they left the car. A stream off in the distance smelled somewhat dirty, but the spice of evergreens permeated everything. Maybe it was only the grass is greener effect, but Andrew liked the West. Back before he'd become Roanoke's enforcer, back before Spain, he'd loved visiting, but of course all that had come to an end. Probably not even Alaska would give him permission to cross territory just for a vacation at this point.

"This is a great place, you can't see very far at all from the parking lot or the beginning of the trail." Tom pointed, and pulled a pack from under the accumulated fast-food bags and soda cans behind the seats. A good idea, since it smelled like the ground would be damp, and a stashed pack attracted less notice than a random pile of clothes. If this trip had been planned, Andrew would have brought his bag. At this point, he didn't really care. He pulled off his phone and his wallet, dumped them under the passenger seat and called it good.

Tom led the way down the switchbacked trail from the parking lot for a little ways, and then diverged from it. He hopped over the tree-branch barrier placed to stop the erosion created by people taking the straightest path down. "I don't get why everyone is afraid of you. I mean, you are a dick, and a hard-ass, but it's not like you randomly kill people." He cut off as if he was only just then considering that Andrew might not want to talk about it. "I mean—"

Andrew stepped in before he could flounder too long. "It's more complicated than that. You're better staying out of it. I'll either get the permission I need to cross or I won't. You being a character reference won't make much difference."

"I wish you could have pounded Craig into a pulp." Tom snapped a low-hanging branch aside with a little extra violence. "I want to."

"Give it thirty years. It'll help with understanding about picking your battles." Some people avoided learning that lesson indefinitely, of course. Andrew wouldn't wish Tom to have an awakening like his own when it came to the consequences of giving in to the rage.

Before Tom could broach any more awkward topics, Andrew pulled off his clothes. He folded them into a compact bundle, Tom held out his pack in invitation, and he dumped them in with the boy's. Shifting took perhaps a minute, with the full getting closer. The seesaw of man to wolf swung with the ease of nearly even balance, rather than feeling weighted down as it did when the moon waned. Time to hunt.

8

When Andrew told Silver's story to all the Portland Were who managed to squeeze into the living room the next morning, their frozen silence made him see her injuries all over again. Time had dulled the shock for him, but even Michelle looked sick, and she'd heard part already over the phone. Tom's girlfriend pressed her face into his shoulder and covered her ears about halfway through the explanation. Tom kept his body language strong for her even as his expression grew young and lost. Only Craig remained bland; impossible to tell if it was lack of reaction or camouflage for one. Silver herself looked so calm it was probable no one was home at the moment. She sat with her bad arm draped open on her lap so people could see.

Andrew could use everyone's shock, as guilty as it made him feel. "She needs somewhere to stay, while I find the one who did this," he said, and sensed the pack's emotional tide flow where he channeled it. Michelle lifted her chin in slight annoyance, but then nodded to him. He'd have liked to know more about the reasons behind her agreement, but while the potent mixture of scents from the dozen pack members crowded into the room allowed him to guess at group emotions, individual signatures were lost. A useful sort of privacy, in many situations. They wouldn't be able to get a good handle on his emotions either.

An older Were scooted closer to Silver on the couch and patted her hand. Maria, Andrew remembered belatedly, the name coming back to him from an introduction last night. Maria had asked for details about Silver's condition as the closest thing the pack had to a doctor.

At least Andrew suspected Maria was older. Age was hard to judge in werewolves, more manner than crow's-feet. Her skin had a Mediterranean tint to it and her black hair was pulled up in a severe bun. She started to help Silver tuck away her arm into a new hoodie someone had donated, but Silver pushed the woman's hands away.

"Death said you were trying to get rid of me." Silver glared at Andrew. "I stopped running, I stayed with you. I trusted you when you dragged me back toward the monster. And now you just leave me?"

"Death?" Maria knelt before the couch and cupped Silver's face in her hands, olive skin against sickly pale. "She mentioned that before."

"Who knows what she's seeing," Andrew said. "She seems to talk to them, the Lady and Death."

Silver made an inarticulate, angry noise. "I no more talk to the Lady than you do, warrior. Perhaps you have chosen Death, but it was not a choice I made. The Lady turned away from me and now I can't find Her or my wild self." She gestured to the empty air beside Andrew's feet. "At least you still have that."

Most of the Were made the Lady's sign automatically, Maria with marked reverence. Michelle let her hand fall, and then gave Andrew a sardonic look. He could tell the "chosen Death" comment hadn't slipped by her. He focused on Silver. "You can't come with me, Silver. I'm hunting your monster, remember? Coming with me will take you even closer to him. Why not stay here?"

Silver clenched her good fist on her knee. "The real question is, who gave you the right to decide where I do or don't stay? You're not my alpha. This isn't my pack, so she"—she gestured to Michelle—"isn't my alpha either. I appreciate the protection you've offered, but I was doing fine on my own— shut up—" Silver broke off to say that to the air beside her, as if someone had interrupted.

"Turned away from you? Why do you say that?" Maria asked.

Silver rounded on Maria, anger rising at what she apparently took for an attempt at distraction. Something about the way Maria asked it made Andrew suspect that she truly meant it, however. Perhaps her religion was so important to her that she did rate that crisis of faith highest.

"I can't feel Her." Silver moved so her injured arm fell back across her lap, and stared down at it. "Her light shines but I

can't feel Her presence with me." She looked upward, presumably at the sky rather than the ceiling. Not that the moon
was out at the moment either. Craig snorted at all the talking
to the air and left. The rest of the Were drifted after, probably
reading that this conversation was a bit more private, though
Tom's girl had to tug him out to overcome his curiosity. After
a few moments, only Michelle and Maria remained with him
and Silver.

"That doesn't mean She chose to leave you. She's just as lost
without you, if there's something that's put itself between
you." The older woman held her palm flat between them: a
barrier. "Tell me about what you see. Maybe we can figure out
what it is."

Andrew pressed his lips together to suppress a sarcastic
comment. Religious discussion annoyed him at the best of
times. It was all superstition. Look where it had gotten the
humans. The torture they'd inflicted on the Were paled in
comparison to the scale of the torture they'd inflicted on
themselves. Even if the Goddess did exist, why would she be
concerned with just one Were, Silver or him or anyone?

"This den shines." Silver tilted her head up. "A happy pack.
Smells of clean water and new growth in the trees. The mist
makes it hard to see farther. I can't smell the monster's trail."

"You're in Her realm, puppy. She's searching for you. She
just can't find you with this in the way." Maria took Silver's
bad hand.

Silver's attention on the other woman intensified. "Can
you speak to Her for me? Convey a message? Ask Her for Her
help, if She can't speak to me directly?"

Michelle gestured for Andrew to follow her, and he jumped at the chance to escape and leave the other women to their conversation. She maintained silence until they reached the master suite upstairs. Andrew hesitated in the hall, wary of trespassing on her personal space even if invited. But her scent was too weak to be personal, so he followed her in. With only her living in the master suite, a desk and TV fit easily, and the place was tidy enough to seem like an office that happened to include a bed. Maybe she slept in a lover's room instead.

"I suppose, viewed in a certain light, it does sound like she's describing the Lady's realm." Michelle spoke mostly to herself as she half sat on her desk's edge. She made a calming gesture when Andrew's expression darkened again. He'd rather stick to business. "I don't know that she'd want to stay here long term, even if I was ready to take her, but she can certainly stay as long as it takes to find her relatives."

Michelle pushed out her computer chair and propped one foot on it, twirling it. "And you may have the permission to cross until—" She held up a finger. "You find out who did this."

Andrew gave her a half bow. No harm in laying the formality on thickly. He'd gotten what he wanted. "If she's right, and she had a whole pack once that was killed, do you have any idea who it might be? Sacramento, Denver, and Seattle haven't returned my calls. But considering I'm persona non grata—"

"It's still my territory at this point, but I wouldn't go south of Eugene if I were you. Sacramento likes to push the border

around there, and he'd probably make your life pretty uncomfortable if he got hold of you." Her delivery of the under-
statement was desert-dry. "But he's alive and kicking. I talked
to him the other week."

She grimaced, and Andrew suspected it was something to
do with the ongoing battle over that territory. "Denver's far
enough away that I don't really have too much to do with
him. Sacramento was whining about him, though, so I presume he's also still all right. Seattle—"

She hesitated long enough that Andrew drew in a deep
breath, trying to read what was worrying her from her scent. It
was low-level concern, not sharp fear. "Seattle, though. He's
been . . . weird. I mean, I've talked to him, but he was constantly trying to get into my pants from the time I made alpha,
only to stop maybe six months ago."

"Maybe he fell in love," Andrew said, mimicking Tom's
earlier cadence with a small smile.

Michelle gave a sardonic laugh. "It's not just him, though.
The whole pack pulled in and stopped calling to chat or coming to visit as much. I mean, packs like Alaska are like that,
but Seattle used to be different." Michelle crossed her arms
and shrugged. "So. For what it's worth. I've been thinking
about it since you first contacted me, and it's the only thing I
can think of that's the least bit out of the ordinary. And it
wasn't weird enough that I've particularly been worrying
about it these last months. It's been a relief, actually. But I
thought you should know."

Andrew nodded. She was right, it wasn't definitive. Seattle
could just have decided he was tired of chasing the prize he

couldn't catch, and clammed up from wounded pride. But put it together with Silver's situation, and it raised questions. "I'll head there next. Stop on the border and see if I can find anything nosing around while I wait for permission to cross." He hesitated, trying to find the most tactful way to ask for the next favor.

"I'll warn him you're coming," Michelle said with dry humor, getting there before him. "Since he does at least still answer my calls. I'll show you where the current borders are before you go, too."

"Thank you." Andrew offered his hand, and they shook on both that and the territory permission he now had. "I think it might be best if I go now, grab a cab to the rental car place. Silver seems like she's objecting to staying anywhere at all, not so much that I'm leaving her behind. You can talk her out of it just as well without me, I'm sure." It felt a little strange to leave without her at this point, but Andrew reminded himself that she wasn't his responsibility anymore. Now it was time to concentrate on hunting and forget about her.

Michelle nodded. "Good luck."

9

She needed to leave as soon as possible, Silver knew. Though it had been sweet relief to sleep without worrying the monster would find her in the night, or Death would steal her voice while she wasn't awake to resist him, she couldn't stay here. This pack had cubs. Besides that, they were too soft, too kind. The monster would tear them into tiny shreds.

Too patronizing, also. One fancied herself a priestess of the Lady, but she had no more of the Lady's light about her than the others. It took Silver a little while to realize it, but the more words the woman spilled into the air, the clearer it became that they were made of mist. Silver had stayed with the warrior because he'd asked her to like she was someone who could think for herself. She would not stay for this pack who assumed she would follow directions like a child.

Rain filled the air, like at home, and the Lady's light grew steadily brighter. It angered the snakes, making them writhe more and more often. Each time Silver got to her feet to escape the den while the pack's attention was elsewhere, the pain brought her right back to her knees again. Death sat by and panted. At least he wasn't urging the fire on this time, calling it down with a borrowed voice. Perhaps that meant she would survive this, like all the other times when the Lady's light had seemed to burn her away, leaving an empty shell.

It hurt. It hurt until nothing remained but pain. Silver wished the warrior was here, to goad her into hanging on through pride. He never gave in to pain, she was sure. It was easier to stay with the world when he was watching and would be impressed by her control.

But he wasn't here. Just Death laughing at her. He wouldn't want her voice now, too raw with screaming.

Seattle didn't answer his phone. Andrew chewed over that fact as he drove north, trying to keep from speculating too wildly. What was Seattle up to? Refusing to talk to Andrew could be simple rudeness, but he had Portland's misgivings to consider. Michelle had talked to him the night before, so he was still alive. But if Seattle was up to something he shouldn't be, it would be much less suspicious to deny Andrew permission to cross flat out, rather than screening his calls. Andrew couldn't figure it out.

When he finally wrenched his mind from the same ruts

about Seattle, the scenery seeped in. Every patch of woods called to him to run. He hadn't realized that the freeway from Portland to Seattle could present such an untamed illusion, given the cities' sizes. Huge evergreens flanked the road's shoulders, even if development lurked immediately behind them.

He stopped south of Olympia, right off the freeway. It was inside Seattle territory as Michelle had shown him on the map, but not insultingly so, yet. Every territory had official borders that lay beyond what could be patrolled regularly, so this was more a "hey, morons, pay attention to me" sort of trespassing. He'd wait here until someone showed up. There was a mall—of course there was a mall—but he couldn't make himself pay attention to anything inside. He wanted to run on four legs. Full moon was soon.

After he'd circled the entire mall twice without feeling the smallest desire to go into a store, he gave up. Suspicions or not, knowing Seattle was alive, he didn't want to trespass any farther without waiting another few hours at least. Hunting and killing anything on Seattle's territory would be a slap in the face he wanted to avoid, but he could run at least. It felt better to have a purpose, even when it seemed he'd been driving forever without finding an end to development.

The place he stopped wasn't a park, but it looked densely forested enough he'd have the privacy he needed, and he'd hear or smell anyone coming in plenty of time. He stepped over a rusting barbed-wire fence to get in, and started piling up his clothes. Since it would be such a short run, he left his wallet and keys in the pile with them rather than hiding them somewhere. The phone went on top so he could shift back and grab it quickly if Seattle finally called.

Finding the wolf was like falling, so easy. He'd just dropped to four feet, shaking to settle fur into place, when the phone's chime assaulted his ears. It sounded even more tinny and strident in this form. What timing Seattle had. At least it wasn't near the new, when the shifting process was too exhausting to begin again immediately the other way.

He shifted back and flipped the phone open with one hand without looking at the screen. He tried to pull on his boxers simultaneously, with little success. "Dare."

"Thank the Lady. How far away are you? She won't stop screaming." Michelle's voice was breathy with stress. "Did she do this with you? Did you hold her still or let her flail? What should we do? We don't want her to hurt herself, but she was bruising from where I was trying to hold her—"

Andrew swore, set the phone down, and used the pause to pull on his pants and then shirt, leaving it untucked for the moment. He managed shoes and jacket well enough one-handed. "What happened? She seemed to be in pain before, sure, but nothing that bad. I wouldn't have left her with you without saying—"

Michelle brushed past the apology. "We have no idea. She was sleeping, and most of us were getting ready to go out on a run."

"All right." Andrew winced as all the needles his shirt had picked up from the ground skittered down his back. "Leave her free. I might be as long as two hours."

Michelle fell silent for a moment as she digested the snap

of command in his voice. Andrew grimaced. He didn't have time for the careful dance to avoid a dominance fight. He wasn't going to challenge Michelle, and if she couldn't figure that out herself, that was her problem. She was the one who'd called him for help. Apparently she was intelligent enough to realize it, however, as all she said after the silence was "Hurry."

It took what felt like days to get back, even speeding anywhere everyone else was, taking refuge from the police as one of the crowd. The irony of being a herd member hiding from the predator would have amused him more in other circumstances. Any time he stopped concentrating on driving, he could feel wolf form hovering near the surface. His impatience, like any strong emotion, was an unceasing pressure on the balance between wolf and human form, trying to push it over. His jaw ached from clenching it by the time he reached the Oregon border.

He heard Silver the moment he opened the car door in front of the house. The noise was low enough that he suspected that the neighbors would mistake it for the television, but it cut straight to something instinctive in him, twisting. It had the whine of someone who'd been in pain too long to spare the strength for real cries.

He didn't bother knocking, just raised a hand to the knob, but the door opened out from under him. Tom stood aside to let him through, anxiety on his face smoothing to a naïve faith in Andrew's abilities. Michelle appeared at the top of the stairs. "She's not thrashing so badly," she said tightly and jerked a gesture to a bedroom.

Andrew sensed other worried Were behind the nearest

doors, but the only person besides Silver inside the bedroom was Maria. She radiated tension from keeping herself still just inside the doorway, watching Silver pant on the end of the bed. A few angry red patches showed on Maria's arms. After a moment to puzzle out the angles, Andrew realized that Silver's thrashing must have brought her welts into contact with the older Were's skin. In exchange, Silver had fingerprint bruises on both her wrists.

He stepped forward, and Maria grabbed his arm in a tight grip. "Don't. You'll make her worse again."

Andrew spread his palms flat. "I'm not going to touch her. I'm just going to talk to her. Silver?" He raised his voice, and called her name several more times, but she gave no sign she'd heard him. Maria's hold slackened when she got a pointed nod from her alpha, and Andrew shook off her hand.

He sat to put his eyes level with Silver's and tried to hold hers. He couldn't put the true command of dominance behind it because she didn't return the gaze, but it was better than nothing. "Death. Tell her she has to talk to me. She has to tell me what's wrong. What made it worse." Might as well make her delusions work for him.

Silver's whine drew out until she ran out of breath. Her lips started to shape words but it was a moment before she put air behind them. "Her light brings it back. The children's voices. He uses the children's voices to hurt me." She sobbed, and her gaze finally focused, but on Michelle. "And your baby. It just cries." Then she curled into a ball, losing the thread of her words. Her low whining began again a moment later.

Michelle made a choking noise. "How could she know—?"

Andrew gritted his teeth. What hadn't these people told him? "A child was killed . . . ?"

Michelle made a violent gesture, cutting off the topic. "Miscarriage. Early-term shifting. Nothing to do with this."

Andrew winced and bowed his head, offering the gesture of submission as an apology. Miscarriages were less common now that women could discover their pregnancy quickly and stop shifting, but they still happened. Some werewolves could shift throughout the entire first trimester, some would lose the baby with even one shift after conception. One couldn't tell.

"But if she's really speaking to Death—" Maria's voice had a note Andrew recognized. True belief.

"Her light—too bright—" Silver distracted them all by reaching out with her good hand to clamp onto Andrew's. She went into something that looked like a seizure, back arching helplessly, while the marks on her arm seemed to blaze red.

Andrew knew that arch. Oh, he knew that arch. He should have realized it before. He had once seen a Were tied down with silver chains on a full-moon night. His back had arched like that when he'd tried to shift. Under the full, the balance tipped into the other form with the slightest push of strong emotion. Then, when the silver halted the shift before it could begin, panic forced him to try another shift, and another.

The only way to stop it was to remove the silver.

But that was what the doctor had said he shouldn't do. It seemed so deceptively simple, just slit the welts and let the poison bleed out. He couldn't sit here and do nothing. Her seizure went on and on. He could cut shallowly, couldn't he? Minimize the bleeding?

Maria made a whimpering noise, unable to bear it any longer, either. "Can't we do something?"

Andrew grasped Silver's elbow, dragging her arm out straight. He felt for his pocket knife and flipped it open awkwardly. Michelle made a noise in her throat and jerked a step toward them, but Andrew looked down at Silver's arching body and then up at her. He didn't need Portland's permission, but it would help if she wasn't trying to stop him. "Trust me." Michelle's jaw clenched and she dropped her head in assent.

Cutting the first line was relatively easy, and the seizure eased as blood seeped out. Silver's face grew confused at the new pain, however, and she struggled weakly. Andrew's courage wavered, seeing her fear. What if he was killing her? After all she'd survived, what if she died of his simple stupidity?

Silver's struggles eased after a second, but the blood flow did not. It seeped steadily. Andrew's lungs started to burn before he realized that he was holding his breath waiting for it to stop. It should stop, for a werewolf. Long before he used up one breath.

He sucked in a deep breath. He couldn't stop halfway. If Silver was going to bleed out, it should take all the silver with it. He cut along the next welt, and again. He cut and then squeezed out the blood until it no longer burned over his fingers.

The tension in Silver's muscles lessened as the burning of

her blood did. She gave a sob of relief when it was all gone. "You killed the snakes," she said, eyes drifting past his face, unable to focus. "Thank you." Then she slumped into unconsciousness.

Andrew gathered her onto his lap. He knew he should get up, especially with the silver-tainted blood soaking into the mattress, but he wanted to hold her a little longer, to make sure she was really done. His burned hand screamed with pain, but he wiped it on the blankets and clamped it to her arm to stanch the blood. It didn't burn him further, which he figured was a good sign.

"How did you know that would . . . ?" Michelle came to the bed, face twisted with worry at the way the blood continued to flow. By now, the wounds on any other werewolf would have healed.

Andrew added his other hand clamped higher up on Silver's arm. "I've seen it before, during a punishment. It's a vicious circle—panic forces you to shift and silver stops you."

"Seen it? Were you involved with the punishing?" The acid in Maria's voice was subtle but there. She seemed less discomfited by the blood than the two of them, and she moved as if she planned to take Silver from Andrew. He suppressed a snarl to make her back off, and concentrated on his hold on the wounds. The blood seemed like maybe it was dripping more slowly now.

"The European packs used silver for punishment long before I ever joined one." Andrew didn't bother explaining further. Slow or not, the bleeding continued. "Bandages."

"Why would we have those?" Maria bristled again at the

commanding tone, but after a beat of hesitation and a glance at her alpha she disappeared from the room. She returned a few moments later with a cotton sheet, cream with an occasional dark green diamond. It tore easily in her hands. It took some glaring to get themselves organized but they worked it out so Andrew peeled away his fingers as Maria wrapped, leaving nothing uncovered for too long. When his hand was free, Andrew wiped it off, leaving a sodden crimson smear down his shirt, and pressed down on the bandages again.

When they were done, the bandages turned pink and then red in lines over the wounds, but didn't stain further. Maria looked around them both, measuring the pool on the sheets. "I think it looked worse than it was."

Andrew settled Silver's arm against her chest and then lifted her. Even as a dead weight she was light. She felt like nothing but bones when he held her like this. "Where am I putting her?" She obviously couldn't stay here. They needed to haul the silver-tainted bedding and likely even the mattress to the dump.

"This way." Michelle led the way down the hall. The room she ushered him into had dirty clothes all over the floor. The scent-marking hit him more aggressively because of that, but at least it was from a low-ranked female. He set Silver down on the bed. Her bandage, where it wasn't darkening to brown, matched the sheets, cream and green to green and cream. Andrew smoothed her hair, and waited a few minutes to make sure she was sleeping peacefully. Eventually he made himself leave the room, closing the door gently behind him.

"Thank the Lady that worked," he muttered. The phrase

came to him by long habit, but he regretted it the moment he saw Maria press her thumb to her forehead. He hadn't meant literally.

"The Lady takes care of her own. Silver is blessed." Maria's voice had that true belief tone again, and Andrew eyed her with tired hostility.

"She's hallucinating," he said. The scent of blood from his shirt twisted its way into his nostrils with every breath, so he pulled it off. "Don't let your imagination run away with you."

"How did she know about the baby, then, if she had not spoken to Death?" Maria crossed her arms. "No one but the pack knew."

Michelle made an uncomfortable little noise. She looked conflicted, like she was trying to talk herself out of agreeing with Maria. "A few friends in other packs knew. You know how people gossip—"

"Exactly." Andrew spoke quickly to cut Maria off. "This Death seems like an expression of her unconscious, and we knew she was probably living out here somewhere. It's perfectly possible she came into contact with the information before, and is incorporating it into her hallucinations."

"But—" Michelle said a little weakly. Where Maria had her arms crossed, the alpha more hugged herself, probably thinking about the child.

Maria gave Andrew a pitying look. "I'm sure it's frightening to be confronted with someone who sees more than we do—knows more than we do—"

Andrew shoved past her, purposely jostling her shoulder. His clean clothes were down in the car. "You're welcome to your delusions, but leave her out of them. We want to pull her out of the madness, not encourage her in it."

Andrew made it halfway down the stairs only to meet Craig coming up. "What in Lady's name have you been doing up here?" he snarled. "Killing her?"

Andrew looked down at himself and realized what a picture he presented, stinking of silver-tainted blood with his shirt a crimson mess balled up in one hand. He could practically see the thought on Craig's face: Butcher. Scents from the rest of the house filtered into his attention, fear and discomfort from the rest of the pack as well. They had chosen to hide from it instead.

"I bled out the poison." Andrew shoved past Craig. The sooner he got his change of clothes, the sooner he could get cleaned up. He could only hope the pack calmed as the smell dissipated.

10

Empty. The snakes were dead, and though her arm throbbed, it did not burn. But everything was still so empty where her wild self should have been. Silver called for her wild self, screamed for her into the new silence that the snakes had left. It was safe for her to return. Silver sobbed, and begged, but couldn't find even the drifting scent of her wild self on the breeze.

She found the warrior's scent instead as she became more aware of her surroundings. Death was gone, but the warrior's wild self had his head in her lap. He had fallen asleep while guarding her. She smiled and used her good hand to ruffle his ears. "You killed them."

"You survived the full moons before. He should have guessed you would survive this one too," Death complained from the entrance to the den. His voice was familiar to Silver, male and warm, but she couldn't place it. Memories of everything before the fire were partially burned away, and those that remained were slippery when she tried to hold them.

"You're angry because he took me from your grasp," Silver told Death, and the warrior stirred. His tame self sat up from his slump against a tree, and reached first for her arm. He examined it, turning it this way and that. He was clumsy in his attempted gentleness, like he wasn't quite sure how to go about it.

"The fire no longer burns," Silver told him, gritting her teeth against the pain he caused.

He set it down, watching her face. "I think you're healing a little faster than a human. That's something, at least." His eyes caught hers. "Can you shift?"

Silver broke the gaze, turning her head and biting her lip so he couldn't see her tears. "I still can't find my wild self. She ran too far to know it's safe to come back now."

"It's up to you." The warrior's hand on her cheek turned her head back. His wild self licked her good hand, encouraging. "But the silver's gone. And shifting would help you heal . . ."

Silver drew in a deep breath. Maybe he was right. Maybe she needed to do more than call. If she reached for her wild self, reached as far as she could for her, maybe she would be there in the dark beyond the edge of the Lady's realm.

So Silver reached. Reached into the nothingness and strained with every ounce of her being to even brush her fingers against a hint of fur. Her muscles screamed with the effort, cramping, but she just couldn't. Couldn't reach, couldn't hold on. She let go, falling short. She had failed yet again, and now the pounding ache from her arm pulsed through her abused muscles.

"Can't," she gasped, and fell back into more comfortable darkness.

Andrew swore at length as Silver slumped from her seizure back into unconsciousness. Going to wolf form and back should have jump-started her healing, and it had seemed logical that she would be able to shift now—but that was idiotic. The silver hadn't been in just her arm, not if her brain had been affected. Some undoubtedly remained throughout her body and in her bloodstream. He was lucky his idiocy hadn't pushed her back into the dangerous circle of the night before.

He checked her arm again, but the seizure didn't seem to have caused any fresh bleeding. "I'm sorry," he said, then lifted his head at the sound of someone approaching.

"How is she?" Michelle paused in the doorway, muscles taut. Andrew could see that having an unfamiliar Were in her house was beginning to tell on her. He didn't exactly like being the unfamiliar Were. Avoiding any assumptions about another Were's relative status made every single interaction an exercise in painful neutrality. Michelle ran a hand through her hair, and then stretched her posture into something more casual. "I heard her voice."

"She knocked herself out again trying to shift." He nudged Silver's shoulder so she was lying in a position that was a bit more comfortable. "If bleeding out the silver didn't help, I'm starting to think she might never shift again."

Michelle looked nauseated. "It's cruel that she's still alive, trapped that way." She lifted Silver's injured arm and let it fall back limply. "I don't think I'd want to keep on living on those terms. I'd want someone to take care of me." The words fell into a sudden dead feeling in the room, like a stone tossed into a well that didn't splash.

He felt the same way, to be honest. But it wasn't about him, or Michelle. Silver had made it across the country, traveling on foot. Two feet, not four. Now the panic of the moment was gone, he realized there had to have been full moons before this one, and she was still here. How much easier would it have been for her to give up long ago? That wasn't a strength of resolve he was going to argue with. "She seems to feel differently, though."

"True enough." Michelle smoothed Silver's hair. "We got real bandages. But is it better to not mess with it?"

It took Andrew a beat to realize she was waiting for him to answer. How was he supposed to know? Silver seemed to be healing like a human and he had no more experience with humans than she did. His lack of a true pack had forced him more into their company than some Were so as to not go mad, but nothing more. "They were shallow cuts. It's been all night. I'd think we could chance it." That would clear some of the stink of blood that lingered on her, too. It was better in the rest of the house, but sitting next to her, it set him subliminally on edge. He felt like he should be hunting the injured prey to finish it off.

Michelle nodded and scooted over like she expected Andrew to move so she could take his place at Silver's side. "We'll take good care of her."

Andrew didn't get up yet. "I was thinking I might take her with me. Seattle's not that far away. They might recognize her in person when they wouldn't from a description." The arguments seemed thin when laid out like that. But he couldn't leave her here, not when the Portland pack had proved themselves incapable of taking care of her. He didn't know any more than them about injected silver or human injuries, but at least he'd done something instead of standing by. "Maybe she'll recognize somewhere herself."

Michelle bristled, apparently able to guess what Andrew wasn't saying. "Last night caught us by surprise, that's all. It's not going to happen again. She'll just slow you down, you know that."

Andrew tilted his head at the last second so they didn't lock eyes in a challenge over Silver's still form. She would slow him down a lot, dammit. But. He scrubbed at the stubble on his cheek, using the movement as an ostensible reason for avoiding Michelle's eyes. "We can decide after breakfast," he said, pushing himself to his feet. He'd appreciate a shave, too. Maybe the best course of action would become clear when he'd had time to wake up a little.

He bolted his food standing in the kitchen, tension thick as other Were came in and out, sneaking glances at him. Andrew wondered if they were thinking "Butcher" too. Tom bounded in like a breath of fresh air. "Is she okay now?"

Andrew speared an egg chunk with his fork. "She's out of

immediate danger, anyway. I don't know how okay she really is."

Tom made a *pfft* noise with an exaggerated face to go with it. "Thanks, though. It was hard to listen, and not be able to do anything. I'm glad you could." He dodged the light punch Andrew aimed at his shoulder and left him to his food. Andrew sighed. If only he really was whatever heroic version of himself Tom seemed to see.

Andrew scraped up the last of his eggs and put his plate in the dishwasher but didn't manage to escape before Craig appeared. The beta brought a sense of congealed anger with him, though it seemed less directed at Andrew than the night before. Michelle must have filled him in on the details of what Andrew had done.

"I suppose Michelle is still determined to keep her?"

"She's right that it doesn't really make sense to keep her with me when I'm hunting her monster." Something about Craig's tone made Andrew want to poke at the subject. He sounded like he was less than supportive of his alpha's wishes. That was worrying.

Craig snorted and slopped coffee into a mug. "It doesn't make sense to keep her, period. Girl needs putting down. She's never going to heal, and just think about her babbling like that in front of humans. She'll be hemorrhaging Were secrets like she was blood."

"Lucky for her, you're not going to get the chance to 'put her down.' She's coming with me." Rage rose in Andrew, but he channeled it into purpose rather than violence toward Craig. If that's the way things were, no way he was leaving

Silver here and giving Craig the chance to wear Michelle down. No way.

Craig's lips started to curve into a sneer, but Andrew curled his fingers into a fist meaningfully, and the other man seemed to recall what had happened last time. His face fell blank and he moved aside.

Michelle met Andrew in the hall as he left the bedroom, the sleeping Silver in his arms. She planted herself, feet a little spread, hands on hips. "I thought we'd discussed this."

"I discussed it a little with your beta, too." Andrew clenched his jaw so he didn't speak too loud and wake Silver, though she seemed to still be more unconscious than asleep. "He seemed a big fan of mercy killing. She'll be coming with me."

"Lady. Craig!" Michelle spat the name as she turned. "I *can* control him," she said without turning back to him as she jogged down the stairs. Most of the resistance faded from her tone, however, leaving resignation in its place. Andrew followed her down, and as he expected she didn't stop him from detouring to the front door.

It worried him to load Silver into the car in daylight, but the neighborhood was quiet and modern enough that few knew their neighbors. And Andrew never underestimated the power of an authoritative manner to convince humans that he had every right to do whatever he was doing.

At some point in the drive, unconsciousness seemed to pass into true sleep for Silver. It was more peaceful than he remembered from their night in the hotel, no quiet whimpering from presumable nightmares. She turned onto her side on the backseat, injured arm tucked underneath her. She left her good arm a little outstretched like she was embracing something.

The smell of fast-food tacos for lunch didn't wake her, and neither did shaking her shoulder after he'd finished. Maybe with the silver drained from her blood, a small portion of her natural werewolf healing had returned, keeping her asleep as her energy finally went to ease old injuries. Andrew picked another mall parking lot, child-locked the back doors, and left another message on Seattle's phone. This time if he didn't hear in a few hours he would keep going north and knock on Seattle's door if he had to. Seattle could just deal with it.

His phone rang five minutes later, but it identified the call as from Boston, not Seattle. Andrew answered, and his tension eased as they exchanged greetings. "Is Rory pitching a fit about my being gone too long already?" Andrew asked after updating the older man on Silver's condition. "It's been two days."

Benjamin chuckled. "Give him another day or two. But no. I need your permission as enforcer to take care of some business." He paused, and Andrew filled in the rest. If it was just permission he needed, not action, he wasn't surprised Boston was avoiding going through Rory. Andrew could give that easily enough over the phone.

"There's a male lone who popped up around our northern border. I know checking him out would usually be your job, but under the circumstances I thought perhaps I could send one of my own people after him."

"Please do," Andrew said. There were other alphas he wouldn't trust to kick a lone out of their territory without antagonizing him, but not Benjamin. He could handle it. Better it not wait until Andrew returned, too. The lone might get settled in.

"Thank you." Andrew filled in a silent bow of Benjamin's head. "And how goes your own search?"

"Seattle's got something to hide, that's clear enough. Whether it's to do with Silver's monster remains to be seen." Andrew glowered at a point out on the blacktop. "I'm starting to think I should just go up there, permission be damned."

Benjamin made a neutral noise that Andrew nevertheless could tell meant he disagreed. Andrew waited him out, and he finally explained. "Do you have any evidence Were are in immediate danger? Otherwise, you'll have destroyed your chance of getting information from them for nothing. Your reputation is bad enough as it is."

Andrew growled. He'd thought as much himself. It still helped to have a second opinion, though. "No, if anything, it sounded from Portland like the rest of the pack were in on the effort to hide it, not frightened. I'll wait out the full polite interval."

Benjamin's chuckle held sympathy for Andrew's impatience. "Good luck."

After their good-byes, Andrew checked Silver in the rear-view mirror—still sleeping—tossed the phone on the passenger seat, and settled in to nap himself while he waited for Seattle's call. He hadn't gotten much sleep the night before, after all.

The cell phone jerked him from a tired floating rather than true sleep. SEATTLE, the screen said this time. Took him long enough. "Dare," he said into the phone, then muffled a yawn in his hand.

"Portland said you wanted a meeting." The male voice on the line was flat enough it took Andrew a minute to match it to his memory of Seattle from the last time he'd accompanied Rory to the North American alphas' yearly convocation. "Portland said," huh? All Andrew's messages must have slipped the man's mind.

"That's right. I'm looking for the pack that—"

"You have something to write down the address?" Seattle's voice stayed just as flat as he cut Andrew off. Andrew grunted his readiness, pen and an old gas receipt found, and Seattle rattled the address off almost too quickly to follow. He added an exit number off the final freeway and a couple turns and then hung up. Andrew was left to stare at the little message about how long the call had lasted. Michelle hadn't exaggerated.

Andrew twisted to look back at Silver. Still sleeping. "I hope for your sake he had nothing to do with what happened to you." Silver murmured in her sleep and turned over, tucking herself against the seat's back.

Andrew checked the car's clock as he started the engine, and frowned. He hadn't realized how late in the day it was getting. Tonight was true full, and no one would be at their most emotionally stable if he forced them to stay in human and discuss Silver. But if he stayed here and shifted, he'd end up hunting, and he couldn't hunt on their territory without them. Better he get there and get permission to hunt. There had been full moons he'd sweated through entirely in human before, just to prove he could, but he had been younger then. He felt no particular need to show off now.

He headed east from the urban area, to someplace called Issaquah. An Indian word, he supposed, like so many place names he'd seen on signs on the freeway. The foothills of the Cascade Range loomed high and green over the road, surface rounded by a blanket of trees.

The directions took him not to a housing development, as he had expected, but up increasingly steep and narrow winding roads. The only turns seemed to be blind driveways. He missed the one he needed at first, and had to travel quite a way to find a stretch of gravel shoulder wide enough for a U-turn.

Then, when he turned up the right driveway, a metal gate stopped him. Was this not the pack house, then? He couldn't see any buildings up in the trees. Perhaps it was private land they'd purchased for their hunting grounds. It would make a certain sort of sense to direct him out to those if they'd end up there anyway when everyone went out running for the full.

He got out of the car and took in the layered Were scents. Many people came in and out of here regularly. Hunting grounds, definitely. He found a couple more recent scents, but no one immediately in evidence. Andrew came around to the back of the car and opened the door, resting his arm on top as he looked in at Silver. She didn't stir. "Now we wait. More. Polite, aren't they?"

Footsteps crunched behind him, from downwind at the gate. Andrew shut the door and turned. He had to remind himself not to make it too quick. It might be a human. Broken beer bottles and an empty cigarette package littered the side of the gravel road, so kids clearly used the place.

A moment later, it was clear the man was a Were. Even without a scent, Andrew could tell by the way he moved. His dark hair was carefully styled, and his face had a fineness of line that made it pretty. But that prettiness was matched by a grace that suggested he'd be a strong opponent. "Looking for someone?" the man asked, with a parody of politeness.

"Seattle's a hard man to get hold of. Where is he?" Andrew watched the man. He was like a coiled spring, thoughts beneath the smiling exterior winding him up tight enough to snap. Something was definitely wrong here. What was a low-ranked Were doing meeting him? The alpha himself should be here. Especially if he had something to hide. He'd want to make sure his Were didn't let something slip.

Something snapped into focus suddenly for Andrew. What if Seattle had been coerced? It would explain why his manner had been off. Kill much of the pack, leaving only enough to keep contact to allay everyone's suspicions. If Silver hadn't escaped, the killer—or killers—might have been able to get away with it for quite a bit longer, until far-flung relatives started to question the lack of contact from the lower-ranked were.

Or worse, what if the alpha had been in on it? Andrew could hardly think that without a growl rising in his throat, but betrayal was part and parcel of their human blood. Wolves were never so inventively cruel or wasteful of life.

"He'll be here soon. I'm Pierce." The man didn't offer a

hand. Andrew wouldn't have taken it if he had. Whatever the alpha's state, this man was certainly not to be trusted.

"Dare. What's keeping him, then?" Andrew dug into his pocket to find the key fob and beeped the car locked. It wouldn't keep Silver safe from a determined Were, but it would at least give Andrew time to stop the man without a hostage thrown into the mix. Andrew circled to keep himself between Pierce and the car. Was this man alone? Had he taken out the pack on his own, or had he had help? If he was alone, Andrew would take him down immediately, but it might be better to retreat and get reinforcements. Andrew was good, but not enough for more than two-to-one odds.

Pierce craned his neck to look in the car window behind Andrew. "I thought I smelled—" He drew in a sharp breath, and the smell of shock then rage bloomed on him. "She is. She is alive. Lady." His next breath was deeper as he shoved the emotions down again. "So you brought her back? Ballsy of you. What, did you get tired of her?"

So he did recognize Silver. Was he pleased to find her alive, or just surprised? His scent was muddy with general aggression. Andrew watched Pierce tightly, but after that first burst of emotion, the man made no move that would telegraph the first blow in a fight, or pulling back to shift before true combat. He seemed content to talk. That wasn't good. He could be stalling for those reinforcements. "I suppose you were overjoyed I found your loose end for you."

"Inconvenient, isn't she?" the man sneered.

The need to kill the man rose up to choke Andrew, and he lunged. After that first poor blow, his composure returned as he found a fight's quiet mental space. But that first lunge left him open, and Pierce took advantage of it, hammering a blow into his jaw. Andrew had to retreat and begin again, circling, always moving to keep the other man off balance.

Pierce's problem was that he was used to fighting humans, with their slow reactions. Andrew had figured out long ago that beyond ritual combat in wolf form and beating up human morons in bars, few Were had the first clue about fighting on two legs. This guy was better than many, but he still lacked finesse and put too much power behind each blow.

Andrew felt an energy drain as the bruise on his jaw healed. He couldn't waste too much time. He needed to take the man down quickly. Pierce lost his patience and launched himself at Andrew, trying to grapple, and Andrew chose his moment. He grabbed behind the other man's head, slamming his knee up into Pierce's face at the same time.

Pierce made a keening noise, stumbling back and pressing fingers to his broken nose. If he didn't shove it back into place within moments, it would start healing that way and need to be rebroken later. "Butcher," he said thickly. "Where's your weapons now? How could you do it? Use silver on another Were?"

Andrew stopped halfway to Pierce and a planned blow to smash his head against something and knock him unconscious. What? What was the man talking about? It didn't ring false like a cheap distraction tactic.

Speaking of distractions, instinct screamed at him, and he started to turn—he shouldn't have gotten so caught up in the fight as to let Pierce turn him until his back was to the downwind direction—and something smashed into the back of his head.

Andrew managed to catch himself on his hands as he went down, but his vision blurred. "Took you guys long enough," Pierce whined. "Lady. That hurt. He might have killed me while you were fucking around."

Andrew didn't hear the reply because the weapon fell again in another blow to his head. Something cracked. He wasted a little time clinging to the wash of light and pain and voices above him, but the darkness won out in the end.

11

Andrew woke with difficulty from the strange, disjointed dreams that came from healing a concussion. He'd had ample experience with them, and they were just as hard to shake this time as he fought his way to consciousness. Rory would be furious he hadn't finished whatever job had gone wrong— only this wasn't just another enforcement job, he remembered. Silver's talk of Death seemed to have wormed its way into his unconsciousness, and he blinked away the illusion of lights like eyes in the darkness wherever he'd woken.

He tried to shove to his feet, but the cool metal bite of handcuffs held him to a wall by one wrist. He collapsed seated again and jerked the cuffs harder, trying to break them or whatever they were attached to. They rang against some metal ring, presumably set into the wall. False fireworks swam in the darkness when he moved his head too quickly in a last yank. His concussion wasn't done with him yet, but he had to get free and find Silver. His stomach clenched as he imagined what they could be doing to her right now.

No matter what he did, the handcuffs didn't give, however. Andrew leaned against the wall to save his strength. He checked his pockets with his free hand to find they'd taken his phone too. He'd have to tempt someone in close enough to get a hostage to force his release. He could only hope it was in time for Silver. The knowledge that he'd failed to protect her settled sourly in the pit of his stomach, joining the throb in his head and the ache in his now bruised wrist.

While he waited, he took stock. The stony scent of concrete was pervasive, but covered over with paneling and carpet. The faintest of gray lines marked windows on the other side of the room. His blindness spoke to how well the windows were covered—his night vision could do a lot with a little light, but he needed at least some. A daylight basement, then. Empty of anyone else for the moment.

He would have at least three opponents, he figured. Pierce had said "you guys." Was one the alpha? Or was the alpha another victim? No matter how Andrew tried to keep his mind on his plans, it circled back to Silver. What were they doing to her?

Steps on the floor above. Andrew sat up straighter and braced his back against the wall. Judging by the sounds, the door was across from him. He looked aside so as not to be blinded by the light as it opened. Someone flicked a switch and light flooded all around him, rendering the effort useless.

"You're sick." A man's voice, but not Pierce's scent. Andrew hadn't gotten a good sense of his two other attackers. This might be one of them, or it might be someone else. Then a bell rang in his memory, and Andrew squinted up as his eyes adjusted and the silhouette filled in with features. The alpha of Seattle looked much the same as Andrew remembered him from the last convocation. What the hell was the man's name? Andrew couldn't remember, as alphas so often went by their titles.

Andrew used the time as Seattle came down the stairs from the door to glance around the room. A broken-down couch took up the room's center. Utility shelves, one with a crappy TV on top, leaned against the walls at staggered intervals. Nothing much to use as a weapon should he get free.

"Where's Silver?" Andrew asked.

Seattle sneered. He was built along typical werewolf lines, but lankier in his muscle, rugged cowboy to Rory's linebacker. He still out-bulked Andrew. "We're civilized. We don't need to keep stocks of it around for torturing our enemies, much as the poetic justice of that appeals to me. Where's yours? I would have thought the Butcher would carry his arsenal with him."

Andrew growled. "The woman. I don't know what her real name is. She was too far gone to tell me."

"Selene." Seattle bent and grabbed Andrew's shirt, gathering up the fabric, ready to choke him. Andrew let the humiliation of this position coil into his muscles, ready to move in another moment. Seattle shook him. "Lady bless her mother's strange interest in human stories. Her name's Selene. Why did you do it? To her and the others?" His voice vibrated with intensity. "Did you think coming back here to dump her like trash and disguising it as concern would throw us off the scent? Make us discount you as a suspect?"

This was what Andrew had been waiting for, someone close enough to grapple, but Seattle's words stopped him. They thought he—? Andrew started to laugh, but it made him feel ill. "Not me. We found her, wandering. I came out to track the one who did it. Your version doesn't even make sense. Why would I bring her back?" He tried to focus on the alpha through the throb in his skull. "Why don't you tell me why your Were have started avoiding contact with surrounding packs. What are you trying to hide?"

Confusion broke through Seattle's anger. "The Bellingham pack, Dare. Selene belonged to the Bellingham pack. I don't know what you're talking about with avoiding contact, unless Michelle has been exaggerating again."

A Bellingham pack? Andrew had never heard of the city, never mind a pack there, and Rory wouldn't have hidden it from him. But the Western packs changed so quickly, who could keep track?

Something smelled fishy about the whole statement—perhaps Seattle knew Michelle had cause. But the man didn't smell as guilty as Andrew would have expected, confronted with a crime of this magnitude. The man should be able to smell the same thing on Andrew, but he seemed too caught up in his anger.

Seattle's grip tightened to the choking point as he simply

discarded the confusion. "What'd you keep her for? A plaything? And then you got tired of her? I suppose we should be grateful you didn't just cut her throat with silver."

Andrew tuned out the man's idiocy and let the burning in his lungs fan rage to life. Seattle would have to listen to reason if he pounded him flat. He launched himself at the other man.

Seattle straightened, stepped out of reach, and lashed out a kick to Andrew's stomach. Andrew doubled over, sucking air for several moments. Some of his ability to think logically returned with the oxygen. He needed to convince Seattle, not beat him up. The alpha had too much physical advantage at the moment. But if Seattle wouldn't take his word for what had happened, whose would he take? He doubted Seattle would entirely trust Rory even if Andrew convinced him to call the other alpha.

Voices from upstairs intruded. Andrew recognized the cadence of Silver's voice after a moment, if not the exact words. As she came closer, he caught the gist. "Where is he? Death says he's here. What did you do to him? No, I don't want to rest. I want to talk to him."

Someone slammed against the door at the top of the stairs—doorknobs were beyond Silver, Andrew suspected—then jiggled it open by accident. Silver stumbled through, a little unsteady. Her eyes widened with relief when she saw him.

"Death tells me you can usually take care of yourself," she said, brushing past the alpha, who was frozen in confusion again. She knelt beside Andrew, and slid her hands into his hair to feel the side of his head.

"Usually I can." Andrew growled at her when her fingers

found the lump. All his healing energy had been soaked up over the night by knitting his skull, so a bruise still remained. And it hurt like a bitch. Silver didn't pay any attention to his growl, and he let her fuss.

"Maybe you'll warn me next time you prod my snakes," she murmured. Andrew grimaced at the dig, but the alpha just looked even more confused. Andrew supposed Silver did make more sense on longer acquaintance.

"Stay away from him," Seattle said, teeth gritted. He strode forward and put a hand on Silver's shoulder, voice gentling to the point of patronization. "Come away. Come upstairs, and we'll get you something to eat, and you can rest. Please, Selene." He smoothed her hair off her shoulder like he would a child's.

Silver's face was turned away from the alpha, giving her a sense of privacy, but Andrew could see it perfectly. He watched it crumple like someone had raked claws into her guts and twisted.

"No." She whispered the first word, but was screaming by the next as she smashed his hand away. "No, that name's gone. Lost. She's dead. Her, and her family and everyone she knows and Death stole her name in all their voices and locked it away with them." The screaming pushed tears from the corners of her eyes. "Lost! Let her be lost!"

"Silver." She didn't hear him, so Andrew said it again, putting an alpha's whipcrack of authority into it. "Silver. Stop it." He took her with his free arm and pulled her against his chest. Seattle jerked forward but hesitated, maybe worried Andrew would hurt her if Seattle came for him.

Andrew held her close, not to comfort, but like squashing a wild creature. You controlled it until it felt the security to control itself again. Silver's breaths and heart were as fast as a frightened bird's, pounding against his skin. They slowed, gradually.

The alpha clenched and unclenched his hands. "I don't know what you've done to make her trust you, but it's not going to work. Sel—"

"Don't be stupid." Andrew tried to glare the other man down. He had to hold his temper. It was the full tonight, he could feel it. If he didn't control the emotions washing through him, he'd start to shift. Not a good idea with his arm restrained this way. "Forcing her to think about whatever happened makes her worse. Thinking about anything before then seems to have the same effect. Don't push it."

The alpha sneered at him, but didn't finish the name all the same. "Even if you're telling the truth about your involvement, she's no concern of yours any longer. You've brought her back to her birth pack, and now you can return to your territory."

Silver took a deep breath and drew sarcasm around herself as she pushed out of Andrew's hold and turned to Seattle. "It wasn't him. And good luck with getting him to leave just like that." She stood and explored the handcuffs with her fingers, treating them like something she could untie. "He's not one for doing things other people tell him." She growled in frustration, maybe over the metal having no knots.

The alpha raised his eyebrows at Andrew, making the question clear. Would Andrew leave?

"You're a help," Andrew told Silver, and then concentrated

on matching the alpha's stare. If only he wasn't held in the lower position. It made his blood boil. "I'm not leaving this coast until I catch whoever did this to Silver. But you can't keep me chained up down here."

"Well, if you won't give your word you'll leave, I don't have much choice."

Andrew barked a laugh. Don't shift, he reminded himself. Be amused at the man instead. "And then what? You can't keep me here forever. And it'll be pack war if you kill me unprovoked. You can't take Roanoke, even if you could convince Portland and one or two others to stand with you."

That hit a nerve. The alpha turned with werewolf quickness and yanked open the door to the stairs. "We'll see how you feel in the morning."

Andrew lunged to his arm's length without meaning to. "It's full tonight."

The man turned back with a nasty smile. "Oh, I'm sorry. I forgot." He went to a shelving unit along one wall, cheap particle board with a faux stain, and picked up a collar attached to a length of chain.

The reason for the ring set into the wall became abruptly clear. Most packs had a method to contain and isolate anyone who lost themselves in wolf form. Andrew readied himself to jam an elbow into the man's groin when the man got close enough, but the alpha slammed a hand into Andrew's throat to hold him against the wall before he could complete the movement. A couple of smooth clicks sounded as he locked the chain to the ring and snapped the collar around Andrew's neck before he could draw breath properly again.

Andrew tried to bring his arm up for a blow again, but the alpha laughed. "I can leave the handcuffs if you want." Andrew subsided, unable to keep himself from spitting curses, and the alpha unlocked them.

"Come on, Se— Silver." The alpha waited at the door for her, arm open to fold over her shoulders.

Silver regarded him expressionlessly. "No." She repeated it when he started to speak again. The alpha waited a moment in frustration, and then left. At least he didn't turn off the lights.

The bastard. Andrew was still coughing from the blow to his throat, but he had to test the strength of the ring and the concrete it was set in. He slid his fingers under the collar and lunged with all his weight.

The chain had no hint of give, that first time, or any of the dozen subsequent times. He couldn't stand it. He was barely able to pull off his clothes before the shift came over him, violent this time, yanking muscles to screaming pain.

He ended it panting on his side. Somehow, it was even worse now, instincts that couldn't bear being trapped now ascendant. He lunged, and lunged again until he could hardly breathe, and then snapped at the chain. Control. Wait. Stillness. Patience. Control, he told himself.

It didn't work.

12

Death howled to the Lady's round, heavy shape in the dark sky, and Silver watched the warrior's wild self thrash its way to the surface even as she prepared herself for the pain of Death's howling. Silver's muscles tensed, waiting to twist into her wild self. Before, when they couldn't twist, they burned.

But burning never came. The snakes were dead. The longing for the Lady's touch hurt, but it was no longer a pain of the body, only another ache like her grief for her brother and all the others. She curled up on the ground and let her muscles relax. If she was not to lose herself in the pain, perhaps it was time to take stock and figure out what to do next.

Her mother's pack were idiots. They meant well, but it was like being smothered in honey, thick and cloying. They were so sure they knew what was going on. They couldn't be more wrong. The warrior was the one whose assistance had allowed her to stop running. The one who had killed the snakes. And now they'd restrained him, the same way she'd been—

Her thoughts skittered away from that memory like a rabbit from her wild self's jaws. She had more pressing problems here and now. The warrior was hurting himself. She hadn't heard it properly at first, she'd been so caught up in waiting for the burning to begin. He had let his wild self out because it was the wild self that wanted most to be free, only now it was free to be the one restrained. He was trying to make himself hurt so much he could stop fighting, Silver supposed.

"No," she told him. Simple, so his wild self would understand. He snapped at her hand. She caught his jaws anyway, holding them shut. She held him that way for a moment and then let go to smack him on the nose. "Stop it. Follow your own advice."

He looked at her, eyes wide and accusing. It made her laugh. "Lady above, you're a liar. That didn't hurt." She smacked him again to prove it. He whuffed in protest. Silver kept laughing, helpless laughter until suddenly it was tears and she didn't understand why.

"He came here because of you," Death said, in her brother's voice. He'd found a rabbit somewhere and was gnawing on the entrails. "It's your fault he's tied up."

"I know," Silver said, and it made the warrior look confused, since he couldn't see Death. She drew in a shuddering breath. Oh, the grief ached. But her brother was gone, and the warrior was here now. "I'm trying. I'll try to help you hunt your prey."

The warrior dismissed that by shaking his steely gray

head. He turned to his bindings again, snapping at them. Clouds drifted away from the Lady's face, and Death looked up. He raised his muzzle to howl to Her once more. Even knowing it would be different, Silver went just as tense from fear.

No. She refused to make it happen anyway by tensing in expectation. She needed to distract herself.

"Idiot. You're all over burrs—" Silver reached out to pluck at the warrior's ruff. There was nothing there, but it distracted him too. He shook his ruff as if to dislodge invisible stickers, playing along. Perhaps he was grateful for the pretense.

She drew her hands through the fur, reveling in the sensation. Just there, the nap was different, over his shoulder blade, and then thinner and softer on his underbelly. His muscles tensed like he was getting ready to pull away, but any wild self could eventually be undone with scratching in just the right spot. Finally he sighed, and relaxed beneath her hands.

Andrew didn't mind being used for a pillow—he fondly remembered doggy piles for naps from back when he actually belonged to a pack—but there was something ignominious about being petted in someone's sleep. Silver was light, no burden at all, but clutched like this, he felt like a child's stuffed toy. But he'd seen her begin a seizure caused by her inability to shift only to pull herself back from the edge out of that odd concern for him. He'd endured enough humiliation already at Seattle's hands; he could sacrifice a final shred of dignity to keep her safe in this.

Silver murmured something in her sleep and petted his shoulder again. How long had it been since he'd curled up with someone like this, without sex beforehand? That was the closest he'd gotten to the intimacy of a pack doggy pile in a long time. No question of naps with the Roanoke pack.

So that would mean the last time had been in Spain—no. That wasn't something he chose to remember.

He growled and wiggled out from under her. Time to be human again. He didn't want the alpha seeing him in the defenseless, personal moments of shifting. And he didn't want to give Seattle a power bonus as the only one able to speak.

Silver reached out as if trying to pull him back again, but then subsided. The collar made dressing awkward, and he discovered he'd popped off a button last night in his hurry to undress. When he finished, Andrew scrubbed at his rough jaw. Unwashed, unshaved, and yesterday's clothes. Damn, he wanted a shower.

"Are you feeling better?" Silver asked, blinking her eyes a few times to clear away sleep. She propped herself up with her good arm to look at him.

Andrew had to smile. That was his line. His concussion was long gone, but Silver didn't seem to realize the irony of the injured party inquiring after the healthy one's state. "Are you?"

Silver wrinkled her nose and didn't answer. She levered herself upright. Andrew motioned her closer and waited this time for her to give him her arm. He alternated watching her face for pain with examining it. She winced once, but otherwise seemed unaffected as he moved it this way and that. No new blood had soaked through the bandages.

"As soon as Seattle comes to his senses, I'll be going to where it happened," he said, laying Silver's arm back against her chest. "I assume they know where, and aren't just inventing a crime scene whole cloth from some mysterious disappearances." He paused a beat. "There's no reason for you to come."

"No," Silver said. "I don't think I should."

Andrew let out a relieved breath and looked into her eyes. There did seem to be more sense there than before he'd drained some of the silver from her blood.

Footsteps on the stairs, and they both looked up. The night's sleep had knocked the alpha's name loose. John. Denied other options by being chained up, Andrew supposed he was down to the stupidest of dominance games, so he pretended that John was too unimportant to bother cutting short his conversation with Silver.

"Do you trust them? I could take you anywhere you wanted to go, if you'd rather not stay here," Andrew said. Games aside, this was important. He didn't want Silver stuck here if she wasn't completely comfortable with it.

"My mother belonged to this pack, before she died. They'll take care of me. Even if they're supremely misguided." Silver didn't ignore John, turning instead to give him a glare as he came down the stairs.

"And your father? Was he not part of Seattle? Would you want to go to him and his pack instead?"

Silver laughed and turned back. "He roams. I don't know where he is or even how many children he has. We have no ties."

Seen from the corner of Andrew's eye, John's expression was getting thunderous, so Andrew stood, chain rattling. The tension between the two men instantly tilted a little more equal, and Andrew relaxed a little. That was better. He was no longer the captive chained to the floor. "So?"

John ran a hand through his hair, dislodging a pine needle. Someone had been rolling in the dirt last night. It annoyed Andrew afresh to think of John running free. But some of the alpha's confidence from the night before had gone. "Sel— Silver seemed to think enough of you I called Roanoke this morning."

Andrew's lips quirked. The man's ears were probably still ringing. Rory tended not to remember in the heat of the moment that he couldn't reach out through the phone and strangle someone. "And how is Rory?"

"Apparently you were both in Ottawa when it happened. And Ottawa vouches for you, not just Roanoke."

The man didn't sound entirely convinced, so Andrew said what he already knew John was thinking. "Unless I hopped a plane. But I do fail to see how I could be gone for something like twenty hours round trip and still have time to do"— Andrew glanced at Silver—"whatever was done. Which, I might remind you, I still have no idea about. I'd be touched if you'd share." John bristled at the tone, but his eyes went to Silver too.

"I'm hungry," Silver announced. She pointed to Andrew.

"And he is too, even though he's too proud to say. C'mon, Death." The last was directed at the air beside her. She headed to the stairs.

The men stood in silence without her for a while. John finally came forward, taking a key from his pocket. "Don't try anything."

"That would be stupid." But tempting, Andrew had to admit. They could see how the alpha liked being chained up. He lifted his chin and stayed perfectly still as John fitted the key into the padlock. He rubbed at his neck once the collar fell away. John offered Andrew's phone silently and Andrew slotted it into its holster.

"You want something to eat too?" The offer was so grudging, Andrew was surprised it didn't stick in the man's throat on the way out.

Silver had been correct, in both respects. Andrew wasn't going to admit he needed anything from this man. "We can wait for her to finish." Andrew nodded upstairs. It was clear enough Silver meant them to talk now when she wasn't around to be hurt by the memories.

Now he was free, he took a look around. Besides the couch and shelves he'd noticed the night before, an amorphous mass of blankets and pillows, thoroughly coated with hair, took up the other corner. If not for Andrew's presence, the pack would undoubtedly have slept down here in wolf form last night. Andrew eyed the couch, but stayed standing.

John made no move to sit down either. He leaned on his hands on the couch back. "The Bellingham pack splintered off five or six years ago, when my uncle was still alpha. Selene's brother was the pack's alpha, she was the beta, and they took about a dozen other young were. We kept in pretty close contact, until four months ago when they went quiet. We waited a little and then went up to investigate." John paused, struggling with the words. "They were all at the alpha's house. It was—like a horror movie. All of them tied up with silver, and then one by one—" A growl rose in his throat. "We found all the bodies but Selene's, but her trail petered out—we assumed she'd died somewhere else, after escaping."

"Selene was the only one missing?" Andrew wished he dared ask if any of the Seattle pack had been coincidentally not around at the time. Someone the Bellingham pack trusted would have had an easier time getting the jump on them, but now was not the time to risk Seattle's anger that way. He could find out later on his own.

"Yes." John shoved himself away from the couch, and started pacing. "You think we haven't investigated this? We combed the woods for trails for weeks. We found gallons of scattered bleach, a few small brush fires. No scent trail left. The house was more bleach and blood. A lot of blood, none of it a stranger's." John slammed his hand into the wall. The paneling cracked, but the concrete beneath didn't care. Bruises appeared across his knuckles and slid through the colors of healing before fading out.

"Why didn't you tell Roanoke?" Andrew flexed his hand against his opposite palm. Hitting things would be a lovely idea, but he was running low on resources to heal another injury if he didn't eat soon.

John snarled. "What business is this of Roanoke's?"

"What business is this of any of us? What if he'd gone to Portland next? They had no idea when I talked to them that they might even be in danger. Or Billings? Or Sacramento?" Andrew didn't give a damn what the Western packs wanted to do with themselves, but he hadn't realized any had gotten to this level of isolationism.

"He was our problem. If we'd caught him—"

"But you didn't." Andrew put a whipcrack into his words, one alpha-powerful Were to another. "You didn't even fucking find Silver. A smart man knows when to call in *help*."

"Meaning you?" John's lips twisted into a sneer.

"Me. Or the next pack over. Or Roanoke, because whatever else you say about us, we can get a network of people looking within hours, without fucking around with people who don't feel like answering our calls."

John made a grudging noise, wanting to agree without losing face. Andrew reluctantly allowed him that and changed the subject. "Silver said she'd stay here while you take me up to see the scene."

"Yeah." John turned to go, leading the way up to the main floor. "We brought your car. So you can get your stuff and change." He sniffed pointedly.

Andrew suppressed a snarl. Obviously, it was his own fault he'd been chained up all night without access to a shower. "But these clothes were just getting properly broken in."

The rest of the pack wasn't in evidence when Andrew left the bathroom, washed and dressed. He couldn't even count them by scent, as the house had been aggressively treated with scent-disguising cleaning products sometime in the last few days. Probably just before he'd been brought back here. The products made his sinuses ache. Clearly, John didn't want him smelling the pack's metaphorical dirty laundry, which made Andrew even more determined to find it. He still hadn't figured out what had caused the pack's behavior toward Portland. He lingered in the hall outside the bathroom as long as he could, and finally caught a whiff of a human woman. Worn in, not ephemeral, so she'd been around quite a lot.

Someone's fuck buddy, he suspected. He could understand the appeal in an abstract sense—he'd had his one-night stands—but he'd never seen the point of starting a relationship guaranteed to end sooner rather than later.

Dishes were piled high in the sink when he entered the kitchen. A couple days' newspapers lay scattered over the kitchen table under the coffee cups. The pretty boy—Pierce—slathered cream cheese on another bagel for Silver as ham slices sizzled in the frying pan. She already had a plate piled high enough to feed three werewolves on the bar counter before her, and she gave Pierce an exasperated look as he set the bagel down next to the mountain of food. Pierce didn't seem to notice. He glanced at Andrew and pointedly rubbed his nose, which was a little bit crooked now, spoiling the pretty line. Served him right. Andrew ignored Pierce and kept conversation with John to a minimum out of consideration for Silver.

"Leave her with Yuri if you're going to work," John directed Pierce when he and Andrew had finished bolting their own ham. "We're heading north."

They took John's truck, a workhorse of a Ford. They maintained silence for most of the drive. John seemed to think that a lot would be self-evident once they got to the scene. That, or he was too squeamish to talk about it. Watching the man's set face in profile, Andrew doubted it was the latter.

It was a comparatively short drive. Just a little over an hour until John turned off the main freeway onto a small state highway. Tight hilly curves flanked the road, though the land had more denuded logged patches than on the way to the pack's hunting grounds. This was the humans' world, if it so happened he had forgotten.

"Why'd they split off?" Andrew asked at length, staring out the window. "This is awfully close to you."

John snorted, eyes tight on the road. "Their mother only accepted my uncle's authority as alpha because she liked him personally. Selene, Ares—either of them could have run a pack on their own easily enough. They could work with each other, but not with my uncle, or me. Too many strong wills."

Andrew choked. "Ares? You're kidding me."

John managed a noise almost like a laugh. "I think Selene's grandmother wanted to name them after the Colonists. Very traditional. Selene's mother went too far the other way."

Andrew smiled, remembering Ginnie and her obsession with Virginia Dare. Silence settled around them again.

When they arrived, the house was nothing much to look at. One story, set back in the trees on a fairly large property, a child's bike leaning against the picnic table in the front yard. John checked the mailbox and cleared some advertising flyers that had been stuffed half under the door.

"We only cleaned up the outside," he explained. "And gave the pack the proper rites. Took some fast talking, convincing their employers and the school that they'd moved back East suddenly to take care of ailing relatives. Haven't decided what to do about the house. Power's cut off, but nothing else to make the authorities come sniffing around yet."

"Well, she's never going to live here again, is she? You could help Silver sell it once we catch the guy."

John didn't pause to unlock the door, just yanked it open and shattered the wood frame. "You'll see," he snarled. "You're welcome to try to clean it up if you want." He gestured Andrew inside with a bow, tension twanging across every visible muscle.

The front room was dusty, filled with the detritus of young adults living together, though there were a few toys, small plastic people scattered around their house. A big TV, a video-game guitar on the couch.

The smell of dried blood came from the kitchen. Seven mismatched chairs stood inside, some from the kitchen set and some from other rooms. There wouldn't have been room for them, but the kitchen table was on its side against the wall, three legs broken away.

One chair was in pride of place, the other standing ones watching it. Several more were tipped over. They all had silver chains wrapped around their arms or back slats. Those who had removed the bodies hadn't done more than get the silver out of their way.

Andrew was no forensic expert to find weapon and injury signatures in the Rorschach patches of dry brown spray on the walls and dripped puddles on the floor. So much blood, splash layered over splash. It all blurred together in his mind.

The kitchen counter finally broke through the numb haze he'd retreated into. He'd seen the blood that remained on the walls after a challenge fight to the death. He'd seen a punishment in a European pack, silver used to bind Were, or placed against their skin for a length of time commensurate with their crime.

He'd never seen so much silver as he saw jumbled on the counter. Knives. Needles, like those used for body piercing. The worst was the jewelry, like a woman's bracelet, one side of the C-curve stained brown as if it had been used for gouging. Necklaces were tangled in knots or laid out like garrotes. To the side, a crucifix, clean and untouched. Being near so much silver was like standing in front of an open oven with the killing heat on your skin, waiting for the stumble or push. Then you'd sizzle and scream.

Andrew retched, controlling himself before more than a mouthful of liquid reached the floor. The acid smell seemed small next to the fear and horror that had soaked into the walls. No wonder Silver had refused to sit on the kitchen chair in the Roanoke house. "What was it like when you arrived?"

"We found them too late to be able to tell much from the bodies. The adults were all tied—" John stood among the chairs and swept his hand to them. "The kids were a mercy, one strike, no torture. Over at the side of the room." He took a stride in that direction. "The others were injected, like her." John held fingers around an invisible hypodermic to his own elbow. "Then tortured. Or maybe the other way around."

Andrew slammed a flat palm into the counter. A tile cracked and a silver knife wobbled and came to rest pointing at a different angle. "This is beyond territorial sovereignty. *You should have swallowed your Lady-fucking pride and called for help.*" It was hard to get the words past the rage vibrating in his chest. "From anyone. Everyone."

John flushed with anger of his own, but something about the curse made him hesitate before speaking. It didn't keep him from speaking at all, unfortunately. "Thought you were familiar with this kind of thing."

Andrew crossed to John in two strides, and clenched a hand around the other man's throat. "Not this. And even if I was, all the more reason to stop the poison here before it begins. The Europeans have always delighted in killing each other. No reason for us to follow in their footsteps." He met the other man's eyes and shoved the two of them into a full challenge, gazes locked together until someone's strength won.

John choked, but didn't fight, putting all his energy into the nonphysical struggle. Andrew hardly registered the effort. Not here. Not like in Spain, where so many were dead because each pack looked only to their own. Not again.

Then John broke, turning his head aside. Andrew opened his hand, and Seattle fell to his knees, coughing. "Why aren't you alpha of Roanoke, Dare?"

Andrew started opening drawers, collecting dish towels. "Don't want the job." He wrapped one around his hand, and laid another several flat, loading the silver onto them piece by piece. When he was finished, he folded it up into a neat package. Maybe the silver could tell them something about the man who'd used it, but Andrew would also be delighted to show it to anyone else who doubted the situation's seriousness.

"I'm checking the rest of the house." He left the silver on the counter and stalked down the hall to the bedrooms. They were dusty too, left in a state of life interrupted, covers rumpled and dirty clothes in the hamper.

The house smelled like the ghost of people. Happy people. People and the tang of bleach, then dust and disuse settling in a layer over all. Here and there someone's scent seemed familiar to Andrew, but he couldn't pinpoint it under everything else, even to tell male from female. A faint trace of what Silver had used to smell like, maybe. Selene.

"There was nothing outside?" Andrew came back, and asked the question of John's back as the man looked out the kitchen window. The garden visible beyond was overgrown with weeds. "Nothing else you can remember seeing?"

"No. Things were almost too normal when we got here. The bleach and the blood, but nothing disturbed, other than in the kitchen."

Andrew grabbed the bundle of silver and turned to the front door, hurrying suddenly. He needed to breathe fresh air. He could trust John's word about the rest. John's footsteps followed closely.

"What now?" John asked as he opened the door to his truck. He kept his head down and avoided Andrew's eyes now, the failed challenge hulking between them like a third party in the conversation.

It struck Andrew that the man was glad to drop the

responsibility on someone else's shoulders. Andrew slammed the door behind himself harder than necessary. Coward. "We spread the word. He won't be able to take anyone else off guard that way." He gave John a grin with too many teeth. "You get to canvass the Western packs, see who knows of lones who have gone missing over the last few years, ones who could have been other victims. I doubt this came from no-where, and they'll be more likely to talk to you than to me."

John turned the key and the truck roared to life. "You have a certain charisma of your own." The delivery was desert-dry, but a seriousness lurked under it that Andrew couldn't understand. Anyone could throw authority around. Andrew was no different.

13

Death began to use a new voice while the warrior was gone. It was no one Silver knew, nor anyone she felt she'd once known and forgotten. It wasn't the man's voice from centuries ago that Death used most often as his own.

It was a woman's voice. "So what do you think? Will he run like you did, *mi loba pequeña*?" Her accent was musical.

"She's not one of my voices," Silver said, ignoring the question and the words she didn't understand. The set to Death's ears, pricked forward to follow her, was jaunty to match the new voice.

"*Sí.*" Death laughed the woman's laugh. "I am one of his. Will you do me a favor? Ask him if he remembers me."

Silver threw a pinecone at Death's head. He ducked, avoiding it easily, though he looked insulted. "The warrior has no need for me to taunt him on your behalf, Death. Haunt him with his loved ones' voices yourself."

Death laughed, back to the deeper tones of the man's voice he used the most. "So you protect him now? He doesn't need your protection, Silver."

"And I don't need his. But he offered, and I accepted. That's what living people do." She threw another pinecone at his flank, missing by an even greater margin now that he was expecting it. "Why are you still here, anyway? The snakes are dead. You cannot rouse them. Your easy kill has escaped. Go and chase another."

Death settled back onto his haunches, going nowhere. "He's back. You should go answer his questions."

The warrior's steps crunched on the blanket of dry needles, then, heavier than necessary so that she did not react to sounds of attempted stealth. Silver stood and ran a hand through her unruly hair, tucking it behind her ears.

She could see written all over his face the memories it took all her strength not to remember—or was it that it took more strength than she had *to* remember? But not pity. It helped her keep her chin up and not run and hide from the memories, that she saw only understanding. The alpha of her mother's pack pitied her. It was choking.

"So," she said. "Were you impressed?"

The alpha's face creased with discomfort, and his blocky wild self paced beside him, a few steps and then back. "Sel—"

Silver's growl cut him off. It was bad enough the man held a key to unlock her memories, but he stabbed it carelessly into her gut with every other sentence.

The warrior regarded her steadily. "I can't think of anyone else I've ever known who could have survived that. Even myself."

Death prowled behind the warrior's legs, shouldering the man's unresisting wild self aside. "He's right." The woman's voice again, making the words strange and singsong. Death prowled back the other direction. "I think he likes you."

Silver stared at Death. She knew the others didn't like it when she acknowledged how close Death was—she could hardly blame them—but his words made no sense. The warrior didn't think of her that way, did he? "What?" But Death just smirked, and settled down, black legs long out in front. "I'm sorry," she said, bringing her eyes back up to the warrior. "Death is trying to provoke me with words now he can no longer reach me any other way."

Andrew knew he'd been around Silver for too long when he guessed where her eyes would go to find Death before she even spoke to him. Something about her body language telegraphed the presence of someone she considered to be there.

"But if I'm going to track your monster, I'm still going to need something, Silver. Anything. What was his name? Where did he come from?"

She gave him a look tinged with dry humor. "I've lost my own name. What makes you think I can remember his?" She shivered and the sense of a frightened creature hiding its bleeding to discourage the predators came back into her body.

Andrew clenched his hands together until the knuckles popped and began to ache. Was finding this man sooner worth destroying the only survivor?

He turned away to allow her space. She'd set up in the basement while he was away—he couldn't help but eye the ring on the wall every few seconds, judging John's position relative to it and him. But she seemed to feel more secure down here, returning to a cup formed in borrowed blankets on the couch where she had been curled up earlier.

John tilted his head to the stairs, probably suggesting a conference upstairs now they'd failed to get anything more from Silver. Andrew nodded and took a step to follow Seattle when his phone rang.

"It's Rory," Andrew told John and waited with his cell in his hand until the other man got the hint and left him to the basement's comparative privacy. John's footsteps retreated far enough that there seemed a reasonable chance he wasn't listening in.

"What the hell are you doing out there, Dare?" Rory didn't even bother with a greeting. "I get Seattle crawling up my fucking ass about something you were supposed to have done months ago—"

"I thought you liked my exaggerated reputation. You can't complain when I become the easiest target for anything that happens anywhere in the country." Andrew made his voice sharp, to cut through Rory's bluster. He wasn't in the mood tonight to allow the other man to wear himself out naturally.

"So what in the Lady's name is going on?"

Andrew glanced at Silver, but it was hard to tell if she was listening, or off in her own world again. He supposed he'd have to risk it. "A few months ago, Silver's monster somehow got to a splinter of the Seattle pack that had set up in Bellingham. He restrained the whole pack and tortured them with silver. Inventively." Andrew gave the last word a brutal twist, and was rewarded with a wordless exclamation from Rory. "Then he injected all of them too."

"After." Silver's voice wavered. "He hurt them after. He was angry they weren't strong enough. Weren't strong enough for the fire he poured in their veins and they died. One by one, and after each he—" She was on the floor, curled around her injured arm, and now her lips parted like she was trying to scream without a voice.

"Dammit," Andrew hissed under his breath, going to his knees beside her. He kept the phone to his ear with one hand, and used the other to awkwardly maneuver her against his chest in the same tightly pressed position he'd used on her before.

"I don't understand. I'm not strong like they were," Silver murmured against his chest, and then fell silent, just trembling.

"I need you back here, Dare. If someone like that is on the loose." Rory's voice was controlled, but Andrew suspected he smelled of fear. What a coward.

"I'll keep you and the pack safer by catching the pussy. The way I catch him is I follow his trail out here rather than try to protect everyone in Roanoke at once out there. Your faith in

my abilities is flattering, but that's far beyond one Were."
Andrew suppressed as much of the bite he wanted to put into
his words as he could.

"You have a trail to follow there, then?"

Andrew drew in a slow breath to stall. He could lie over
the phone without Rory smelling it, but the man was still his
alpha, however cowardly. "At least there's the chance of picking it up again. There would be no chance of that back there."

"And by that you mean you don't have anything. No. Leave
the girl there or put her out of her misery and come back
here." The order was phrased too directly for Andrew to
wiggle out of it. If he disobeyed it, that was it, he'd be out of
Roanoke.

Andrew swallowed his rage, trying to think. "Roanoke.
Don't force this choice on me." There was no way he could go
back. Rory was even more guilty of burying his nose in the
sand than Andrew had just accused John of being. To a certain degree, individual packs could afford to look only to
their own safety, but Rory's territory was half the human
country. He had a greater responsibility to show the Western
packs you couldn't stand idly by while a threat worked its way
through fellow Were just because it hadn't reached you yet.

"I won't say it twice," Rory snapped, his fear lending fuel
to the rage in his voice.

And if Andrew went lone over this, what then? Roanoke
hadn't been a real pack for him, but it had been better than
the crushing loneliness of living completely packless. He'd
tried that. The eastern half of North America would be closed
to him, and he doubted the Western packs would allow him

on their territories. Not when the "Butcher of Barcelona" was no longer controlled by an alpha. But he saw no other choice.

"You'd have been strong in my place," Silver murmured, and pushed away. It took a moment for Andrew to make the connection to her previous words. She must have tuned out the conversation in between, though she seemed to have picked up on his anger. She granted him the space to move by curling back up on her blankets.

"I'm afraid I'm going to have to refuse that offer, Roanoke. Find yourself another enforcer." Andrew ended the call, and turned the phone off so he wouldn't have to take any further calls from Rory. His hands shook from the effort of not smashing it into the wall. He compromised by throwing it into the couch.

It took only a couple paces to reach the other wall, then Andrew turned violently and went back. Damn Rory for putting him in this position. Damn Silver's attacker to the deepest oblivion for even existing. Where would he go when this was all over?

Andrew's muscles tightened with the beginnings of a shift, and he jerked his thoughts to a stop. He was going to find the monster. Anything else could come after. And the first step to tracking the bastard was to go upstairs and pretend this conversation never happened, so Seattle didn't evict him from his territory now he'd lost his patina of legitimacy.

Silver roused herself when he put his foot on the bottom stair. "Are you—?"

"I'll be fine. You'll want to stay down here; John and I are going to discuss things you don't want to think about."

Silver nodded, and subsided back into her curl. Andrew took a deep breath to try to control his emotions, and headed upstairs.

He found John in the dining room, the dish towel–wrapped bundle on the center of the long, solidly built table. All the adjoining rooms were empty, as if everyone but John had scattered to a safe distance from a ticking bomb. The stench of bloody silver was more psychologically overpowering than literally present, but Andrew felt it too. With any luck, it would help camouflage his scent from John.

"Everything all right at home?" John asked.

"Fine," Andrew said. "He was just checking on my progress." John frowned at him, and Andrew's heart sped a little. He concentrated on his revulsion at smelling the silver to hide the scent of the lie. It seemed to work, as John looked away again after a moment.

"I've been thinking." John pulled on one leather glove and folded the top layer of fabric away to expose the crucifix on the top of the pile of silver implements. "That's a human symbol. Wasn't it monks that were supposed to have experimented with injecting silver, a couple centuries ago?"

Andrew used a corner of the towel to turn the crucifix over. "A couple centuries ago in Europe, sure. But you know as well as I do the Catholic Church doesn't go in for that sort of thing anymore." The crucifix wasn't particularly well made, probably available at dozens of Catholic stores.

"But you know human crackpots. Any one of them could have followed in their footsteps. They could have even researched old records." John used his gloved fingertips to stir the other silver objects, but nothing else seemed distinctive either.

Andrew called up the scene in the Bellingham house in his mind again. "Can you imagine how many humans it would have taken to overpower a whole pack? But they weren't overpowered. You said nothing was disturbed. Human or Were, there had to be some reason the pack didn't see it coming."

John drew his hand away from the silver. "If it was a Were, someone they knew, they'd have let him into the house."

"More than that, there had to be a reason they didn't fight him. If only she could tell us." Rage boiled up in Andrew again, and he swept the pile of silver off the table to clatter to the floor. One butter knife made a dent in the opposite wall. If it *had* been someone Silver had trusted, someone she knew . . .

John winced. "Maybe she'll be able to, given time." He came forward to clap a hand on Andrew's shoulder, and Andrew realized his reaction must seem out of proportion to anyone who didn't know about the other worries bubbling at the back of his mind.

"It means we don't have to go chasing a gang of humans, at least." Andrew drew in a calming breath, and snagged the extra glove to pick up the silver. All this could go out with the trash. "Narrows down the possibilities."

"Not by much. Say it was a Were they knew. We found everyone in the pack in the house except Silver. I can't think of any other friends of theirs that have gone missing lately."

Andrew set the silver on the table and straightened. He owed it to John to look him in the eye when he said this. "Someone wouldn't necessarily have gone missing. Someone could have helped the man Silver talks about who did the actual deed. Or the man could have just cleaned himself up and gone home. Someone that unbalanced, he wouldn't smell of guilt. I thought of it when I first got out here, and it still fits."

Suspicion flickered into John's face. "What are you implying?"

"Could be one of yours helped," Andrew said, letting the stark words fall into painful silence.

"No." John growled the syllable, straightening his shoulders so their muscled bulk was even more obvious. "Impossible."

Andrew took a step back. "Or maybe one of them knows something about him passing through. Something they wouldn't admit to their alpha for fear of punishment. The killer had no reason to travel directly to Bellingham by human means. It's just another random human city unless you know a pack is based there, which you seem to think no one did but you. So unless it is one of your pack, he must have traveled through somewhere. It's unlikely he came through Alaska, or he'd be hamburger by now, not walking around killing packs. I'll talk to the members of the other packs one by one if necessary. I'm just starting at the closest."

"No." John got up in Andrew's face as he growled it this time. His scent soured with fear. Fear of what Andrew might find out? "I'm not letting you treat my people like criminals because you can't think beyond your enforcer habits. Track the killer however you like, and I'll help, but leave my people alone." John turned and stalked from the room.

Andrew stared at the pile of silver on the table, eyes unfocused. That could have gone better. It might be time for a strategic retreat. There was no way he wanted to stay the night here anyway. He should find a hotel.

When he raised the possibility that one of John's pack was involved, he'd just been following the train of logic. Now the idea started to chew at him, especially given the way John had smelled. He couldn't leave Silver here if someone in the pack had been involved in her torture. It would be much safer if he took her with him.

Andrew took the long way around the circular path through the ground-floor rooms to avoid encountering John on his way back to the basement door. Silver's head came up at his footstep on the top stair. "Come on, we're going somewhere else for the night."

"Good." Silver uncurled smoothly and joined him at the top of the stairs.

They reached the entryway before John arrived, face thunderous once more. "What in the Lady's name do you think you're doing?" Pierce thudded down the stairs to back up his alpha a moment later.

Andrew glanced back at Silver to stall before answering. Her face looked set and he couldn't smell anything more specific than frustration. He returned his attention reluctantly to John. The whole point of a strategic retreat was to retreat, not begin a fight about a different subject. He couldn't just let this go, though. Silver needed to be safe. "We're going to a hotel."

"She's not." John moved to take Silver's arm and she

backed up into Andrew's chest. He gritted his teeth and tried not to touch her. They needed to keep this from turning into a physical fight, especially with Silver in the middle. He wished she'd let him talk his way out of this first. Somehow. What to say would occur to him any minute now.

"And if I decide to leave, what will you do to stop me? Will you tie me up? Chain me up?" Silver gave the last question a vicious twist. John and Pierce flinched. Even Andrew's stomach lurched. Apparently Silver could take care of herself quite well without his arguing her case.

John stepped silently out of the way, face drawn and arm outstretched to herd Pierce to do the same. "Why him?" he asked softly when they were on the threshold. "We can take care of you—Silver."

"Why?" Silver didn't bother to turn around. "Because he doesn't look at me and see only someone I'll never be again." She strode for the car, leaving John and any other questions he might have behind. Andrew walked through the lingering frustration of her scent as he followed. Having seen the pack's attitude, he couldn't blame her for her reaction. Yet another reason to get her away from them for a while.

14

Silver was glad when she and the warrior finally managed to leave her mother's pack's den. It cleared her mind to breathe in air untainted by memories of what she once was. Worry for the warrior pulled her farther from the mire of her memories. The mist had pulled close in on her, but she'd still heard the argument he'd had with his alpha. Something had happened, and now he smelled of desperation and the stress of a wolf who didn't know his place in the hierarchy.

She watched him secretly as he ran, looking for a place safe enough for them to stay the night. She kept waiting for Death to crow that it was her fault, her fault that the warrior had been taken from his life and forced away from his pack. But Death just ran with them, tongue lolling. He must think Silver was blaming herself quite well without him.

When they reached a clearing and stopped running, Silver

lingered beside the warrior where he stared into the trees without seeing. "Why did you follow your alpha for even this long?"

"What's that supposed to mean?" The warrior kept his teeth covered when speaking to her as he had the whole trip, but his voice still snapped.

"You could have been an alpha—his alpha—long since, except that you won't fight for it. You're strong enough to hold a position even as a lone, except you don't seem to want to be alone." Silver stepped around him so she could see his face better. He was still too much in control for what she had planned. The impulse to hit her for implying he was weak barely danced behind his eyes.

Silver met his eyes. "Are you a coward? Did you follow his authority because it's easiest? Do you want to crawl back to doing it now, or are you going to stand on your own and get something done?"

That provoked him into movement and the next moment he was nearly nose to nose with her. His hand was tight and heavy and warm on the back of her neck, keeping her looking at him. He needn't have bothered. She wasn't going anywhere. This was what Silver had been trying to get him to do. She wanted the coming dominance challenge. She let him feel in her muscles that his strength didn't frighten her.

"You don't even understand—" His next words slipped by her while she watched the interplay of expressions on his face. "Why are you lecturing me on pack hierarchy?"

"Because you're off balance. It's tiring to watch you. And what you seem ready to do will only make it worse." Silver reached back to put her good hand on his, more gently. "I can't help but think I'm not helping that. I can take care of myself. You don't have to do any of this." It hurt to say, hurt to consider facing the monster alone again, but it was true. The warrior owed her nothing.

"Take care of yourself. Ha." With the two of them standing so close, his scent filling her lungs with every breath, it was only a surprise that the spark of a dominance struggle waited so long before flaring to life.

She'd always suspected he could have been an alpha, but knowing it and feeling it were two different things. That kind of strength had a visceral beauty all its own. This was a man who knew himself, even if that knowledge was buried somewhere for the moment.

"Well spotted," Death said, breaking the moment. Silver jumped and the warrior broke the stare. Death sat back on his haunches and looked up at the warrior's face. "She's feisty, Dare. Are you sure you want her?"

"Go away," Silver told Death. The warrior laughed a startled laugh. Whether it was at her speaking to those he couldn't see, or whatever he'd found in the contest of gazes, she couldn't tell.

"Silver." He let his hand fall from her neck. He said the word like he was trying to fit a new rhythm to his new sense of her. "Being an alpha is about responsibility, not just power. Knowing the consequences if I fail, I can't take that on again."

"Too late," Death said in the female voice that belonged to one of the warrior's ghosts.

Silver was unsettling, pure and simple. Intellectually, he'd known that there must have been something about her that allowed her to survive when the others had not, and John had said she was strong-willed as a young woman. But he hadn't expected to see a full alpha's strength in her. It was deep, deep, like at the bottom of a well, but there nonetheless. Having found it, he saw it in her movements now, even under her uneven white hair and fine bone structure.

He hadn't thought she'd even registered that part of his conversation with Rory. Andrew stood beside the car, where he'd parked against the thin tree screen at the hotel parking lot's edge, and watched as Silver wandered to look up into their branches. Her words had planted a seed in his mind, and he couldn't seem to stop it from growing. What if he challenged John? He was already in water so deep he could barely reach the surface, why not push off and try to swim? He'd have to run when the other Western packs found out he'd done it, or they'd tear him to shreds. But if he could command the Seattle pack temporarily and keep people from finding out for long enough, he could use that power to track the killer without fighting John at every turn.

Of course if he challenged and lost he'd be even worse off. He'd have nowhere to go, but that seemed inevitable at this point. More important was that he'd be unable to chase the killer through Western territory. The risk of a challenge was all or nothing.

Andrew put a hand out against the car's cool metal to

ground himself with the sensation. The idea was unbeliev-
ably stupid, and yet. Silver might be right. If he was going to
catch the killer, he couldn't do things halfway. He couldn't sit
around whining about how Seattle was limiting the trails he
could follow. He'd have to challenge, and he'd have to *win*.

Andrew shook himself. He couldn't make a decision like
that tonight. Better to sleep on it, see if he'd come to his
senses in the morning. Silver followed him when he touched
her shoulder to regain her attention and led the way into the
hotel.

The room smelled like every two- or three-star hotel room
Andrew had stayed in across the country. Cleaning products
couldn't erase the ground-in scent of hundreds of humans,
but the layered effect made it easier to bear, because no individual scent stood out.

"Can I wash—?" Silver said once he'd dead-bolted the
door behind them. He nodded to the open bathroom door
on his way past in invitation, but after a moment remembered she would probably need help. He dropped his shoulder bag on the nearer bed and returned to the bathroom.

When he arrived she was already standing in the shower,
turning the taps. Her clothes got soaked in the first rush of
water. The movements seemed habitual, like her hand knew
the motions without her mind quite directing it.

She raised her eyebrows at him, lips quirking in something that looked like amusement, and then waited. Andrew
removed himself and closed the door behind him.

The running water rumbling in the pipes made a soothing
background as Andrew dumped out his bag on the bed and

sorted through. He was nearly out of clean clothes, but he didn't feel like doing anything about that at the moment. His stomach grumbled, and he stopped to search for any local restaurant information compiled by the hotel so he could order pizza.

Someone turned on the TV in the next room and an evening news anchor's strident tones intruded. Andrew couldn't even really blame thin walls or the human's choice of volume, since you couldn't do much about werewolf ears other than get a house well buffered by land. That was the worst thing about hotels.

The rumble of water ceased soon after he finished ordering. Andrew cocked his head, listening to the noises of her puttering around rather than turning on his own TV. He should check her arm once she was done.

She peeked around the bathroom doorframe at length, towel held over her chest with her good hand. Her hair lay flatter when wet and the moisture darkening the color made it look more normal. Without anything to tuck it into, her bad arm looked even more pathetic, dangling lifeless by her side. She'd managed to soak the bandage thoroughly in the water.

"C'mere," Andrew directed, motioning for her to come closer so he could deal with the wound. Now she wasn't half hidden by the doorjamb, the towel was awfully short, part of Andrew's brain informed him. It revealed a lot of leg.

And curves. She was still scrawny, but the towel swelled slightly at chest and hip. He swallowed, and reminded himself that he was interested only in checking her arm.

Her scent changed when he touched her and it was hard not to respond to the femaleness of it by drawing his fingers more slowly than necessary along her undamaged skin. Soaked, the bandages peeled away easily, and the knife scores underneath looked healthier. They were still scabbed over and red, but it was a healing red rather than the angry red of a fresh or infected wound.

"How's the pain?" he asked, probing lightly with his fingertips along her arm. Silver sucked in a breath once when he got too close to a scar's edge, but otherwise shook her head.

"Can you do anything with it?" Andrew switched his grip so he could curl up her fingers with his other hand, repeating the motion and then letting them flop back several times.

"I—" Silver hesitated on the edge of an immediate denial. "I think maybe—"

Her middle and ring finger twitched. It was slight enough that Andrew wondered if he'd shaken her hand by moving himself. She gasped and they twitched again.

Silver let out a ragged breath, holding either tears or laughter just before the threshold of sound, and then threw her good arm around his neck. "I felt that!"

Andrew almost couldn't move, though his arm came up and fitted around her waist without conscious thought. Her scent was all around him, filling every breath.

She shivered, the crackling tension that had sprung up between them finding form in the movement. The towel had been tucked, but it was coming free. Andrew was about one more shiver from getting an eyeful as he looked down between them. Her breath was hot against the side of his neck. They were frozen that way for who knows how long—breathing, feeling, towel clinging desperately to friction.

Silver's next breath came husky, and she nipped at his neck. Andrew shoved her away, suddenly sure that if he didn't stop this now, his body would take over entirely. He retreated behind the closest bed instead.

"Oh," Silver said, flushing. Her towel puddled on the floor and she snatched it up. Wrapping it again one-handed was a long and awkward process. Her scent muddied to embarrassment and anxiety.

Andrew knew he should say something, but the silence stretched. What was he supposed to say, though? He wanted it as badly as she apparently did, but she was crazy? That he didn't want to take advantage, but then again, hadn't she proven herself pretty hard to take advantage of? And she'd started it!

"Thank you, Death. I'd figured that out for myself." Chin tilted up, Silver returned to the bathroom and her clothes. Andrew exhaled in relief. It was just the long dry spell talking, that was all, confronted with the scent of an interested female Were. Better than a cold shower, he needed to get out of the hotel and into fresher air.

Silver stayed in the bathroom, and Andrew stayed in the main room, pacing until the pizza guy arrived. He paid the boy, subtracted a few pieces to take with him, and left the rest in the box open on the bed. "I'll be back in a few hours," he told the room generally. Time to go see what kind of wilderness Seattle could muster for him to run in.

15

"Idiot." Silver straightened from sitting with her head in her good hand. She could smell Dare still, though only dimly. "Idiot. As if he didn't have enough to worry about." She wasn't speaking to Death for the moment, but the habit of organizing her thoughts out loud did not die so easily.

"Oh, he always has this effect on *las chicas*." The accented female voice was back again.

Silver pointed to Death. "You. Will be quiet, or I will tear out your throat with my teeth, whether my wild self is here to help me or not."

Death made a gesture much like a shrug, ruff fur bristling up and smoothing down as the muscles underneath moved. His silence was mocking, but at least it was silence.

"We can always pretend it didn't happen." Silver returned to her earlier train of thought. "I'm sure he'd be as happy as me to do that." She squirmed as a flutter below her stomach reminded her she hadn't started this out of nowhere. She hadn't felt that flutter since her wild self ran away. But it wasn't like she needed him to take care of it, anyway.

That was best done under running water, though, or he'd smell it the moment he came in. Silver sighed and stood to go find some.

The run helped a little, letting Andrew lose himself in the exertion, but the park was small, and he found himself not ready to go back when he'd done a couple circuits. He ended up at a bar, not really watching the game on TV, and intimidating any humans away from sitting near him.

When his phone rang, he considered ignoring it. He checked the ID first, at least, and frowned down at Benjamin's name. Dammit, he didn't want to talk to anyone right now, but he owed Boston better than a snub.

"Yeah?" Andrew could hear from Benjamin's silence that his greeting had come out sharp.

"You've certainly dropped a bomb in Roanoke, boy." Benjamin's voice was dry. "May I ask what you were thinking, breaking with Rory?"

Andrew swallowed a growl. He really didn't need this right now. "He didn't leave me any choice. He ordered me back there—to guard him personally, probably, the pussy. I'm not leaving her here. I don't trust any of these people, they all either want to put her down, or they're completely incapable of protecting her." He didn't realize how loud he was getting until the nearby humans glared at him.

Ben's silence after that was thoughtful, and Andrew realized he'd sounded much more sure of himself than he had been at the time. He couldn't think of any other decision he could have made, even with the time he'd had to think it over and regret it, so perhaps he'd made the right decision after all.

"I've been waiting for you to find the thing that would bring you back to yourself, boy. After Spain. You took your time about it, I must say. A waste of talent."

Andrew gritted his teeth. He didn't need the voices of his past haunting him yet again. "Don't."

"As you wish."

Andrew considered bristling at the soothing tone, but he knew Benjamin wasn't being patronizing. "It's been a long day," he said in a sideways apology. "And I don't know where I'm going to go once I catch the killer." That was more than he'd planned to admit, so he hurried to cover it over with a subject change. "Any progress on that lone?"

"Nothing yet." Frustration seeped into Benjamin's tone. "I haven't heard from the woman I sent after the lone. It's unusual for her to not report in promptly. But it's only been a day. She's probably hot on his trail in wolf, hasn't had a chance to get back to her phone."

They said their good-byes after that, the conversation too strangled by subjects Andrew was avoiding to continue. Andrew set his jaw as he put his phone away and ordered another drink. He wasn't going to think about any of this right now.

Silver was asleep on the far bed when Andrew returned to

the room. Her breathing changed as he entered, so she'd undoubtedly heard him and was awake, but she didn't open her eyes, so he politely pretended she was still asleep.

It was later than he'd intended since he'd wasted a lot of time walking himself sober. Usually werewolf healing resulted in a better alcohol metabolizing rate, but one could always swamp it if one really tried. Those last few whiskeys after talking to Benjamin had probably been a mistake.

At least he hadn't drunk-shifted. He'd busted plenty of young Were for playing stray doggy along the freeway because they thought it would be funny when smashed.

He ran himself a glass of water in the bathroom to kill the hangover—fast healing didn't do much for dehydration in the absence of water—and stood in the entryway to watch her as he drank. He could see perfectly well in the room's darkness, but colors were washed out. Silver looked almost normal when her white hair was seen only in the context of light and dark. He wanted to stroke it.

Her wounds showed dark on the arm flopped beside her, the lines curling over the pale skin. Snakes indeed. He could see their shape now in the contrasting light. Tiredness washed over him. He needed sleep if he really was going to challenge John tomorrow. And yet he was standing here trying to find the features of the strong woman she must have been underneath the stress and blankness the silver had washed over them.

Water. Bed. He pulled himself away and padded to the other bed, drinking as he walked.

Silver smelled like she might be awake when he looked

over at her the next morning, but her breathing was still even. It was possible she was dozing, close to the surface but not quite awake. They smelled much the same. Either way, the shower's noise would wake her more gently than he could.

The shower smelled a little off from Silver using it the night before. Andrew pushed that thought away and dressed and shaved quickly. They could raid the continental breakfast on the way out through the hotel lobby.

"You ready?" Silver asked from the doorway. Rather than shove it inside her jacket, today she'd tucked her bad arm into her jeans' hip pocket. It still didn't sit quite right, but it looked more natural. She used her other hand to settle some of her hair's fluffiness.

"As I'll ever be." Andrew gripped his rental car keys until they pressed painfully into his hand. Sleep hadn't changed his decision. He had to do what was necessary to catch the killer, including risking challenging Seattle. Even if that meant he was taken down by the other Western packs afterward, when he could no longer order the Seattle pack to keep quiet about what had happened. He needed to find Silver's attacker as soon as possible; having to find him before the Western packs found out about the change of alpha was no more time pressure. He couldn't think about losing the challenge. He'd just have to win.

He spotted a Denny's on the drive to the pack house and pulled in on an impulse. Better to face this after a proper meal. After seating them, the plump waitress eyed him with distaste when he ordered Silver's drink for her. Andrew stared the waitress down until she went away.

Silver's attention was caught by a small child at a nearby table. The girl banged her neon green plastic spoon on the neon purple dish her parents had brought with them. They were no fools, either, as the dish contained about three molecules of scrambled egg, hardly enough to bother wiping up should they reach the table, the floor, or her hair.

Andrew clenched his jaw, jerking his own eyes away. His daughter would be a teenager by now, he reminded himself. A teenager who probably hated him. It was only in his memory that she lingered at that age, and a few years older.

"Tell me about your mother's pack," he said to break the silence. Silver had her chin cupped in her hand to watch the child, and she looked up in surprise. It was a calculated risk—he didn't want the memory to drop her into the madness, but this might be far enough from the trauma to be safe. And she might have some insights that would help him in dealing with them this morning.

Silver's eyes flicked across his face, and her expression remained lucid. "The former alpha always had a sense of honor, like you. Not many would have ceded my brother territory rather than beat the disobedience out of him. His nephew, the current alpha, is very like him. You two might get along well, if not for the competition for power." The waitress delivered his coffee and her juice, and Silver dragged a finger along the condensation on her glass without drinking. "The pack raised us. A human hunter took my mother by accident a little after our Lady ceremonies."

Andrew waited a moment, but that seemed to be all the information that was forthcoming, so he slipped in to fill the silence. "They seem like a healthy pack. No fear. Other than of me, of course."

Silver sipped her drink, lips curving in their press against the glass. "You're very scary," she teased. Andrew blandly raised his eyebrows at her and she laughed outright, then sobered. "It would go better if they weren't afraid of you."

Andrew slumped back in his chair. Wasn't that the heart of the matter? "I wish they weren't, but if wishes were rabbits, everyone would feast. It wasn't anything I planned, it was a side effect."

"Because of those you killed?"

Andrew clenched his jaw. "Mostly, yes. And the fact that no one likes an enforcer."

"Because it's his job to carry out punishments." Silver's lips twisted as she said it, as if she wasn't quite sure what to think about it.

"Someone had to. Rory probably . . . couldn't have kept Roanoke together without me. I don't know what he's going to do now." He tapped the cutlery napkin roll against the table. He couldn't afford to worry about that at the moment. After he'd found the killer, and after he'd extricated himself from the West without permanent injury. Then he could think about that.

Silver reached out to still the fidgeting. "I do understand," she said with a half smile. "But you're not an enforcer now. Stop expecting that they will fear you, and maybe they won't."

Andrew looked down at her hand over his. "Easier said than done, even if you're right." She probably was. He was learning to trust Silver's instincts about pack dynamics. It was as if her twisted perspective on the outer world made her see inside people more clearly.

When the waitress returned to take their orders, Silver saved him from further server censure by pointing to one of the large, bright pictures decorating the menu's side. The parents and their little girl left, and Silver and Andrew ate in silence.

When they arrived at the pack house and rang the doorbell, no one answered for some time. Andrew frowned. They knew he was here. They would have heard him drive up, smelled him at the door. His first thought was that John was trying to avoid the fight, but that made no sense. No one but Andrew knew what he'd planned. What else was going on?

Finally, the door opened. Pierce glowered at them. "John's out for the moment." He wore only pants and was unshaved, his hair still tousled from sleep. Andrew could smell other Were in the house, but they must have nominated the beta to deal with him. Everyone else was keeping out of sight. Andrew almost smirked when he noticed Pierce's nose was still crooked. He caught the expression before it formed. Unprofessional, especially since he might have to work closely with Pierce soon.

But where was John? Andrew thought back to Michelle's words about the alpha's strange behavior. John had read so straightforward in person, it was hard for Andrew to believe that he would be in on anything. But what was going on, then? John had to have known that Andrew would be back the next morning, so he was either trying to be rude, or whatever was going on was so important it couldn't be put off until another time.

It probably had nothing to do with Silver or her pack's killer, of course. It could be perfectly innocent. And yet the small suspicious voice at the back of Andrew's mind was hard to squash. "I'll wait," Andrew told Pierce. Wait, and try to get some information from the beta.

Pierce started to shut the door in their faces. They would wait outside in the alpha's absence, apparently. Silver put her hand on the jamb so he had to stop or smash her fingers. "Can I at least get some breakfast?" Andrew couldn't see her expression, but her body language was one pathetic droop. He'd watched her eat not fifteen minutes ago, and the protective instincts he felt around low-ranked Were stirred anyway.

Pierce's face softened and he opened the door to usher her inside. He glared at Andrew as he invited himself along behind but didn't object. Andrew kept his head down to hide his smile. Well played, Silver.

Pierce strode ahead to reach the kitchen first, where he rummaged around and handed Silver a huge chocolate muffin from a multipack on top of the fridge. He watched solicitously as she devoured it.

As he entered the kitchen, Andrew sniffed, trying to find anything unusual or something that had changed since the day before. Under the cleaning products it was just a lot of Were, some male, some female, some children, all mixed with the scent of the human woman. No accounting for taste. If something was out of place here, he couldn't tell without knowing every pack member by scent.

"How long do you think John'll be?" Andrew asked. Pierce's shoulders set, and he remained silent. Andrew drew in a deeper breath of the man's scent. If he wanted answers, he'd probably have to beat it out of the man, and he didn't need the information that badly.

Silver gave a shiver, the single violent kind from long-term cold, and Pierce's attention snapped back to her. She made a show of looking exasperated at the concern. "I'm a little cold. I'm not going to break into pieces."

"I'm sure one of the girls has something warmer you could borrow." Pierce left Silver to her muffin, and strode off to appropriate something. Andrew watched Silver the moment Pierce's eyes were off her. No way she was that cold, not with how she was standing now, never mind the fact she'd been fine all morning on the way over here.

Andrew came to stand close to Silver, exhaling in amusement and stealing a muffin piece. "Aren't you the switch?" he murmured. Some Were were low-ranked, some were high-ranked, just by pure nature, though the fine gradations of hierarchy changed based on circumstance and packmates. Of course one could always attempt to act like the other, but most often it just didn't smell right in some metaphorical way. Andrew had assumed he'd discovered Silver's dominance as her madness receded, but she'd roused Pierce's protective instincts by seeming truly weaker than him. She smirked at Andrew now, changed her posture, and he was struck anew by what a vulnerable little thing she was.

At least until she punched him in the side. He expected to find her laughing, but the teasing that had prompted the blow faded from her face almost immediately. "Survival is a harsh mistress. It's better to be able to both fade from notice and bully away the bottom-feeders, rather than be limited to one or the other no matter the situation."

He'd made a promise to himself last night to keep his hands off her, but Andrew slid a hand under her hair to squeeze the back of her neck anyway. She sighed, releasing some tension with the sound.

Andrew stepped back. "I just want to get this over with. Then I can order people to answer me."

"Well, you certainly weren't doing very well coaxing him even when I had him distracted," Silver said, dry. Her body language curled back in on itself as Pierce returned with a leather jacket. She pushed Pierce away when he tried to pull the jacket on after guiding her dead wrist into the sleeve. Her dexterous wiggle to settle the jacket made for good watching from behind.

Andrew jerked his mind back onto the matter at hand. Enough of this. "I'm going to call John." He pulled out his phone. It rang four or five times before John picked up, growl already running under his voice, even in the greeting.

"Having fun wherever you wandered off to? I think your beta's getting twitchy, having me here without you." Andrew kept his tone light to offset the baiting phrasing.

"Fuck you, Dare. I'm practically there." The call cut off, and Andrew imagined that the end button had been pushed harder than was good for the phone.

A car turned into the driveway and they all looked toward the front door. A car door slammed, locks beeped, and John's half-running footsteps reached the house.

"It wasn't supposed to take this long," John snapped as he entered. He smelled strongly of humans, which could mean anything about where he'd been. Humans were everywhere. John tried to brush past Andrew and Silver, but Andrew caught his elbow.

"And what would it be that wasn't supposed to take long?" he said, putting a little command into his tone.

John's lip curled up into a snarl. "I swear on the Lady that it's personal pack business. Nothing to do with the one you hunt. Is that good enough?" He met Andrew's eyes, clearly expecting the other man to step back from the confrontation. Andrew met his show of dominance squarely, shoving down the mental voice that called him a fool for taking this risk. He had no choice. No choice but to risk it.

They stayed, locked in the stare, until John broke first. "You gave your word," he growled. "I invited you into my territory, and now you betray me and try to take it for Roanoke?" He put a hand on Andrew's shoulder and shoved. Andrew rocked to absorb the blow and stayed where he was.

"This isn't for Roanoke." Andrew hesitated, hating to voice the painful fact. "I'm no longer affiliated with that pack. And I don't want your territory for myself either." No going back now, win or lose. That thought brought a fighting calm with it. "But you won't let me do what I need to do to address this threat to all North American Were." He unbuckled his belt and started unbuttoning his shirt as John stared at him. He nodded to the living room, since the entryway didn't have enough space.

The man's growl died away into an edged laugh. "If you insist." John kicked off his shoes and started undressing too as he moved into the living room. Andrew might have scored a few points in their verbal confrontations over Silver before, but John knew he had the advantage over Andrew in physical power. The confidence in how he moved, the smirk buried in his expression; they said he knew Andrew knew too. He rolled his shoulders, showing off the play of muscles beneath the skin.

Since it was a Sunday, the majority of the pack was home, and they pressed around three edges of the room and into the den beyond. Someone moved the love seat, someone else the coffee table, until only an empty swath of carpet surrounded by the bookcases against the walls remained. Andrew felt the press of their contempt mixed with a whiff of fear of the Butcher like the worst summer humidity he'd ever experienced. He had no doubt they'd love to see him pounded into a pulp, love every minute. Whatever you said about Seattle, he inspired loyalty. They arranged themselves behind John, leaving the wall behind Andrew and the arch into the entryway empty but for Silver.

"Even if you somehow manage to win, Portland and Billings will take you down," John taunted, once he was down to his jeans. "They won't let the Butcher of Barcelona take a Western pack."

Andrew clenched his hands. It was only a nickname. It had no power over him. "I find it ironic that you'd all pull

together against me, but let a more heinous butcher go free."
He forced himself to stand still as John circled him, sneering.
He couldn't show that he was physically intimidated—couldn't
be physically intimidated. They were still in human, still talking. This was when Andrew had the advantage.

"You say one of my people might know something—what
about *you*, Dare? Selene says it wasn't you, yes, but you know
silver. You know Europeans. Maybe it was one of your little
friends from Spain. Why don't you question them instead?
Or do you know they wouldn't tell you anything after everyone you slaughtered in cold blood?"

Andrew couldn't see for a moment, rage's wildfire rush
through his muscles showing as a red mist before his eyes.

"Or are you afraid of yourself?" John tossed out the words
like arrows shot blind, trying to overwhelm the target with
quantity. "I've talked to Were in Roanoke. They say you're
more of an alpha than Rory, but you won't do anything about
it. Why is that? Are you afraid that someone will die and
you'll end up dripping with blood and surrounded by people
with torn-out throats again? Why should my pack be your test
case?" John's scent was off. He had to be working from logic,
not from real knowledge. All Andrew had to do was not react.
Keep his muscles leashed into stillness so strained he nearly
shook.

Cold fingertips against his back. Andrew jumped, his
muscles were wound so tightly, but his subconscious knew
Silver's scent so he didn't touch her. "Calm," she murmured.
If he'd been properly listening to the word, he might have
growled at her presuming to give him advice, but sensation

was what grounded him. The coolness stood out against his anger's heat and focused him.

John's lips drew back from his teeth at seeing her touch. He snapped his fingers at his side. "Selene, get over here. You're no loyal member of Roanoke. Stand with Seattle."

"I'm alpha of my own pack of one, wild self or no wild self, before I'm a loyal member of yours," Silver said, leaving Andrew to stalk over to John. "The warrior is speaking sense, but you're not *listening*."

"I know you want to be kind to your people, John. To protect them," Andrew said, when he was sure his voice would come out evenly. "But I've been an enforcer for nearly a decade, and it's taught me that sometimes you have to do the things people will hate you for. You have to let them hate you, if that will keep them safe."

John shook his head, contempt in his expression so deep he couldn't have heard a word. "Selene," John said again, and grabbed Silver's elbow to yank her over to him. The unexpected threat startled a whimper from Silver.

Andrew didn't give him a chance to finish the motion. Thought left him at Silver's whimper and he was just motion, any motion at all, as long as it carried him to John to pound him into a screaming, bloody pulp.

John growled and blocked Andrew's blows as easily as Andrew usually did when fighting untrained Were. "I'm not hurting her—"

Silver hissed in rage, and slammed a kick into John's knee. The man staggered out of Andrew's reach, eyes wide with shock. A few gasps slipped from the watching pack. "I told you not to use that name, I told you to pay attention to what the warrior says, and yet you still don't *listen*. Why don't you listen?" Silver retreated to stand behind Andrew. Her voice reached down through his rage and caught at his attention too. He needed to listen, to think, not just react. He'd handed John the advantage.

John pressed a hand to a shelf of the bookcase behind him and panted with pain as his knee healed. "Well?" he sneered. "What are you holding back for now?"

Andrew drew in a deep calming breath and inclined his head to the injured leg. "It's not a fair fight right now. I'm not trying to win by cheating, Seattle." Good tactics to make sure the pack stayed with Andrew if he did win, but it also gave him welcome time to regain control.

John snorted, and leaned weight onto the leg to test it out. "You're not going to win at all. You talk big, about doing what has to be done, but no one believes you. Let's do this."

Andrew dipped his head in acknowledgement, pulled off his jeans, and shifted. Residual anger gave him all the strength he needed, so it came as easy as the night of the full.

They circled each other. Andrew's lupine instincts urged him to useless gestures, snapping in John's general direction, but he suppressed them. John lunged forward a couple times himself, but then fell to circling too. True wolf fights were highly ritualized, since too many deaths didn't serve the species. Werewolves could heal a lot more damage, but still stopped short of death, except in the worst European packs.

As Andrew had expected, John was the first to break, a dark shape barreling toward him to sink his teeth into Andrew's neck. Andrew danced aside, snapping his own teeth down as John's momentum carried him a little past. Andrew tasted blood, but couldn't get a grip. John turned and slammed into him again, and again, both men falling into the whining growls of true wolf fights. Andrew made it back to his feet by thinner margins each time. Here and there he felt the sting of scrapes from Seattle's teeth healing over.

The next slam carried him onto his back, and Andrew held John's snapping teeth from his neck only with the rigid strength of his forelegs. He couldn't hold that for more than a few moments; he could feel the strain each time John lunged and snapped.

With the last snap, Andrew rolled, writhing out from under John's weight as the man's teeth closed on his ruff's loose skin. Pain seared through Andrew as he ripped free and danced back to stall until the tears healed. Blood seeped through his fur and down his shoulder. He couldn't keep fighting defensively like this. He was more maneuverable than John. That should count for something, dammit.

John dropped his jaw in a triumphant canine grin at the blood and body-slammed Andrew. This time he didn't snap for Andrew's neck, but used his weight to smash Andrew's bloody shoulder into the wall. The joint screamed in agony, and Andrew nearly fell when he tried to put weight on it to dance out of John's reach. Now. He had to do something now, or John would wear him down and smash him into the ground.

On John's next lunge, Andrew let him close, close enough his instincts screamed at him that he was about to die. When John's teeth were nearly in his throat, Andrew twisted and rolled up and got the grip he needed on John's ruff. Deep, so John couldn't pull free. Now Andrew just had to hang on. John slammed him over and over into the wall, bad shoulder first, but Andrew kept his teeth locked through the pain. He sawed his head back and forth to worsen the wounds and John's agony.

That was when Andrew felt the turning point and began to believe that he might win the challenge. They were both injured, both exhausted, but Andrew could feel the pain wearing on John faster than it did on himself. Andrew was familiar with pain. He knew all about dragging yourself on through agony. He didn't let his grip loosen, and John stumbled and fell when next he tried to throw Andrew off.

Andrew summoned all his strength for a last heave and John went down. The moment his side hit the ground, Andrew pinned him, letting go just long enough to get a good grip around the man's neck. A grip good enough to kill, should he close his teeth.

John stayed rigid for a couple seconds and then slumped in defeat, rolling enough to present his belly. He whine-growled a last time in rage, then fell silent but for his panting.

Andrew stepped back and stood panting himself with all four feet braced, waiting for his healing to catch up with his shoulder. Silver ruffled his ears. He considered biting her hand for having precipitated this in the first place, and being crazy and hurt and just generally inconvenient, but the rush of winning mellowed the emotions. He'd actually done it. He'd taken John down.

Pierce pushed from the gathered Were and knelt by his

former alpha, helping John sit up after he shifted back. He offered John his clothes, and then rocked back on his heels to eye Andrew.

Andrew shifted back and grabbed his jeans. It was easier to stand on two legs, since his bad shoulder no longer had to take weight. He ignored Pierce. He wasn't going to force the pack to hide their sympathy and continued respect for their former alpha. Pierce could do as he liked with John, as long as he followed Andrew's orders first.

"So now what?" John said, voice a little thin from humiliation and probably some self-recrimination. "What are your orders?" Where do you want me, he meant. Some alphas kept the old one on high in the hierarchy, in the old strategy of keeping enemies even closer than friends. Some busted the old alpha down to omega, or forced him from the pack entirely.

The Were gathered around them were still frozen, no one wanting to be the first to step forward. Even with the fight over, Andrew's heart pounded with residual adrenaline as he buttoned his jeans and stood tall. That posture seemed to be a cue. Pierce straightened too, came forward, and knelt. It was different than the human gesture: rather than bowing his head he tipped it down and to the side, baring more of his neck.

The smell of John's frustration at his defeat was too sour for Andrew to be able to read Pierce's sincerity even when he came forward to stand over the man. The others knelt where they were.

"You know your territory better than I ever could in a few

days," Andrew said after taking a deep breath. "I'll need your expertise as beta." He came over and offered John a hand up. John stared at it for a while, and then accepted it, dropping it as soon as possible. They both knew it would cause the least turmoil in the pack if everyone simply moved one place down in the hierarchy. Whatever else Andrew thought about John, he knew the man wasn't stupid, just out of his depth in some situations. He'd work with Andrew, to minimize the stress on the pack.

Andrew took a step toward the entryway and the illusion of privacy, taking a moment to himself as the last euphoria of victory drained away. If one of John's people was working with the killer, the surest way to make sure Andrew couldn't catch him would be to leak news of the challenge to someone who had it in for him, like Sacramento. Andrew couldn't track anyone if he was defending himself from half the Western packs.

"All right." Andrew turned back to the pack and raised his voice. "Everyone in this room. Cell phones here." He pointed to a spot at his feet. "Pierce, you can call in anyone who's not here, nothing else." Everyone shuffled but didn't otherwise move. The air turned bitter with scent of hostility.

Andrew unclenched his jaw to speak again. He couldn't bark orders often enough to keep people in line if he ran things that way exclusively. He'd have to at least try to persuade. "Look, my only goal in this is to find the man who killed the Bellingham pack. Then I'm gone and everything's back to normal. If any of you tell someone outside the pack about this, I'll be taken out before I can accomplish that. So cell phones. Now." He punctuated the last word with a loud clap. Everyone jumped. Phones clattered to his feet.

It took about fifteen minutes for the last stragglers to arrive, summoned by Pierce. Five minutes in, Andrew wished fiercely that he could drop to a seat as the majority of the pack had, but he continued to stand tall the whole time, no matter how much exhaustion sucked at him.

When the last family herded their toddler in the front door and came to sit with the rest, Andrew drew a deep breath. If he accustomed his nose to the background hostility and fear now, hopefully he'd be better able to read the nuances of changes in a moment.

"Does anyone here know anything about the man who killed the Bellingham pack?" He waited until every Were adult shook their head. The hostility intensified and grew layered with some fear at the talk of Bellingham's fate, but the air held no hint of guilt.

"Does anyone know someone they suspect might know anything?" The same shaken heads, the same lack of guilt. "Were any of you involved in any way with what happened in Bellingham, intentionally or not?" Still negative. Andrew started to breathe a little easier. He'd been afraid of what he might have to do if someone had smelled guilty.

"Keep this to yourselves," he ordered after taking a moment to consider whether there were any other questions he needed to ask. He might be forgetting something, but better not to strain everyone more than necessary by dragging it out. "Keep talking to your friends in other packs, cutting contact is suspicious, but don't say a thing about the change of alpha." With luck that would give him a couple solid days to work before anyone noticed that their Seattle friends were suspiciously strained in their conversation and started asking questions. He was under no illusions no one would notice for longer.

A ragged chorus of agreement reached him. Andrew let his shoulders drop and nudged the nearest phone forward with his toe as a signal the rest could be reclaimed. No one moved until he stepped back. "I'll want to talk to you all individually," he said as they came up in twos and threes. He suppressed an impulse to rub at his eyes. He'd cleared the pack, but he still needed a new lead. One of them might know something. He'd find it if he had to question everyone twice.

"Dare." Silver rocked back a step and beckoned when he didn't immediately follow. Andrew narrowed his eyes at her. Couldn't whatever this was wait?

He strode to her and then beyond, hurrying them into the kitchen. "What?"

"You need to calm down." She brushed her hand down his upper arm and raised her eyebrows at him when he twitched with the effort of not knocking it away. Maybe he was a little on edge, but who wouldn't be? He had a killer to catch, as well as suddenly having the responsibilities of an alpha as well. Silver's expression hardened. "I wouldn't have thought I'd be the one to say this to you, but you need to step away until the voices of your past fade, Dare. It will do the others good too. Let them get used to the idea of a new alpha."

Andrew swallowed. Even thinking explicitly about Spain made all his muscles tighten like he was still in the middle of the challenge fight. Silver was right, he hadn't realized how much of his tension stemmed from that. He didn't relish the idea of spending time alone with his thoughts at the moment, but maybe he could use the time to better craft his questions for the pack. He blew out a breath and Silver relaxed as she correctly interpreted the agreement.

Andrew stepped back into the living room. "Get the master suite ready for me," he directed the pack, concentrating this time on keeping any anger out of his voice. John would be the one moving his stuff, but it was more polite to order the lower-ranked Were than tell John directly to get the hell out. "I'll keep out of the way for a while." He jerked his thumb in the front door's direction. He'd seen a few parks on the drive over here. Hopefully one would provide more than a five-minute circuit.

Once everyone nodded, Andrew strode outside. Silver had to run a few steps to catch up. He picked a direction at random, sidewalk taking him past driveways and the various polite shapes of landscaped shrubs. Just him and Silver and his past, as she'd said.

"Are you going to ask?" The possibility that he'd have to explain pressed in on him. It had been years, he realized, since the last time he'd been able to neither hide it nor use shorthand with someone who already knew the details.

"Would you tell me if I did?" Silver stopped before a gate into a deserted park. The paths along the central stream were a muddy mess only now starting to dry out in the summer weather. No surprise people were avoiding them. She started to reach out with her good hand for the latch and then stopped, frowning at it as if she couldn't figure out how the mechanism might function. Andrew watched the frustration grow on her face for a moment, then lifted it and opened the gate when it was clear she couldn't work it out on her own.

Did he want to tell her? Andrew stopped with his hand on the open gate and considered that. It was like as long as he didn't close them in, he had space to consider his decision. After a moment, he stepped through, shut it with a bang, and jogged to join her on the path. He was occasionally an idiot, but never a coward.

"Probably."

Silver waited in silence for a moment, as if acknowledging the effort of the answer. "How did the woman with the accent die?"

Confusion distracted Andrew for a moment. "Accent?" Of course Isabel had had an accent in English. Before he'd even met her, he'd heard her musical voice across the room at a crowded party and sought her out. But how would Silver know anything about that?

"Death speaks with her voice." Silver grew more hesitant, as if afraid she was reminding him that Isabel was dead.

As if he could ever forget.

But if it was Death that knew, Andrew supposed that whatever part of Silver's mind that had created the character had simply stored away the references to Spain. It was a logical jump.

He found a patch of only partly muddy grass and stood to stare down into the stream and watch the rippling motion of the shallow water. He summoned the polished set of empty words he'd created at the time, memorized so as to have no association with the actual memories. "Fire. It was a territorial dispute, and the other side decided to start making examples of Were homes. Isabel—" Saying her name made Andrew stumble. He'd forgotten he needed to avoid that. "My wife had forgotten something at the house, she went back while I took our daughter on to the restaurant. She was taking so long, and then I saw the smoke—" Too many details again. The words were tearing his throat on the way up. He had to stop and find the polished, meaningless ones again.

"I tracked them down, the ones who had done it. I found a hunting party out running. They said they'd thought our home was empty. I didn't know if they were lying, but I killed them anyway. Seven of them. One was Barcelona's beta. I killed him first—it was half luck, since he wasn't expecting me, wasn't expecting me to fight so hard. The others were scared after that. They didn't coordinate attacks as they should have."

Andrew reached up and pulled a branch off a tree overhanging the stream so he could snap it into smaller and smaller pieces. "The rumors are true. I . . . lost myself, for a while. The last few surrendered. Even in Europe, no one could remember the last time someone had ignored a surrender. They surrendered and I killed them anyway and tore out their throats so Death couldn't find their voices and they'd wander forever, denied their return to the Lady." Andrew didn't believe it now, couldn't remember if he'd truly believed it then, but the words and fear came from his childhood. Wander forever, voiceless.

He dared a look over at Silver and something inside him

sobbed. At the mention of the stolen voices she'd turned partly away, good hand pressed to her face. Andrew swallowed, dry and painful. "Silver, I'm sorry—"

"Death says—" Silver's voice came out as cracked as his own felt. "Death says that we are foolish indeed if we believe that a Were's true voice rests within a small patch of flesh and muscle." She straightened her head and scrubbed tears from her eyes, voice gaining confidence. "They are with the Lady."

Andrew wasn't going to let himself off so easily. He hurled the remainder of the branch into the creek. The shallow water barely mustered a splash. "What it meant to the dead is beside the point. It's the message I sent to the living that mattered. I tore out their throats and then burned the Barcelona hunting lands to the ground."

He let a breath trickle out, but Silver didn't say anything more, so finally he continued.

"Madrid tolerated me for Isabel's sake, never liked me, and when I"—he swallowed—"went after Barcelona on my own, and did what I did, they disinvited me from their territory, and kept our daughter to raise themselves. I tried to get her back, I tried everything—but there wasn't much I could do, one against many. I had to run to North America before they killed me, and no matter how many messages I've sent over the years, I know they're not letting them through."

Silver finally spoke after another stretching silence. "When Death speaks with people's voices, he sometimes claims it is their souls, speaking through him, not simply his words in their voices. I think he lies. But—your wife says that she's happier you weren't there to die with her. That she under-stands you regret what you did after."

"It would have been better if I'd been able to keep her from dying at all," Andrew said. He'd heard all the possible forms of condolence before. Hundreds of times. She would have wanted him to move on. She would have wanted him to be happy. Well, he had moved on, and he was happy after a fash-ion, he supposed. It wasn't anything he put much time into thinking about.

"Mortality is the gift that Death gave to the Were." Silver smiled a little bitterly. "I have not been particularly grateful for it myself. But their voices tell me I could not have pre-vented anything that happened to my pack."

"No, Silver." Andrew put out a hand to squeeze her shoul-der. "I saw your house. You couldn't be expected to take down someone like that all by yourself."

"*You* don't believe that about what you couldn't have prevented," Silver said with a dark slash of humor. "Dirty hypocrite."

"Do as I say, not as I do," Andrew said. A slightly hysteri-cal chuckle bubbled up and he turned back up the path out of the park and back to the house.

Silver sighed and took his hand gently as they climbed up the hill. "Death's very much of the kill-or-cure school of thought—he kept feeding me information to throw at you, like getting it all into the open will help you somehow. After you, you know, finish bleeding from the great wounds it would create."

She said it like Death had told her about Isabel before Andrew had, but Andrew supposed her unconscious was just assembling clues from Craig and John and everyone who'd referred to his reputation. Or maybe she'd heard the rumors herself before silver had taken her mind.

Silver laughed, the sound thin. "I'm not much of an advocate for facing up to things, in any case."

"That's just the silver." Andrew squeezed her hand. Dammit, what did you say in this situation? No, you're not stark raving nuts? Yes, you're crazy, but it doesn't seem likely to change anytime soon, so you might as well get used to it? I'm sorry?

"No, it's not." Silver looked away from him. "Since you . . . purged it, I can feel things at the edges. Names. Memories. I'd have thought you'd be first to sense that I wasn't trying very hard . . . Dare."

She said the word with a twist of effort, like someone pulling a foreign word from deep in their memory and trying to get the pronunciation right on the first try. It was only then he realized that he'd never heard her use his name or anyone else's before.

"Just because I push myself too hard doesn't mean that I expect everyone else to. Leadership 101. Be aware of people's abilities. Don't push them past their limits." He dropped her hand and slung his arm over her shoulders to squeeze her bad arm, reminding her that it still hadn't healed. "We have time. Some, at least. I won't pretend that your attacker's name wouldn't be more useful than mine—"

Every muscle in Silver's body went rigid, but she made no other comment for several moments. The leaves they passed under made shadows flicker in the sunlight across her face. "Not yet."

16

After he'd told his story, Silver let Dare get ahead on the walk back, giving him time alone. His wild self growled and snapped at the air as it followed at his heels. She'd hoped his story would help banish them, but while the voices had receded enough for her to see the new weight of being alpha resting heavy on his shoulders, they had not disappeared.

His need for space suited her in another way too. Lately, she'd noticed Dare looked worried any time she talked to Death. It made her head hurt trying to think about it, but she seemed to recall that it hadn't bothered her once that Dare couldn't see Death. Now it felt wrong. She knew Death was there, was real, as real as the Lady, and yet everyone looked past him. Now she had the chance to speak to Death alone.

"Now you know his secret," Death said in the musical voice

of Dare's dead wife. "What do you think? Do you fear him, now?" Death chose another voice, harsh and filled with the bite of command over the accent. The beta Dare had killed, perhaps. "He could kill again, just as easily. Just as gruesomely."

Silver plucked off a leaf and twirled it between her fingers. "I thought you liked him for that. You told me he wasn't afraid of you."

Death shook his head, puffing up his ruff, and bared his teeth in a laugh. "I meant because he sought me for himself, once upon a time."

"All the more reason to trust him." Silver slowed and looked where Dare had disappeared off into the trees. "He knows the worst of himself, and is vigilant to make sure it stays buried. Better that than to be surprised by it and unable to stop the worst from taking over."

Death flopped onto his side, forelegs out straight in front. He had chosen the darkest patch of shadows in the forest, and it was hard to tell where his flank began or ended, though a flick of his tail broke it away from the blackness for a moment. "You'll just have to hope he'll hear the sound of his enemies approaching over the voices of his past."

Silver growled. "He's doing all this to catch *my* enemy. I think there's no danger of that." She tossed her leaf to the wind, but it only flopped to the ground, upside down. "Is he going to find anything? Now he's alpha of my mother's pack?"

"He's not going to find what he expects." Death turned his head to look off into the distance.

Silver couldn't help but notice that it gave him an excuse

to display his profile. She waited a moment to see if any more information was forthcoming and then sighed. "He'll figure something out. He's a clever man."

"You could always do something yourself, rather than waiting, helpless. Find your monster before Dare finds him by noticing the monster's teeth in his neck." Death gave the last sentence a malicious twist.

"Stop it." Silver pressed her hand to her face. "Please. I can't."

"So you keep saying." Death turned his head back. "It's no concern of mine when your warrior's voice finds its way to me."

"Dammit, Death!" Silver looked around for something to throw but couldn't find anything. He would have ducked it anyway, she supposed. "Why are you still here?"

To her shock, Death looked uncomfortable, avoiding her eyes. After a brief pause, he whuffed a laugh like he wasn't going to deign to answer the question.

Andrew had to remind himself not to knock on the Seattle pack house door. As the alpha, he could just let himself in. As they entered, John strode up to hold the door open formally, the muscles in his jaw tight. "Welcome back, Seattle. Your room's ready."

"Thank you." Andrew dumped the shoulder bag he'd gotten from the car on the floor inside the door. The alpha didn't carry his own luggage upstairs. He opened his mouth to ask about seeing people individually again, but stopped without Silver's intervention this time. Protocol after a successful challenge was that the alpha parked himself—or herself— somewhere and let people come by at their own pace to pay their respects. Now he'd had time to breathe a little, following protocol seemed like a much better idea. Maybe he'd get something out of the informal conversations, and if not, people would trust him more later.

He leaned close to Silver as they headed for the dining room, John trailing awkwardly. Betas didn't carry luggage either. "Think you can keep everyone calm and worried about the poor low-ranked wounded bird again?" he said, low-voiced.

"Of course." Silver nodded to him and turned back to John, smile springing up. "Don't worry, I promise to make sure he behaves." Silver jerked on an imaginary leash near Andrew's neck. Going along with the game, Andrew grabbed her wrist to immobilize the imaginary hold.

The playful mood vanished when Andrew saw John's face. Forget his earlier tension. This was pure fury. Andrew dropped Silver's wrist. "Lady's light, man—"

"What have you been doing to her?" John stepped forward. "Is that why you wanted the power? So you could take advantage of her when no one could stop you? You're sick."

Silver got up in John's face before the man could come any closer to Andrew. "He's been doing nothing I haven't invited. Or allowed. Or is your memory so bad that you can't remember that I'm perfectly capable of taking care of myself?"

"You weren't the last time I checked." John pushed her

aside and launched himself at Andrew. Andrew stepped aside and used John's movement to slam him into the wall, where he held him.

"Silver." Andrew wrestled his voice under control to make it calming. He knew by now what a sore point her sanity was with her—and by the same token, how unlikely to win any argument based on it she would be. She was, after all, not entirely there. "He has a right to be protective." Andrew wanted to convince John he wasn't doing anything, not beat him into stewing silently, dammit.

"But she's right; if I was taking advantage, you have to admit she's at least more than lucid enough to tell you about it." Andrew held John still until his muscles relaxed a little and it seemed like the words had gone in. He let go and stepped back.

Silver snorted, grumbled something inaudible, and subsided. The two men measured each other in silence for a few more moments. John put an arm around Silver's shoulders, and Andrew gritted his teeth rather than react. Silver crossed her good arm across her chest and stood there like a sullen lump.

"Come on," Andrew said to Silver. "Guess we might as well make ourselves at home."

Andrew had never been on this side of the process before, but he remembered the change of alpha in his birth pack when he was about ten. Accordingly, he found himself a cup of coffee and a newspaper to pretend to read, and settled at the table.

Were drifted in and out on various pretexts. He spoke to most of them, collecting names and trying to pick up a detail or two about each. Most disappeared off on Sunday afternoon errands, still tense, but at least reassured he wasn't about to start passing out beatings just yet. The longer it went on, the more Andrew had to bite back pointed questions about any strange Were who might have come through their territory. Soon this would be done, and he could get to the real work.

One woman came into the kitchen holding a shy three-year-old whose curls stood up every which way around his head. They both had the same redheaded complexion, tending more toward freckles in the mother, and hair so light as to seem translucent in the son. The knees of the boy's pants were clean, but had a dingy patina that suggested more constant grubbing in the mud than a washing machine could fix.

It was probably time for the start of an early lunch, as the mother switched her son to the other hip to have a hand free for getting an apple from the fridge. The movement dislodged his toy puppy, stuffed between him and his mother. He whined, reaching after it. The woman sighed, bent to retrieve it, and returned it to him. He dropped it again a minute later.

Andrew stood and picked up the puppy himself before the woman was forced to bend down once more. It was really a bean-filled husky, not a wolf, but it looked as thoroughly disreputable as Andrew remembered his childhood puppy being, nearly half a century ago.

"What do you say to the alpha?" the woman prompted the boy. She set him down, obviously intending him to walk forward and claim the puppy himself while offering his thank-you. Good for her. She was raising him right in pack behavior. The boy refused, however, and grabbed his mother's leg and hid his face behind it. No real surprise, since the alpha he needed to show respect to wouldn't usually be a stranger.

"What's your puppy's name?" Andrew bent to hold out the toy to the boy. The boy peeked out, then hid his face again more definitively. Andrew's heart clenched for a moment as that peek set off a burst of memories of his daughter, but he pushed them away again. The intervening years had washed them out, anyway.

"I have to cut up your apple, sweetie." The woman reached down and tried to pry off little fingers, but he just switched his grip to a different place on her jeans. Andrew sighed and straightened. Apparently he frightened even small children. Lovely.

"Let me." Silver came up behind Andrew and took the puppy. She knelt on the kitchen floor and placed the toy before her, set up on its legs like it was sitting too. The boy peeked out, and continued to watch when Silver did nothing more than watch him back. The droop of her head and shoulders gave off low-ranking signals even to him.

"Hi," she said. "I'm Silver. Are you good at fighting? I bet you are." The boy nodded. "Wanna show me?"

"Sure." The word came out thickly, and the boy smiled. He ran at Silver with arms out. Silver cried out in mock surprise, and slowly toppled onto her back. The boy tried to climb on her, but she gently knocked him to his back and started wrestling with him to get his shirt up to blow a raspberry on his stomach. He shrieked with laughter. When he was well into the game, she scooped him up with her good arm and took him out into the den. There they were within line of sight through the dining room, but not underfoot.

"Oh, Selene."

Andrew had been watching Silver, not the mother, and he looked up in surprise at her words. He could see memories of what Silver must once have been like written stark across her face. "Don't let her hear you say that," he reminded as gently as he could.

The woman sliced into the apple. "I know, John told us. I was just thinking how much she's changed, anyway." She must have read his glance back to Silver, because she snorted. "Not just physically." She subdivided the apple into smaller and smaller pieces. "Her sister-in-law Lilianne was a friend of mine. When they split off, I'd already had my oldest, so I wanted to stay more settled, but once Lilianne and Ares had their children, I visited a lot. We had that in common."

Another shriek of laughter interrupted them, and the woman rocked backward to get a better view of her child before continuing. "Selene was never that interested in the little ones. She loved them, sure, but she didn't have the hunger to have one of her own. You know?"

Andrew clenched his jaw. Oh, he knew that hunger.

"Her brother wasn't that much older, but she just wasn't at the right stage yet, I don't think. She should have been out roaming, trying out packs until she found someone to settle down with. But I think her mother's death left her so close to

Ares she kept hanging around, hoping someone would roam by and stay with *her* instead."

"Maybe someone did roam by." Andrew hadn't intended to bludgeon the woman with all the death and gloom of the pack's fate again, but the words slipped out. "Who actually knew about the Bellingham pack, anyway? It was news to Roanoke. We thought you guys went all the way up to where Alaska ends."

The woman flushed, just visible under her freckles. She stalled, grabbing a plate and arranging the apple slices on it. "Well . . . uh. Portland probably had to have known." Her scent muddied, matching her flush in showing she was hiding something.

Andrew frowned. "Besides them. Anyone else?"

"No one else knows."

That was a lie. A blatant one. Even if Andrew hadn't smelled it, he could hear the woman's voice waver. The woman edged away with a sullen look that told Andrew that the more he pushed, the farther the woman would retreat, leaving no information behind. Maybe he could set Silver on coaxing it from her? Or would that be too close to topics that Silver was trying to avoid?

The woman got very busy with collecting her son and feeding him, cutting off further conversation. Andrew didn't linger. He needed somewhere to think this out. He'd use his newly acquired bedroom, but werewolves couldn't help but hear him pacing through adjoining walls. He was trying to keep everyone calm, not infect them with his tension. The only place in the house without that problem that he could think of would be the basement. Silver seemed to sense his mood, because she joined him and waited at the door for him to open it.

Andrew shut the door carefully, jogged down the stairs, and then allowed himself to pace. He carefully didn't look at the ring set into the wall. "Who'd they tell?" He was just thinking out loud, but Silver tilted her head, listening. He'd have to phrase carefully to avoid giving her flashbacks. "The Seattle pack told someone about where you lived. Someone they shouldn't have. I doubt I'd smell that kind of guilt on her if it was someone like a member of the Billings pack. People have friends. It happens."

Andrew stopped to lean on his hands on the couch back. "So who's shameful to talk to? None of the pack smelled guilty when I asked them if they knew someone involved with what happened in Bellingham. Why react to the one question and not the other?"

Silver frowned at the empty air, and then slapped her hand against the paneling. "If you don't want to tell me, fine! There's no need to be so smug about it!" She grimaced apologetically at Andrew. "Death says we'll find out soon enough. He's been crowing about this all day, in his laconic way—'Dare won't find what he expects.'" Silver's expression twisted. "Cat's bastard."

Andrew pushed off the couch to pace again. "I wanted to avoid ordering people to give me information, but I might have no choice. We're going to run out of time soon and we're not getting anywhere."

Footsteps thundered up to the door, and someone yanked it open. "Mom! Go away. I don't care if the new alpha's down there."

Andrew didn't have to get a look at the sullen expression, or smell the sulkiness. He could hear the teenage tantrum in each stomp down the stairs. The girl making all the noise looked about thirteen, dressed in what Andrew assumed to be the best in current teen fashion. Her jeans were ripped, her top looked like the design had smeared in printing, and her hair was bleached and shaggy.

The girl's mother appeared at the top of the stairs, anxiety clear on her face as she opened her mouth to apologize for her daughter's behavior, but Andrew waved her away. He could handle one teenager.

The girl stumbled to a stop on the stairs when Andrew came over, probably realizing an alpha in person was more intimidating than one in abstract. She dropped her head. "Um. Sorry. Sir."

Andrew nodded to acknowledge her respect, and moved to push past and leave her the basement. He needed to go order that woman to tell him who knew about Bellingham. Silver stopped him with a hand on his wrist. "Aren't you going to ask her what's wrong, alpha?" she murmured, soft.

Andrew stopped. In the normal course of things, she would have been correct. A large part of the alpha's job was keeping track of everything bothering his pack. Temporary or not, he supposed he had a duty to watch over the pack's health while he was in charge, even if it would take a little more time.

He sighed and turned back to the girl. He slid his hands

into his pockets to keep his posture casual. Even knowing his daughter was around this age, he found he couldn't imagine the sweet toddler he'd known transformed into this leggy, conflicted, proto-adult. "What's up?"

The girl twisted to look up at her mother. "Mom says I can't go to the movies until I do my shifting practice, but I usually practice down here, and you're down here, and anyway, I don't see what good it does. People are just able to shift farther from the full naturally, as they get older."

He raised his eyebrows at her. "Are they? Or does everyone get better because of all the practicing they've been doing?"

Her expression grew suspicious. "Well, I don't know, I guess."

"And so when some Were from a neighboring pack is taking liberties, you just roll over, and tell him to wait a few years?" Andrew took the sting from the words with a grin, which made her bristle more. As he'd suspected it might. This was a feisty one. "Everyone has to practice shifting outside the full when they're young. Besides, if everyone else your age can't shift right now, don't you want to show them up?"

The girl looked struck by this for a moment, but then her sullenness started to creep back in. Andrew started pulling his shirt over his head. "Come on. I'll do it with you."

The girl hesitated a few beats, but then she started pulling off her clothes too. "But you already shifted back and forth this morning." Since he was a comparative stranger, she frowned and crossed her arms over her chest before his own nudity made it more like any night of the full among her own pack. She relaxed and let her arms fall.

"But that's what practicing gets you." Andrew closed his eyes, having to search to find the point to push. The bigger drain this morning had been his injuries, not the shifting, but either way he was exhausted. Every Were hated shifting tired, and every young Were hated learning to shift when they couldn't just fall into it like in the full, but it was something you had to know how to do in an emergency.

He gritted his teeth against the pain of twisted muscles and bones. He was tired enough this was almost as bad as shifting in the new. Then the process was like shoving a heavy rock uphill, every muscle screaming in protest. The longer the shift took, the longer his body spent in a halfway configuration it wasn't designed to stand, and the worse it hurt.

It didn't get any easier, either. It hurt all the way until the moment when he was on four feet and the process was complete. A few muscles still jerked, but he shook himself, smoothing soreness out with movement.

The girl was still in human form, and he tilted his muzzle up to look her in the face. The height difference was annoying. He growled lightly to remind her time was wasting, and she closed her eyes, making a low whine in her throat with her effort.

Andrew waited a good five minutes, but her scent stayed static. It suggested that in his metaphor, she couldn't even find the damn rock in the first place. He couldn't coach her at the moment, either.

He dropped his head. Time to start the process all over again. It was worse going back, since he had less energy, and his muscles started out sore. When he was done, he stayed sitting on the floor, trying to look nonchalant about the fact that he couldn't stand.

"That was— Wow." The girl looked at him with big eyes.

Andrew nodded. His voice might betray him by being breathy if he answered. Judging by the smirk she threw his way, he suspected he hadn't fooled Silver. "Be glad the Lady's light is still there for you to find if you search," she told the girl, lips twisting.

The girl looked blank. "What?"

Andrew drew a deep breath. He could probably talk now without betraying himself. "She means it's not just about pushing harder. You're pushing plenty, but it doesn't do you any good if it's in the wrong spot. If you just fall into it every full, you don't learn the exact spot in your mind where the shift starts."

Silver shook her head. "If I'd meant that, I'd have said that. You have to use the Lady's light between the clouds. The light is dimmer, and you can't see your wild self as well. Remember that she's always beside you, you just have to call louder." Her voice wavered at the end, but she suppressed it. "Call to your wild self. Call until she listens. Don't drag her in by the scuff, growling all the way." She gave Andrew a pointed look. When he matched her look for look, she stuck out the tip of her tongue.

"Oh!" The girl concentrated for a moment, then her shift began. It took a full two minutes to complete, and she made panting noises of pain the entire time, but Andrew had never seen such a proud expression on someone in wolf before.

She trotted up the stairs to whuff triumphantly at her

mother. The woman looked just as proud, but hid it better. "Good job. Remember you have to shift back for school tomorrow." She turned back to Andrew, but hesitated before saying anything else. "Thank you."

"Come here," Silver offered. "You should rest a little before you shift back." The girl came to thrust her ears under Silver's hand for scratching and her mother disappeared upstairs, apparently willing to put her faith in the alpha handling the girl alone from here on out.

Andrew left the girl to Silver's petting as he dressed until he heard a panting growl. He turned to find the girl shifting back.

He sighed and crouched beside her. "I'm an *alpha,* and I also have a good few decades on you," he pointed out as she whined and twisted. "No need to show off."

The girl collapsed on her side, wheezing, once she made it back to human. She seemed to be too exhausted and aching to be smug or even nod, but Andrew figured she'd taken his point. He smoothed her hair, and helped Silver slide a floor pillow under her head.

Andrew was conscious of time passing, but there was no way he was going to just leave the girl now. He went to poke around the entertainment equipment to give her some privacy. He turned on the TV to find only static. It was hooked to a cable outlet, but it undoubtedly required some arcane combination of inputs, outputs, and channels to be chosen on each device involved in the tangle. Andrew noticed Silver watching him with interest, though he couldn't see any understanding of the equipment on her face. "Does Death give advice on electronics too?" Andrew chuckled when she gave him a look. "He seems a wolf of many talents, you have to admit."

After about five minutes, the girl pushed herself up onto her elbow. "I've never seen someone with white hair before," she told Silver as she pulled her clothes over to her. Exhaustion had stripped the teenage arrogance from her voice, leaving it much more pleasant. "Are you white in wolf too?"

Silver picked at a loose thread on the pillow. "I can't shift. My wild self got lost."

"Lost?" The girl's face scrunched up in confusion. "You can't lose something that's . . . part of your body, can you? It comes from growing up. Like your period." She paused after pulling on her shirt.

"Oh, that's gone too. I doubt I'll ever have cubs." The bleakness in Silver's words made Andrew's throat tighten.

"Leave it," he said, raising his voice, when it seemed like the girl might say something else.

The following silence felt thick. Andrew racked his brain for something that would interest a teen.

Silver beat him to it, though her voice's cadence was better suited to a younger child. "The Lady is white, you know. Her wild self. And her face up there." Silver pointed to the sky. "Like Death is black. She creates the light and he absorbs it."

The girl pressed her thumb to her forehead, automatic. "Well, Death *is* evil."

Silver laughed. The sound grabbed at Andrew's gut for

some reason, compelling. "I suppose I thought that at one point too, but mostly he's full of himself." She laughed again. "Yes, you are."

The girl gave Silver an incredulous look. "Who are you talking to?"

"Oh, Death follows me. But don't worry. I won't let him near you. It's me he wants. Dare made it so he can't have me, but I think he still follows me just to be an ass."

The girl tittered nervously. "You goth or something? Death betrayed the Lady."

Andrew sat on the couch as quietly as possible, not wanting to disturb Silver.

"Not because he wanted to. It may not make sense to you now, but when you get older you'll understand that sometimes things have to be done. Hard things. But everyone will hate the person who finally does them."

Andrew drew himself up straighter, recognizing the echo of his own words. Silver gave him a tiny smile when their eyes caught, then she looked away again. "But if they do them anyway, that's the mark of true honor." She let her breath slip out in a sigh and her words took on a storytelling cadence. "When the world was young, we couldn't die. Not by sickness or age, or injury. Only fire could destroy us, since fire was where the world began. Fire is how the world rebuilds itself even now. But back then the Lady lived among us, with Death at Her side, Her partner in everything. But the humans and the human gods were jealous. That is how humans exist— they are driven to take everything they see, and destroy it if they can't take it. The human gods gave them fire, and sent them to take what we have.

"But the Lady didn't see it. She thought we were safe. Death knew better. He knew that we were complacent, and if we did not learn of mortality, we would never stand against the humans. So he killed the first of us with his own jaws, so we could know death and fear it, and fight against it when the humans came. He had to do it, and it worked.

"And the Lady punished him, for betraying Her, because She had to do it too. Because he had stolen the voices of Her slain people, She stole his voice, so he must forever after borrow those of the souls he takes and returns to her. She took his name. And worst of all, She barred him from Her side until the end of our time. So he loves Her, but he can never feel Her presence again."

Silver tilted her head up so her tears couldn't spill free. Andrew's instincts screamed at him to touch, to pet, to hold, but the girl was right there, and the moment passed. Silver pulled herself together.

"Little heavy for a kid, don't you think?" he teased awkwardly.

"I'm not a kid," the girl protested. "But I still think Death is evil."

Silver smiled, a little tight, but a good effort. "I know, puppy." The girl bristled further at the diminutive and pushed herself up to finish getting dressed.

Andrew watched Silver, rather than the girl. Her expression was unreadable, but he kept turning her words over in his thoughts. Was he Death, doing what no one else would, or was Silver, barred from the Lady's presence? He supposed to Silver's mind he was barred from the Lady too, though he had chosen that when he ceased to believe.

17

Once Andrew had seen the girl to her mother, he returned to the kitchen where Pierce and another couple Were had gathered, cleaning up after lunch. Now he had a sensitive question, he might as well try it on everyone.

Something made everyone's heads come up before Andrew could speak, however. Unused to sorting traffic on the road from traffic up the driveway for this particular house, Andrew took a moment to realize what had attracted their attention. A car door slammed, and someone's key scraped in the front door.

"John!" Everyone seemed too frozen to answer. A woman's heels tapped down the hall. "Look, I'm so sorry, but there's no one else to take Edmond."

Pierce cast a frustrated glance at Andrew and stepped forward to intercept the woman. The other Were faded back into the kitchen, smelling of fear and more guilt. What the hell was going on?

John's footsteps thumped down the stairs in a great hurry and he skidded into the entryway behind her a moment later. The woman stopped short at John's sudden entrance. She was close enough now that Andrew could match her to the human woman's scent around the house. She looked to be in her midtwenties, with an aggressively fashionable haircut of the kind Andrew associated with women planning to climb the corporate ladder.

The baby in the sling across her front squalled, but subsided when she cupped her arm underneath to bounce him. He needed his diaper changed. Strange choice of girlfriend. Awfully young, and Andrew wouldn't have thought that John was the type to put up with a single mother.

"Susan, not now—" Pierce started herding her toward the door. The scent of panic bloomed from John's direction when he noticed Andrew watching the whole scene. He strode forward like he wanted to block Andrew's view with his shoulders. Andrew just sidestepped.

"I'm just dropping him off. I'll only be here a minute, I promise." Susan pushed right past the beta. Dominant. That made more sense for John. She unbuckled the sling and dropped a hefty diaper bag covered with tulips at John's feet. "Please, just for a few hours." She put the baby into John's unresisting arms.

Andrew rubbed at his jaw. That's how it was, then. John must be the child's father. Was this what John had been hiding? But this was too simple. People would give John shit, sure, but everyone had some human blood somewhere in their family tree. It was like how everyone had a relative among the true wolves if one looked far enough. These things happened, especially when you lived in a world where one had to practically live and breathe human. He presumed this explained yesterday's late arrival. John must have been arguing with her over whatever excuse he was using to keep her away while Andrew was here.

"Hi." Andrew put on a pleasant smile and stepped around John. Might as well introduce himself to the woman. John had no reason to hide her now his secret was out. Andrew didn't want that additional guilt confusing what he needed to find out.

Silver slipped in behind him. Less worried about manners, she stared at Susan with frank interest.

Susan rocked back on her heels like the hand Andrew extended to shake was some kind of threat. "Oh. Uh. Hi." She glanced to John and her baby, and then to the door and escape. Andrew suppressed a frown. He was keeping his dominance as damped as he always did for humans. Was he getting that sloppy, that he was scaring her?

"You smell of fear. Which, as Death says, is odd." Silver prowled over to stand between Susan and the door. "What's to fear? Those of our kind are hardly frightening unless you know."

"Know what?" Susan's hands started shaking, and her fear flared to choking levels. "John said the friend coming to stay was kind of a hard-ass, that's all." She threw Andrew an apologetic smile.

Andrew would have growled at Silver for scaring the woman for no reason, but Susan didn't quite smell of fear of the unknown. She smelled of guilt and fear of being found out. Her and the entire pack. The stink of panic had gathered thickly enough to cloud the hall.

Could she know about the Were? The conclusion seemed obvious, but Andrew couldn't wrap his head around the idea that anyone would be so stupid as to tell a human anything, sleeping with her or not.

"I doubt that's what he really said." Silver dropped to all fours, or at least three, with her bad arm tucked into her pocket. Susan flinched from the movement, a movement that, if anything, should have been less threatening in human terms.

There was no mistaking Susan's flare of fear, either. The human woman knew about them. How could John have told her? How could he?

"No!" John tried to hand his child back to his mother, but quivering tension made her slow to respond. Silver straightened and slipped between them and gathered the baby up, cradling him in her good arm. The moment the baby was elsewhere, Andrew shook off his shocked paralysis and closed the distance to John.

"Have you lost your mind?" Andrew had the satisfaction of seeing John flinch as he spat the words, a few inches from his face. "How could you possibly—"

John put a restraining hand on his arm, and Andrew jerked it off. "Outside. Do this outside." John repeated the motion, and Andrew repeated throwing it off.

"Why? Since she knows already—" Andrew glanced to Susan, and when he looked back, he saw such fear in John's eyes it disgusted him. Disgusted him with himself. He hated that his reputation was so bad people would actually think he'd threaten the life of John's child, or even the human he loved.

Andrew stomped for the front door without saying another word. John's garbled explanations to his girlfriend followed Andrew out to the front step where he waited, door open, for the other man to follow.

"—that's why I said you couldn't ever come to the house. He smelled it on you. It doesn't matter how much self-control you have, you can't hide that—"

Silver made an exasperated sound, and Andrew smiled slightly, imagining the matching expression. "He's not going to kill you. Either of you." Susan's wordless response didn't sound particularly soothed. "However stupid you were." That, too, sounded aimed at both members of the couple.

"John," Andrew snapped, putting an alpha's command into the word. The moment he heard John's steps coming toward him he started around the side of the house. He found the patch of shadows he wanted under the eaves alongside the garage. They'd still have to keep their voices down, but they would have more privacy from neighbors there than in the backyard.

"Dare—" John's voice was practically whining now. He dragged a hand through his hair, spiking it up.

"Look." Andrew brushed away a spider silk strand he'd picked up on his sleeve. The scent of decomposing grass clippings from the bin next door stung his nose. "Was this human woman the one who knew about the Bellingham pack, the person everyone was protecting?" He paused for John's jerky nod. "Do you swear on the Lady no one else but Portland knew about Silver's pack's existence?" For that, he caught John's gaze, to hit him with dominance as he answered, and read the truth in his eyes.

"Yes," John said, voice steady for that at least. Truth, so far as Andrew could tell.

"Fine. If she can swear she didn't tell anyone, I didn't hear anything about her, understand? I don't want to—" Andrew was so frustrated he couldn't figure out what he'd intended with his gesture, so he aborted it halfway. "Deal with this. Any of this. I think you're a moron who should have been castrated if he was going to let his dick do his thinking for him to this degree, but I can't scare the knowledge out of her, can I? So it can wait until I've dealt with the killer, and then you can have your pack back and all these stupid problems with it, and welcome."

John stared at him in silence for several moments. "Oh," he said at length. "Who'd have thought." Andrew speared him with an annoyed glance, and he continued. "That you're that style of alpha."

Andrew snorted. "What, temporary? Sure. Makes life much easier." He set his fist against the garage wall's siding, careful to hold back any force. "We none of us bask in unobscured moonlight. I married a European, of all things. No one was exactly happy about that at the time, as I recall. But that ended badly, and you know this is going to also."

"Susan's intelligent. She would never—"

"She's a young human. 'I won't tell anyone' actually means '—except my closest friend I trust not to tell anyone else.' You see how it starts?" Andrew got up into John's face again. "Or imagine if she was tortured. She can take a lot less than a werewolf could, should the killer decide to dig for a little information."

John barked a harsh laugh. "It's not like Selene could take much either. And yet you've hardly cut ties to her, have you?"

"Silver." The correction slipped out before Andrew even thought about it. "I'm protecting her from the danger she was already in when I met her. You're putting Susan into it."

The garage door machinery in the next house rumbled a warning of prying eyes arriving soon. The two men eyed each other for a moment before heading back to the front door.

Susan sipped a cup of coffee at the kitchen counter as they came in. She looked a little less severe with her jacket hung over the chair back, but maintained a self-possessed air.

Silver sat on a step stool rather than a kitchen chair, the baby in her lap now to save her arm from getting too tired. She made little yipping and growling noises as well as faces, entertaining him with canine baby talk. Susan looked twitchy, showing the usual human discomfort with the Were habit of passing a child around the pack like it belonged to everyone.

Seeing John, Susan picked up a second mug of coffee that had been waiting ready, and came over to offer it to him. "I'm so sorry—I thought I'd just be here for two minutes, and what I know or don't know wouldn't even come up—"

"It was going to come up eventually anyway," Andrew said before John could answer. "Better me than someone else."

Silver balanced the child's weight so she could prop him up for Andrew to look him in the face. He stared at Andrew blankly, lips a little poked out. "You can see his wild shape in his eyes!" Her face shone with excitement. "Even though he doesn't have a real one yet. Maybe that's where mine hid." She continued holding up the baby, like Andrew was supposed to look into his eyes and see—whatever was so important to Silver.

He ruffled the baby's hair instead, and the boy transferred his blankly intense gaze from the opposite wall to Andrew. Andrew's heart squeezed. He missed his daughter like a physical pain sometimes. Silver's arm looked like it was tiring from the strain, so Andrew got a good grip, took the baby from her, and swooped him around to the side. The baby made a sound like he wasn't sure if he was supposed to laugh or not. John flinched, and Andrew handed the boy to him unharmed.

"What the hell is she talking about?" Susan looked from Silver to John and back.

Andrew hadn't realized how Silver had gone from being incomprehensible to sounding almost normal to him until he saw Susan's completely baffled expression. "Silver sees our Goddess a lot. I think she's talking about how your son can't shift yet."

"Yet?" Susan glanced to John. The word had a dangerous overtone.

John winced. "I told you, there was always a chance that he wouldn't inherit—"

Andrew snorted. "And by 'always a chance' he means 'certain unsubstantiated rumors' about crossbreeds—"

"You may not have planned him, but he is the Lady's. Her light is on his face." Silver inserted herself into the conversation as she came up to flick the baby's cheek. "She watches over the smallest of Her children."

"How do you know we didn't—?" Susan's anger turned to focus on Silver.

"Death undoubtedly told her. Come on, Silver. Stop scaring the nice lady." Andrew patted Silver's shoulder and she snapped her teeth at his hand. He wasn't going to explain it in front of Silver, but it was an obvious conclusion. He doubted John would have planned to give himself the trouble a crossbreed child would cause. And he was nearly certain the man would not have lied about the chances of werewolf blood being inherited if he'd been faced with a woman making an informed decision.

Andrew moved around Silver to get a better position to smell Susan's reaction as he asked his next question. Hopefully her confusion over Silver's rambling would distract her and make her answer more honestly. "Did you ever tell anyone about John's friends up in Bellingham? Doesn't matter if you said they were human or not, just that you said they were in Bellingham."

Susan shook her head. "I didn't know he had friends in Bellingham." No lie in her scent.

Andrew let a breath trickle out. That was that, he supposed. Seattle wasn't hiding anything after all. And so the time continued to tick away without him having a real lead.

"I should go back there. Try to find the monster's name where the memories are stronger."

All eyes in the room turned to Silver except Susan's. Her disgruntled expression at having no clue what was going on deepened. Silver crossed her arms, good holding up bad, and looked stubborn.

"No." John spoke the word as Andrew opened his mouth to say the same. Andrew's automatic instinct to oppose John whenever he tried to meddle in Silver's business made him pause long enough to really see Silver's expression.

She looked and smelled frightened, but not like she had been before, at the mention of the killer or going back to the scene of the crime. It seemed like fear that had been harnessed to fuel action, resolve. He frowned. "Maybe she should. There's a lot that would help us if she could remember it."

John's expression started to darken. "No—"

"Death speaks to me in their voices. It's not as if I can escape them even here. You can't wrap me up and save me from what's in my own head and walking beside me." Silver tapped her temple and gestured to the area beside her feet that Death seemed to occupy most often. "Look to your own pack. Look to your child. Dare will need my help if he is to find the monster before the monster finds you."

"So let Dare go to Bellingham, if there's something in Bellingham." John held the baby closer and the boy squalled at the jostling.

Silver started to shake, and Andrew caught her shoulders in case she should start a seizure, but the trembling had the same focused quality as her fear, carrying her to her goal. "Dare doesn't know what I know. I have to help. He'd kill the baby first, you know. The monster would. That's how he caught us. The children. Held a knife to their throats, and we all sat still for him to tie up, no fight. That easy. To save the children from harm.

"And then he killed them. For mercy. Let the Lady keep the innocent soul while he tried to save yours. Only all his knives were silver. So it wasn't a mercy. One clean stroke, but you could see in their eyes that it burned to the last. The last thing they felt was the poison in their blood."

Susan made a strangled, gagging noise and grabbed for her child. The boy cried louder as he left his father's arms. John hissed a curse under his breath. Andrew tightened his grip on Silver, remembering only belatedly to think of bruises. Just when he thought he'd discovered the depth of the killer's perversions, something shook him to the core once more. Using a pack's children against them?

Silver switched her intense gaze to him. "You understand inaction, don't you? Let me do something. Let me go home. Stop him before it's someone else who is listening to silver screams."

Andrew drew in a long breath. She was right. He understood inaction, the emotions bubbling up until they either had to be turned inward, or outward. His had been rage, not fear, but who was he to say Silver didn't have some rage too. She had been a powerful woman and that didn't just go away. She'd want justice even more than he did. "Give me a chance to exhaust every other lead, at least. After that, we'll go." There had to be something he'd overlooked. He'd do everything he could to find it, to save her the need to face her home.

"So now we know why they didn't fight," John said, rage in his voice sliding into desperation. "Lady's light in Her realm above. Using the children. But how does that help us?"

"We know it could have been one man alone," Andrew said, pinching the bridge of his nose as he tried to think. He was no detective—as enforcer, he put his nose to the trail of the perpetrator, and found them for punishment. Easy, clear-cut. "We know he could have been a stranger . . ." He repeated that to himself a few times and got no farther.

What he needed was a fresh perspective. He got out his phone and nodded to John. "I'm going to make some calls." He headed for the stairs. This time, it was less important if someone overheard. It might strengthen the impression their alpha was accomplishing something, even, when he really wasn't. At the head of the stairs, Andrew drew in a deep breath until he found the direction with the strongest scent of John. Silver verified that clue by turning that way without stopping after she climbed the stairs behind him.

John's former room was reasonably spacious, though a lot of that room was taken up by his king bed. A flat-screen TV spanned the entire wall between the windows opposite it. Even with clean sheets on the bed, the place still stank of John in a way that suggested his dirty clothing hadn't often made it into a hamper in the closet. Silver jumped on the bed immediately, pulling over a pillow to lean on.

Andrew remained standing as he dialed Benjamin. The older alpha waited patiently after they exchanged greetings for Andrew to get to his real point but Andrew couldn't think of a way to phrase his question without sounding weak. When the silence drew out a bit too long, he started with the easier thing first. "Any news on that lone of yours?"

"Nothing yet." Again, Andrew got the sense Benjamin suspected there was more to this call than that, and was waiting for Andrew to get his act together.

Better to just say it, then. "I don't know where to pick up this scent, Benjamin. I'm reduced to backtracking, but I keep feeling like there's something I've missed." He summarized all he'd found for Boston. Laid out, it seemed so little. Probably Were, could have been someone alone since he'd controlled the pack with threats to the children.

"Have you called your contacts in Europe to see what they can add? I know it's not anything you've seen before, but the use of silver remains."

Andrew drew in a deep breath against the familiar surge of anger. Why couldn't anyone leave it alone? Of course he hadn't.

"You should have seen him the last time someone mentioned his past," Silver remarked, coming into range of the cell phone's pickup. "You're smart to stay out of reach to bring it up."

"Leave it alone." It was hard for Andrew to get the words out with his jaw clenched.

Silver cocked her head in a listening posture. "Death wishes to point out that you're avoiding your memories as much as I am."

"You're the one who just finished saying you didn't have any idea for what to do next." Benjamin's tone took on a paternal flavor of exasperation. "What, you called thinking I'd give you permission not to do what you're avoiding so hard? No such luck."

"Of course not. But I'm still not going to." Andrew put his hand on Silver's shoulder to shove her aside and out of the conversation, but she proved surprisingly resistant, bracing herself on both feet.

"Death says your wife wants you to man up and stop being such a coward."

Andrew shoved hard enough to throw Silver off balance this time. She smirked and pressed right back into his personal space. "Come. I can take you down easily." She brought up her hand to make a "bring it on" gesture. It was so incongruous, laughter bubbled up from somewhere. Andrew had no doubt that Silver could hold her own in a conflict, but it would be from knowing not to start a head-on fight. This was playacting.

He snorted, and took her good wrist, holding it tightly enough that she couldn't move her arm. She kept her eyes on him calmly, as if she was waiting for him to think it through now that she'd freed him from his immediate, unreasoning anger.

"They wouldn't tell me anything anyway. If they did, they'd lie." It came out as a snarl. He dropped her wrist.

Silver stepped away this time. "You still need to try."

Rich laughter came from the phone. "Well, well."

Andrew snarled again. "What's that supposed to mean?"

Benjamin gave a last chuckle. "It means good luck. Tell the young woman I'm impressed." With that, Benjamin ended the call.

"I'm hungry," Silver said with the bouncy tone she'd used the last time she used the announcement as a stone thrown to disrupt the growing tempest of people's moods. "I'm going to get some dinner. Do you want some?"

"Go ahead." Andrew tipped his chin to the door and she let herself out. Someone downstairs could certainly find her something. He didn't want to deal with people in his current mood. He couldn't hear anyone in the adjoining rooms, so the pack must be giving him privacy, which was nice given the turn the phone conversation had taken.

Andrew stared at his phone for a while and then threw it down on the bed. Benjamin was right, of course. Not about wanting permission for cowardice, but about the necessity of it. That's what he had been promising himself earlier, wasn't it? He'd do anything to save Silver the trip home. Well, this was part of that anything. He glowered at the phone.

Silver returned with takeout Chinese. The bag looked deflated around the three or four cartons inside, so Andrew assumed she'd taken the remains of the household's larger order. She left the bag on the floor, selected one carton, and settled herself cross-legged on the middle of the bed. She drew out food piece by piece with her fingers. She licked her fingers after a broccoli chunk and made a forestalling noise when Andrew picked up his phone.

"Eat first." She left her carton where it was and leaned perilously over the edge of the bed to grab him another. He came to take it quickly so she didn't fall.

"What, now you're telling me to put it off?" Andrew opened the carton and looked inside. It wasn't the highest quality Chinese food but it did smell edible at a time when his instincts were waking up to remind him that his last meal had been breakfast several shifts ago.

He rustled in the bag for a plastic fork, too concerned with speed to bother with the chopsticks, and dug into the sweet-and-sour pork. Silver had chosen well. No extraneous vegetables to slow him down in that. He sat on the edge of the bed.

Silver grinned and returned to her carton. She sat cross-legged facing him and continued eating with her fingers. "You'd have been gnawing on *my* leg soon, the way you were acting. Not the mood to go into a tricky conversation with." She wiped up a drop of sauce on her thigh with one finger. John's bedspread was doomed. "Besides, eating helps nearly all bad moods."

"You sound like my mother," Andrew said, pausing for breath now that his tines scraped the container's bottom. He checked the other cartons to find the rice and then levered in a thick raft to soak up the sauce. "She was always pushing food on people any time it looked like there might be a fight." He frowned in memory. "It worked more often than not, too, I suppose. I was a morbid kid so I was more interested in watching the fight happen. I stomped off to find my own pack fairly early."

"Like my brother," Silver agreed. Andrew caught himself before he tensed, worrying about the memory's effect on her, but she seemed mellowed by the food also. "He started planning his rise to alpha before our Lady ceremonies." She paused a beat and then laughed. Andrew presumed that Death had offered some comment.

Andrew moved on to the remaining General Tsao's. "I was a little shit, really."

"Not little anymore," Silver said, and then leaned backward when he made a threatening movement with his fork.

As pleasant as it was feeling full and relaxed, it didn't take much longer to finish up all the food and clear the cartons into the wastebasket. Andrew picked up his phone and stared at his in-laws' address book entry for a while, making sure the number was correct. He checked his watch. Five P.M. That would make it one A.M. in Spain. Pushing it a little, but Andrew suspected Arturo would still be awake.

Enough delay. He punched in his brother-in-law's number. When Arturo answered in Spanish it took Andrew's brain a moment to dig out a long-disused fluency. The pause stretched long enough the man growled in annoyance.

"Yes? Who is this?" Arturo asked again.

"I am out of practice," Andrew said in Spanish, feeling out the words. "It has been a long time."

This time, the silence was resounding. Andrew grimaced, wishing that he had Arturo's scent to clarify his reaction. Was it rage? Indifference?

"Dare?" He pronounced it with Spanish vowels, dah-ray. Still no hint of his emotions in his voice.

"I need your help." It didn't bode well for the conversation ahead that even those simple words were hard to say. At least his Spanish was coming back to him. "We have a killer—"

"And it's somehow our fault? Not all evil comes from Europe, Dare." The hostility in Arturo's voice was almost a relief to hear.

"It does when he's so well-versed in the more perverse uses of silver, Arturo." He flattened the name with ugly American vowels, a familiar swing in a half-remembered pattern of blows. That was the way it had always been with his brother-in-law.

"Try Alaska. They're too crazy to care about the morality of it."

"Injected silver."

Stunned silence. Andrew couldn't have said how he knew without the scent, but he was suddenly sure that Arturo knew something. "You've seen it before. Who? Where?"

"There was a man." Arturo hesitated. "Early twentieth-century Eastern Europe somewhere."

Andrew waited several seconds. "And?"

"The monks who did it were all slaughtered, of course. There was talk of mercy killing him, but his mate was powerful and so got him locked up instead. He's still there."

"Is he?"

"Of course he is. I suggest you book your flight if you want to talk to him." Arturo's voice grew smooth and oily. He was undoubtedly desperate to have Andrew at least on the right continent so that Arturo could have another chance at beating him up. "He won't make much sense in person, but it's not like he's going to be able to come to the phone."

"You're lying." Something was off about how smoothly Arturo had agreed the man was still there. If it had happened so long ago, how would Arturo know for sure without checking?

Arturo hesitated just too long, and Andrew knew for sure. Another dead end. He couldn't even ask this other victim for information if he had disappeared. Frustration twisted in his stomach, but his mind kept going, prodding at the information. Another victim, at large. At large, smelling like silver—

The realization hit him all at once. There had been another lone, smelling of the metal, before Silver herself. Male. And now Boston's people were chasing a lone in the area once more. What if it had been more than those monks? What if the other victim had come to North America and led trouble here?

"He escaped, and I suppose none of you thought to warn the North Americans? Who knows what followed him over here." Andrew trailed off into a snarl.

"He was never Madrid's problem." Arturo hung up. Andrew could only hope he was feeling a little guilt. How could they? Even if the victim hadn't brought trouble with him, why had no one hunted him down to help him? He had to be in pain, as Silver had been.

Andrew turned, searching for something to destroy that wouldn't cost too much for him to replace later when he handed the pack back. Nothing suggested itself to him. John had removed all the small items, leaving only the solid furniture.

Silver caught his hand, squeezing. He tried to yank away, but she had a werewolf's strength, and he would have to put his whole body into it if he was going to succeed. He squeezed back, and it devolved into something of a mini arm-wrestling contest. The angle gave her enough of an advantage that he didn't win immediately.

"There's another victim. We have to find him, help him, see what he knows." Andrew clenched Silver's hand so hard she squeaked.

He opened his again quickly, leaving hers lying across his palm. The angry red finger marks weren't ripening to purple and then brown and yellow with the speed they would have with a healthy werewolf, and he drew in a breath of anger with himself. "Why didn't you stop me?" He pressed her hand flat between his. Had he broken any bones?

"Another."

The moment Silver spoke, Andrew realized that she was gone. Far gone. He hadn't considered the effect his words might have once he switched back to English. "Silver? Yes, another victim. He was injected like you."

Her eyes wouldn't focus on his. "What doesn't kill you makes you stronger. Stronger. Purified. Purified of the Lady. Not the children. They weren't strong enough. He killed them first. Kinder. Put them out of their misery. Put her out of her misery, Dare."

It took Andrew a moment to recognize the cadence of Rory's words. That conversation seemed so long ago now.

"No." He gave it the weight of absolute certainty, every ounce of authority he had ever held or pretended to. "No." He scooped her up into his arms, feeling the way she was shivering. Not a seizure, but she showed no signs of snapping back to lucidity again.

It would have taken too much juggling to get her under the covers on the bed, but he managed to pull the comforter out from under her and lay it on top. She still shivered, but lapsed into silence. Her hair had fallen over her face, and he brushed it away. She seemed to calm with the stroking motion, only to begin to shiver again when his touch left her.

Instincts, canine or human, urged him to extend that calming touch more widely, and Andrew sat down on the bed's edge and pulled off his shoes before the problem there occurred to him. He put his hand over hers, and she grasped it tightly. Could you cuddle without ulterior motives? Silver was too out of it, but his body was already giving him signals that it wouldn't end up being so pure and innocent on his side.

Her shivers were subsiding even with just that handclasp as comfort, at least. Andrew let her keep the hand and thought hard about the minutia of flight plans. He needed to get a flight to Boston as soon as possible. If he couldn't buy a ticket directly, he'd go and see about standby. He'd have to be careful, too. Rory could come after him if he realized he was on Roanoke territory.

Silver turned over to get more comfortable. She took his arm with her, trying to settle it over her hip so he would be pulled into spooning her.

Andrew jerked away. Silver made a protesting noise and

tried to hold him, but she couldn't do anything about it when he actually decided to break her hold. After a moment she went still and her back took on an accusing tenseness.

"Silver. You're hurt. I can't. Too much temptation—" He swallowed. "We can talk about it later when it wouldn't be taking advantage." *When would that be?* a little voice at the back of his mind asked. It didn't look like she would ever heal entirely, whatever her progress lately. How could anyone with a conscience be with her when she was like this?

"Fuck you," Silver said. She jerked the coverlet over her head, muffling her voice. "Isn't that my decision?"

Andrew leaned over and stopped with his hand short of her shoulder's lump in the blanket. It seemed disrespectful to touch her comfortingly now. "Not when you can't stand to hear your own name, no." Silver maintained a sullen silence, and Andrew straightened after a moment.

Flight plans. He needed to keep his mind on making flight plans. Hopefully before he left for the airport he'd have time for a cold shower.

18

Her world had changed, Silver realized as she searched for anything to focus on besides Dare's lingering scent in her nose. At one time, she'd had trouble telling dream from reality, but for the fact that she sometimes felt the Lady's light when she wished hard enough for it in the dreams. She never felt it when she was awake. In both places, she walked through misty landscapes, unsure of their form and landmarks. Or at least she had.

But the real world was not like that anymore. The Lady was not always full above her, filling the mist with diffuse light. Was that hopeful? It seemed the Lady waning should not be, but it was nice to walk on ground that was solid and not changeable as the mist and be able to speak so that Dare could understand.

If he hadn't already decided to ignore her on a topic. Infuriating man. Infuriating, irresistible man.

"If you could forget your urges long enough, we need to talk, you and I." Death paced to stand before her, but did not fold down to sit on his haunches. His refusal to relax made Silver uncomfortable, along with his use of her brother's voice. Her brother had always said that: we need to talk.

"It's not my fault I'm still distracted by them. If he'd just stop being so damn stubborn and—gentlemanly—" Silver sighed. Was that a compliment or a complaint?

Death snorted. "So hold him down." That was in his usual voice, not Silver's brother's, and she laughed. "But do it later. You have something more important to do now. You no longer have time to avoid it."

Silver ran her fingers along the ground, smoothing out a wrinkle in a fold of it. She supposed she shouldn't pretend that she didn't have an idea what Death was talking about, but not thinking about it was easier. "I told you—"

Death leaned over and snapped his teeth so close to where her injured arm lay, she felt the movement of air. The helpless feeling of being unable to jerk her hand away almost brought tears to her eyes. She aimed a smack at his head instead, and actually brushed an ear tip with her palm.

"So you're content to continue to let him fight your battles alone? The monster is close. You know he is. And if you sit back and do nothing, or only play at finding his name, he'll free your warrior's voice for me too. You know this." Death's voice had a growl now. His eyes appeared disquietingly dark and deep, as if by looking too far she would see all the way

back to the first voices that he had collected when he betrayed the Lady.

Silver lifted her bad arm with her other to hold it in her
lap. "So you've said before. But what good can I do? I'm in no
shape to fight him." She swallowed, mouth feeling dry. She
did know what she could do. Knew, but almost couldn't make
herself say it. "I could lead him away. If the monster chases
me, Dare can take him from behind, with much less danger."

Death let his silence be his agreement.

Dare's scent and that of food reached Silver, carried by the
den's air currents, but she ignored him. She didn't feel like
speaking to him yet. "I know. I know. Just—give me time. I've
been trying to work myself up to it. We spent so long running—" It was strange that Death had been so much a part of
the journey she thought of him as participating in it now, even
though in the beginning he'd helped chase. "I wanted this to
be the end of it. To be able to rest."

Death whuffed, like the matter was settled, though she
could have sworn she hadn't actually agreed to the plan. Silver rubbed her face once more, running her fingers through
her hair to straighten it. Lady help her.

Andrew put off getting his bag from the room where Silver
was resting as long as he could, but it didn't take that long to
inform the pack where he was going, book exorbitantly expensive tickets online, and get directions to the airport. Even
beyond the recent awkwardness, he didn't want her to figure

out he was leaving without her until it was too late for arguments.

He heard her steps on the stairs when he was taking his boarding pass out of the printer in John's office. He froze, but she turned deeper into the house instead. Maybe she would join the others in the kitchen. Andrew didn't wait to see. He jogged up the stairs to grab his bag. He took a moment to check everything was there and tuck the boarding pass away, but it wasn't like he'd had time to unpack in the first place.

Someone came up to the doorway and Andrew turned to find Silver there with a plate with a dozen or so brownies. "For your journey," she said, holding it out with all appearance of being calm.

Andrew stayed where he was, expecting a trick. That was it? No objections? What was she up to? Silver just raised her eyebrows like she couldn't imagine what he was so suspicious about. He reached for a couple of the gooey rectangles, but Silver moved the plate away. "Greedy! One's for you. The rest of these are mine."

Andrew snorted in amusement. "Alpha's share." He made another grab and Silver darted past him into the room and out of range. So that was it. She hoped the game would delay him. Andrew checked his watch. Not a bad strategy, but as long as he kept an eye on the time, he figured he'd be safe to indulge her. It would be nice to leave on a laughing note and the game appealed.

Silver went to sit on the empty waist-high bookshelf beside the bed. She set the plate in her lap and picked up a brownie for herself. Andrew snatched one in his first raid, but Silver thwarted his grab for the next one. She stuffed the last of hers into her mouth and stood up on the shelf, lifting the plate out of his reach.

Andrew grabbed her around the waist and lifted her to the center of the room. She shrieked with laughter and held the plate even higher, though it was tipping badly. "I think your cunning plan has backfired," she told him.

"I'm not done yet." Andrew shifted his hold so it was more stable under her ass, then tossed her. Only about an inch, and his arms were around her the whole time, but she shrieked again and dropped the plate. It landed brownies-down, saving the plate but not the dessert or the carpet. Silver wiggled and clamped her legs around his waist so he couldn't try the trick again, leaving him with—rather than brownies—a generous armful of female Were. His body seemed to think it was more than a fair trade.

Andrew's phone rang, and he dropped Silver to her feet, glad of the distraction. Dammit. What had happened to watching the time and not getting caught up in her game? Where the hell was his control? It hadn't been *that* long since the last time he'd had someone in his bed, even if that had been one of the ill-fated flings with human women.

The phone identified the caller as Laurence, and Andrew frowned at it for a few seconds before answering. The lingering distraction of Silver's presence made it hard to think. What was Roanoke's beta doing calling him? Did he want to crow about his bump in status since Andrew left?

"Dare." Laurence's voice was barely a whisper, ragged with fury and fear. "He's here. He's got Ginnie."

Andrew could hardly think for a second, all his muscles paralyzed. "What? Who?"

"He must have tracked that white-haired rabbit of yours out here. He's got a knife to Ginnie—" Laurence growled a lower oath. "He's not watching me right now, but I don't think I have long . . . don't say anything. He'll hear you." The sound took on the tinny white noise of a cell switched to speaker phone. Andrew's muscles quivered with the need to do something—anything—to affect events three thousand miles away.

"Now, now. I won't hurt the pretty little thing. She's too young for my help, anyway." The new male voice had a Slavic twist to his consonants. Silver folded to the ground at Andrew's feet. She curled into a fetal position and pressed her hand tightly over her ear. Tears streamed down her cheeks. "Just tell me where I can find my Selene." Silver started to hyperventilate, but Andrew was too frozen to do anything about it.

"We don't know any Selene." Rory's voice. Andrew winced to hear how weak he sounded.

"White hair, bad arm? You couldn't miss her. Ah, I see you do know her." There must have been some expression on Rory's face that gave it away, as the stranger laughed. Ginnie— Andrew assumed it was Ginnie—whimpered. "Where can I find her?"

"Put her down, first." Rory's voice grew more firm. "Laurence! No!"

A growl from nearer the phone's speaker. "All of us against him, Roanoke. He won't have time—"

"No," Rory said again, less sure this time. Andrew closed his eyes. He couldn't imagine being forced to make that choice, Ginnie's life or taking the stranger down. He'd probably choose to save his daughter too. But how had Rory let her get captured in the first place? No threat should ever have gotten that close to the pack house. How could he have let his pack down that way?

"We've seen her." Rory's voice wavered.

"But her trail ends here. She traveled somewhere. Drove, flew. You know where." The stranger laughed again, timing all wrong. It was a normal laugh, but so out of place, it sounded mad.

"Ginnie!" A new voice, desperate. Sarah's.

"Mommy!"

"Would you like to tell me where, 'Mommy'?" The stranger's voice moved, farther from Sarah's. Rory's wife began to sob. Andrew jerked as that sound made his instincts scream even louder, demanding he somehow launch himself across the miles.

Sarah drew in a deep breath to smooth her voice from the crying. "She just ran off that first night. I didn't even have the chance to get a real meal in her, she was so skinny, but we don't know where she went."

Even knowing every word was a lie, Andrew found himself believing Sarah. Her quivering terror only lent it credibility. Lady bless her, for taking the risk the stranger would smell it on her.

"And you didn't even notice which way she went, didn't follow? Careless of you." The stranger's voice sharpened.

"She left going south. Rory underestimated how fast she could move and lost her trail near Richmond." Just the right note of suppressed accusation entered Sarah's voice.

Andrew held his breath. Would the stranger buy it? The man chuckled. "Your husband seems surprised by this information, Mommy." Ginnie began to keen. "Where is Selene really, Daddy?"

"Seattle," Rory said, words heavy. Andrew clenched his free hand until it shook. No. No. How could that pussy throw away his wife's bravery and just hand Silver over to her enemy?

Sarah broke in again, panic making her voice stumble like water over rocks. "But it's not our fault if she's not there anymore. Promise you won't come back for us. Laurence flew out there with her, and dropped her off with the pack. They said they'd take care of her. You didn't stay long enough to know she didn't run off again, did you, Laurence?"

"No, ma'am." Laurence's voice came louder than the others again, startling. He must have kept his answer short to avoid an outright lie.

"Much obliged," the stranger said. "Don't worry, sweetheart. I'd be more surprised if she did stay anywhere." He sounded smug at his own magnanimity for not blaming them. Ginnie's second "Mommy!" dopplered, then grew muffled, suggesting a dash to bury her face against her mother's shoulder.

Many voices started up at once, too many to make out individual speakers, until Laurence came back in isolation, speaker phone punched off. "He's gone. Rory won't let us chase—Lady damn it!"

"At least we're warned. And he doesn't seem to think it will be possible to warn her, so he won't expect it." Andrew had a hard time making himself sound like he believed it either. He dropped to his knees to stroke Silver's hair. "It's all right. We know he's coming. I've got to go get Seattle mobilized, Laurence."

"Of course." Laurence ended the call before Andrew could.

Andrew holstered his phone and picked Silver up like a child to put her on the bed. To his surprise, she stirred and struggled until he set her down on her feet again. Her cheeks were salty-damp, but she'd stopped crying.

"I underestimated her bravery," Silver said in a small voice.

"Sarah?" Andrew nudged her to sit on the bed and only moved for the door when it seemed she was content to stay. She didn't need to listen to any of the planning to come.

"I dismissed her as being weak, but I do not know if I could have done the same in her place, deceived the monster that way."

Andrew rubbed the heel of his hand against his forehead. He'd underestimated Sarah just as much. She'd done what her coward of a husband couldn't do, and given them a bit of an advantage. Not much of one, but every piece would help. "You'll be able to thank her yourself when this is all over," he said, and jogged downstairs to tell the others.

19

For all the events back in Virginia had seemed to take an eternity to happen, they took only a few moments to convey to John when Andrew found him in the living room. John bellowed down into the basement for Pierce, and their war council solidified in the dining room. Andrew leaned on a chair back to keep himself from pacing. John and Pierce and another woman who was clearly part of the pack's muscle— what kind of alpha was Andrew, when he couldn't remember everyone's names yet? But he couldn't worry about that now— waited more quietly at the front, heads bowed. It was easier for them, Andrew realized. They just had to follow the orders he gave. A smattering of other pack adults filled in at the edges of the room to find out what was happening.

"We need to get the children safe first. That's the absolute priority. He's proved that's how he gets to people, so our strength of numbers won't do a damn thing if he gets his hands on one of them." Andrew flexed his hands on the chair, cracking his knuckles.

"Where are we sending them?" Pierce asked, running fingers through his dark hair. It eroded the pretty image, taking the style from artfully mussed to just plain messy.

"I'm sure you have property somewhere near the edge of the territory, but if you can manage to mend fences with Portland, I think it would be better to join them. Being with a different pack should confuse the issue for our killer, and that puts our families behind their fighters, without having to draw down our strength here."

John looked blank. "Mend fences? We've always had an amicable border with Portland, but you were there last. Was Michelle angry about something?"

Andrew suppressed an urge to put his face in his hands in exasperation. "Well, she noticed you'd stopped trying to jump her like it was a spring full, and cut most contact. To hide Susan, I presume. But if you let her know you're no longer interested in getting into her pants, I think she'd forgive you."

John coughed, and the other two Were smirked. "I can do that."

Andrew nodded. "Speaking of your girlfriend, have her take your son to her parents'. Coach her in the usual scent trail stuff—shower, new clothes, don't get out of the car on the way to her destination, stay indoors, you know the drill."

Andrew looked to Pierce and the other woman next. "We'll stay here. Silver's scent's all over the place, he'll show up here eventually. I want a few people stationed on likely entrance points, too. Airport and train stations. Maybe we'll luck out and get some warning when he arrives."

Andrew let John point people out, since he didn't know the names—one got Sea-Tac and another King Street Station. Andrew pinched the bridge of his nose. Now they came to the part he hated. "Silver should stay here too, rather than going to safety with all the families. We can't risk her scent bringing the killer down on them."

John drew in a ragged breath, but didn't object, even with a growl. Andrew met the eyes of the other two, checking that he didn't see any resistance. When he found none, he nodded to release them from the meeting.

"Why not set my scent on the wind, to bring him right to us? When we expect him, where we expect him?" Silver startled Andrew by walking into the dining room. She stood straight, all evidence of tears gone.

"No, Silver." Andrew put a hand on her shoulder as he passed her on the way out of the dining room. The basement would probably be safest for her. She slapped his hand away and he stopped and gritted his teeth. "It puts you in too much danger. If you're going to be credible bait, you have to go out somewhere alone. And if you're alone even for a while, he could reach you before us."

"Kind of you to even bother to explain your reasoning." Silver's voice rose. "But you're still not actually listening. You're looking at me, thinking 'Oh, she's crazy. She's just babbling again.' That's an answer to everything. You don't have to listen to me, you don't have to try to understand my arguments,

you just have to remember I'm crazy." She came to stand before Andrew, chin tilted to close the gap in their heights
when she looked into his eyes. "Then you don't have to feel
bad when you lock me up. It's for my own good."

Andrew clenched his jaw, and resisted the urge to reach
out to squeeze her shoulders. Something told him she'd take
it—correctly—as him trying to soothe her out of her burst of
insanity. This level of self-awareness made his heart squeeze to
watch, since he couldn't do anything to help her. He couldn't
make her sane. But he couldn't lie and tell her that nothing was
wrong either. If she would even have believed him.

"I knew it." Silver jerked her head to the side, breaking their
gaze. "You know why I'm offering to do it? Because someone
has to. You know about that, Dare. Someone has to do the
thing no one else will do. And no one will thank them for it,
will they?" Her good hand clenched. "The monster wants me.
He'll follow me anywhere. I'm the one who can lead him into
a trap."

"It's not worth putting you in danger." Since he wasn't going to touch her, Andrew tried to put his concern for her into
his expression. What was so bad about letting him protect
her?

"You can't change what was already done," Silver snapped,
using her working shoulder muscles to hold her bad arm out
wide and accusing. "And you can't stop him forever. He will
find me eventually. I'm tired of running from that truth as well
as him. He might as well find me on our terms." She slammed
her good fist against his upper arm.

"No, Silver." Andrew took a good grip on her upper arm

this time and propelled her to the basement. Whether she was crazy didn't matter. Her idea was too risky. She was going to stay here where they could protect her. "You're not to try it anyway on your own."

Silver didn't struggle, just gave him a look of pure frustration and disgust, and went where he pushed. "I understand." Her eyes flicked down like Death had said something, but otherwise her manner didn't give any hint as to what she'd felt she'd heard.

Andrew winced. He knew better than to think this would be the end of it. She hadn't given in, she was just biding her time. They'd have to keep one eye on her while they kept the other out for the arriving killer. Dammit.

20

Silver ignored Death as they descended into the deepest, most defensible part of the den, not wanting Dare to hear that she had no intention of following his directions. It was madness to let the monster choose his time and place to attack them, to choose his strategy. Better to entice him in quickly, before he had time to think.

"You really think he believed you?" Death commented, curling up near Silver's feet. He used his favorite male voice, leaving Silver's ghosts alone for now.

When Silver didn't answer once more, Death let his tongue hang out in a long laugh. "I know you better than that. I think he does too."

Silver rounded on Death once Dare had left her. "He can't stop me. I'm going to do it. I promise you that. I just have to choose my moment. They can't watch me every breath of every minute. They need to look to their own plans. Then I'll run, and draw the monster away, so they can capture him from behind."

"I know."

Silver felt wobbly, as if she'd aimed a blow only to meet with no resistance. Death sounded almost . . . concerned? The taunting tone had left his voice. Silver stared at him, but there was nothing to read in the black fur of his face. He put his chin on his paws and settled in to wait, same as her.

Andrew had never been particularly good at waiting. He could sweat through it, same as he would sweat through staying human in the full, but it took most of his attention for the effort. If the killer found a commercial flight immediately, it would take him hours to reach this coast, longer if he couldn't. But if he was related to the European victim, he'd gotten to North America somehow, so Andrew wasn't willing to bet on him taking the bus now.

Andrew took the first watch, wandering around in wolf in the backyard to keep a nose to the air currents. The currents got more boring as the flurry of everyone packing up and calling in sick to work and school died away, and the pack's noncombatants left for Portland. The young, single Were who had remained behind that weren't out by the airport mostly stayed inside, waiting for their turn on watch.

The hours stretched on into the night, and Andrew took

his turn inside to eat something and stretch out in front of the TV in the living room. He checked on Silver, but she was still sulking down in the basement.

His phone's ring startled him from a doze in front of endlessly repackaged sports highlights. He squinted at the number on the screen, realized it belonged to the woman out at Sea-Tac, and woke up very quickly. "Dare."

"I've got a Were here, but he surrendered quietly. No smell of silver. Claims to know you?" The woman sounded a little breathless with excitement. Andrew scrubbed aching eyes. Ah, to be so young. Who could be so stupid as to show up on Seattle territory now, of all times? Was the stranger playing a deeper game? He'd sounded far too crazy on the phone not to stink of it.

"Dare? I'm not trying to cause trouble." Andrew recognized Laurence's voice after a beat, distorted by the distance from the phone's inferior microphone.

"Let me talk to him," he told the woman, stuffing down his anger until he heard the phone being passed over. "What in the name of all that's holy in the Lady's realm are you doing here? Are you working with our killer?"

"No, Dare. I swear it on the Lady. I'm here to help." Laurence's tone was uncharacteristically subdued, and Andrew could just imagine his tail-between-the-legs posture.

Andrew put his face in his hand. He'd have to check Laurence out by scent in person to be sure he was sincere. They could use the support if he was. He was a capable enough fighter, given the right orders. "Are you insane? Did Rory seriously give you permission to come out here?" Andrew couldn't imagine that the man had defied his alpha. Not Laurence. That would mean thinking for himself.

"Rory's going crazy. He knows we all think he fucked up, letting that guy get to Ginnie, and he's getting paranoid about his position and the rest of the sub-packs, and he's just—we need you back, Dare. Please."

Andrew got to his feet to turn on the overhead light. The single lamp he'd left on was casting annoying shadows. Better for his eyesight for things to be either bright or completely dark. "You should know why I can't do that." He snarled. "Especially now."

"No! I know." Andrew could hear Laurence tucking an invisible tail again. "That's why I came to help you. To . . . get away for a while, and allow you to come back faster."

The hesitation was heavy with something unsaid, but Andrew was too worried about a dozen other problems to bother figuring it out. Should he have Laurence come straight here to check his story, or somewhere unrelated? But picking him up from somewhere else would thin their strength even more. If Laurence gave anyone the pack house address, it wouldn't get them here that much faster than following Silver's scent. He growled for Laurence to hand him back to the Seattle woman. "Shove his ass in a taxi back here, so you can stay at your post."

Andrew ended the call and went to warn the others and find some coffee.

When Laurence arrived and turned away from paying the driver, he moved like he was in pain. Andrew let him come up to the house rather than meeting him on the driveway, both to allow the cab time to turn out of sight, and also to verify his initial impression.

The longer the man walked, the more unmistakable it was. No bruises were visible on Laurence's skin, but that meant nothing on a werewolf. If Laurence was still in any pain, however minor, it meant the damage had soaked past his ability to heal it all at once. And it had been a long plane ride over from Virginia.

"You working with our killer?" Andrew planted himself on the path downwind from Laurence. The man's head shake smelled legitimate. "He the one that worked you over?" Another shake. John and Pierce slipped into the doorway, arms crossed. It reminded Andrew of how Rory liked to have a couple thug types standing by whenever he met someone. He must be starting to look like a real alpha. It disgusted him. He waved them back, but not before he caught Laurence noticing their body language.

"Rory did this, then?" Andrew growled to distract him. He held the door open to bring Laurence into the entryway, shut it, and then crossed over to the man. He put a hand on the side of Laurence's neck, to keep him still and calm, then ran a hand down the man's side. Laurence winced when Andrew found the cracked ribs. If those were left, it meant the energy of healing had probably gone into something like a punctured lung.

As Andrew kept his hand on Laurence's neck, a corner of his mind noted how the man relaxed into the gesture. Dammit, he wasn't part of Roanoke anymore, and he didn't want the pack he had, never mind another follower. "Laurence," he said sharply, reminding the man that he'd left a question unanswered.

"I told you Rory was going crazy. Paranoid. I think he's got the other sub-packs under control, but he's feeling so unstable, he takes it out on me." Laurence lifted his chin. "I came out to where I could follow someone sane." His attention went again to John and Pierce, both watching silently. "Seattle?" John didn't move, Andrew winced, and Laurence looked like he'd gotten his answer. It only strengthened his worrying expression of loyalty.

Andrew let his hand drop. "That fact absolutely doesn't go beyond this pack, understand? This is temporary, and I don't want anyone riding in to beat me down when I have a killer to catch." Only temporary. He was going to hang on to that with everything he had. "I'm not going to crawl back to Roanoke afterward. I doubt Rory would take me back even if I tried." He sighed. "Come on. You need to eat and rest and heal up if you're going to be any good to me."

21

Silver put Death on watch for Dare as the Lady's light gave way to sunlight the next morning. They brought her food down in the den, and she made sure to stay silent and cowed, avoiding Dare as much as possible. Death was right, he knew her too well. The others saw a weak, broken thing, and dismissed her.

She kept her eyes on her food, and waited. "He's out of sight," Death said. "Chewing the same bone again with talk of plans, since there's nothing new. Only the new one left to watch over you."

Silver stole a glance at the man she vaguely remembered from Dare's not-pack. She hated to use his kindness against him, but she had little choice. She pushed to her feet. She wasn't cold, but it wasn't hard to find shivers anyway. Just thinking about the monster made her muscles feel weak and she courted the shaking. Weak. Weak and needing protection.

"Are you cold?" the new man asked, concern settling onto his face. He came closer.

Silver shook her head. "No. Just sometimes I can't help but think about—" She drew in a breath, making that shake too. She lifted her useless arm to hug it across her chest, tight. She saw the idea of a hug enter his expression and prayed to the Lady's clouded face it would continue to grow. She needed that protection, didn't she?

The new man enfolded her in an embrace to help damp the shaking. "Don't worry, I'm sure Dare knows what he's doing." He was slight and hardly taller than her. It made her feel even more dishonest. She leaned into the gesture and took a deep breath. Death panted in amused anticipation.

Silver slammed her knee into the new man's crotch and ran when he doubled over. Up, out of the den and for the entrance. She could only pray speed was enough, combined with the others' surprise. They'd hear her steps, but maybe they wouldn't understand at first what had happened. Her legs weren't injured. She could run fast enough. She hoped.

Then she was through. They might still catch her, but at least she'd gotten that far. "And now we run again." Silver didn't let herself think about the monster, just concentrated on running as fast and as far as she could.

"And now we run," Death echoed.

Andrew pushed up off the couch at the sound of running footsteps. Those sounded light. Silver? But Laurence had promised to guard her. "Laurence?" he shouted as he ran for the front door himself, John following. It hung open, Silver already outside. A wheeze from the basement was the only answer he got. John thumped down to check on Laurence as Andrew strode out on the front step. No sign of her, just her lingering scent on the air.

"You moron." Andrew strode back to smack the back of Laurence's head as he came up from the basement, still wheezing and hunched over. "I told you to watch her."

"But—she was so upset—" Laurence hung his head.

"She does that." Andrew scrubbed his face. All right. They still had time.

"I'll go after her on foot. Easiest and fastest way to track her, and she listens to me slightly more than she does any of you. She might actually come back with me rather than making us drag her."

Andrew nodded to Pierce as he arrived from the bedrooms upstairs. "You and John follow in the car. We can take her back that way, and I'll keep in contact in case I need backup. Laurence, you stay put here. Stay out of the others' way." Laurence whined in further apology, but didn't otherwise argue. Andrew couldn't really bring himself to blame the man for being fooled by Silver. She was good at that trick. Andrew paused to collect nods at his orders, and then pounded out the door.

It gave Andrew a strange sense of having come full circle to be chasing Silver again. The background behind her scent was different, composed of evergreens and the nearby bodies of water and a particular tang to the air that made Andrew think of mountains whether they caused it or not. But it was her and him and the quiet noises of a suburban neighborhood as he tracked her.

Her trail crossed a couple major roads at crosswalks, which stilled at least one of Andrew's worries. He had to remember how much more lucid she was now than when he'd first found her. He reported the first couple intersections to John on his phone, but he moved faster when he didn't have to hold it to his ear. After that, he called only when she made a major change of direction.

Houses got closer together, then condo buildings got taller, and he started having more and more trouble following Silver's exact trail. Her scent was on the wind, but that left far too large an area. Pedestrian traffic picked up as he grew closer to downtown businesses.

He lost the trail entirely somewhere in the middle of a courtyard between several high-rises. A fountain splashed in the center and silver-colored concrete blocks marked a pattern of lines among the red brick. The crowd of people walking in every direction was thick, far too thick for it to do any good even if Andrew bent as if to tie a shoe and got his nose closer to the ground.

It was hard to smell anything other than humans, their perfume and deodorant and sweat swirling together. Andrew paused to give John his location, hung up, and pushed toward the courtyard's edge. He'd have to pick Silver's trail up on the other side. He'd never find it in here.

A blond man coming from the other direction jostled Andrew and caught himself on his shoulder. Andrew lifted a hand to sweep him aside, but froze when he saw what the man held shielded between their two bodies. A gun barrel and silencer flashed with a sliver of sunlight, and the smell of metal and acrid gunpowder drifted up to Andrew's nose, sharp over the Were man's own scent.

"I'm so glad to meet you. I'm Stefan. You must be the delightfully protective male scent I found all over Selene's trail in the east and in her home. These are silver bullets, by the way—I know, how clichéd, yes?—so you might want to come with me to discuss this somewhere else."

Andrew recognized the voice immediately. He stayed frozen for several seconds longer as his instincts screamed at him to pounce, and he overrode them. Not here. Not with a gun on him. If those were silver bullets, he'd probably be dead after the first shot, and who knows how many others after him when Stefan caught up with Silver. "Can't say I return the sentiment. What do you want?"

"Just to talk." Stefan ground the silencer's barrel into Andrew's side. "Let's go this way."

Andrew twisted to try to get a better look at the man's face, to read anything more about his intentions. Now he was close, he had the same poisoned, infected stench of silver metal that had underlain Silver's scent at the beginning. Same as the scent of that lone in the east, so long ago, and that half-familiar scent at the Bellingham house, Andrew realized. How could he have been so stupid, and not linked the two before now?

The man was fair in an Eastern European way, lank hair

falling into his eyes, and gaunt to the point of emaciation. One arm dangled free. Like Silver's. He was the other victim. Andrew gritted his teeth until he felt they would crack. As long as Stefan was here, with a gun on him, Silver was safe.

Stefan jabbed the barrel again, into the center of Andrew's back this time. "Faster, please." He laughed, an even, pleasant sound with the same mad lack of context. He shoved Andrew into an access road between two buildings, Dumpsters along its length. Several cars and small delivery trucks sat at service entrances.

Pain burst in Andrew's back and his legs collapsed beneath him. He didn't register the sound of the silenced gunshot until after the pain, though it had come first. He'd been shot before. He knew what it felt like, or at least what buckshot in the flank or leg from rednecks taking potshots at "coyotes" or "stray dogs" felt like. This was worse, but not so much worse. It didn't burn like silver.

Stefan grabbed him by the back of his shirt and dragged him into the shadow of a compact car. Andrew tried to summon breath to call out and attract human attention, but the pain made it hard to breathe. How far was Silver? Could the others find her before Stefan did? The pain swelled up again as Stefan hoisted him up into the trunk. When he had his hand free, Stefan pulled out a crowbar that had been tucked at the front of the trunk. He smashed it into Andrew's temple. Darkness.

22

Silver stopped to drink at a small spring that bubbled up when she leaned her weight on the soil around it. She raised her head to check the wind. Was the monster on her trail? She couldn't find his scent. What was taking him so long?

"The trap falls apart if he doesn't take the bait," Death said in her brother's voice. She could almost see her brother's frown in her mind, so caught up in the thinking of a thing that he forgot about its why. The why was all Silver could think of. The trap was to save Dare and her mother's pack. If she failed in this, she failed them.

She hesitated a long time, until the spring's water built up and dribbled over her fingers, painfully cold. "We're going back," she told Death. "Maybe the warrior was right. The monster's too smart for such a trap. I need to warn my mother's pack."

Death dipped his head that he had heard, but his manner was too bland for Silver to tell if he agreed. "If you think you can find them in time."

Silver snarled at him. "If I didn't think that, I'd give up. I'm not giving up." Her next breath twisted into her throat and choked her. The monster was here. Closer than she'd realized, hidden as it had been under the forest's normal scents. Lack of breath made her weak, which was good. She couldn't just run, she had to think. Had to strain her nose to find Dare's scent, or those of the pack. She had to go to them.

She found the former alpha first, strong and solid. The thought of that loosened her throat, let her breathe again. He was circling around toward the monster, which let her move away from the monster. Thank the Lady.

The former alpha tackled her when they intersected, and she let him have that feeling of victory. Now it was no act that she needed the grounding of strong arms around her. Dare's would have been better, but she couldn't smell him any longer. Perhaps he'd ceased to follow her and now followed the monster, as had been her first intention.

"Where's Dare?" the former alpha asked her, settling his fingers as a tight band around her good wrist. "He said he'd lost you and we haven't heard anything since. I'd have thought I'd find him coming around this direction, not you."

"I was looking for you. One of you." Silver twisted to look back over her shoulder. Death padded behind alone. Where was Dare?

Andrew drifted into consciousness as the car slowed to a stop. It felt like the bullet hole in his back had healed, but it was still hard to focus his thoughts. Silver. Was she all right? He should . . . should do something. More than just lie here. Then the trunk lid lifted and the sunlight blinded him.

"Welcome back." Stefan smirked down at him, and manhandled Andrew from the trunk once more, ending with him sprawled facedown on the concrete of a sidewalk or path. Andrew's thoughts moved faster as each moment healed more of his concussion. Silver wasn't here, but he'd been unconscious. Stefan could have done something to her, left her somewhere else. He had to warn the pack. His phone. He curled up to hide the motion from Stefan with his body. John was on speed dial. He just had to get to a couple buttons—

Stefan slapped Andrew's hand away. He patted Andrew's pocket until he found the lump of the cell and jerked it out. "Now, now." He dropped the phone on the path, retrieved his crowbar, and smashed it down. "We have no need of interruptions." The metal glinted in the sunlight, like silver instead of steel. Silver-plated? But Stefan held it in his bare hand without apparent pain.

Andrew pushed to his hands and knees. "Where's—Selene?" Wherever they were smelled familiar. He recognized the scent as that of the Bellingham house a moment later.

Stefan kicked him viciously in the stomach. Andrew's head swooped and swam from the concussion and he retched onto the concrete. "You're keeping me from her, it's true. But I thought it might be best to pause and teach you a quick lesson." Stefan bent to snarl into Andrew's face. "Selene is *mine*.

She knows that, too, she's just lost her way a little. I'll have to remove the obstacle, that's all."

Then he laughed. His face cleared like a switch had been flicked to a pleasant, smiling manner. "But you're lucky." He stepped back and Andrew made it to his knees again. So Stefan didn't have her? He needed to stall, then. He took a deep breath to calm his roiling stomach, fanned his rage to make it to his feet. How could this psychopath claim Silver as his?

Stefan took out Andrew's knees with a sweeping kick before Andrew's head could clear from the change in elevation. Back to hands and knees again, palms abraded against the concrete. The futility of it stung like the acid left in his mouth. He had to get up. Had to do more than stall, had to take this man down, so he couldn't return for Silver. Maybe humans would notice the disturbance if they were out on the path long enough. Call the police. He remembered the house and driveway as all too wooded and obscured from the road from his first trip here, though.

"Help—" Andrew raised his voice, getting barely a word out before Stefan kicked him in the stomach again, stealing all his air. Any humans on adjoining properties were probably still too far to hear anyway. It still all came down to him. His muscles spasmed from the recent kick and his head swam, but he gritted his teeth. No way he was going to give in.

"You know why you're lucky?" Stefan's voice was poisonously smooth. "Because even if you tried to steal my mate, I'm going to give you a chance to repent before you die."

"She's not your mate." The words bubbled up before Andrew could stop them, soft from his lack of breath. But maybe he could distract the man, giving Andrew time to heal a little more, and stay on his feet the next time.

Stefan laughed. "What, you don't believe me? It's true, she might not remember our . . . time together. She was a little out of it, once I helped her purify herself in God's sight."

The anger this time was so white-hot it obscured Andrew's vision. It wasn't true. The man hadn't done anything of the sort to Silver. He couldn't have, and Andrew was going to torture him with his own silver before he killed the bastard. He panted, pushing back the anger to summon words. He had to find words to keep stalling. "Purify? Is that what you call it?"

Stefan swung the end of the crowbar like a pendulum. "God's favor does not come without a price for those such as us, it is true." Stefan shrugged. Only one shoulder moved, making the resemblance to Silver not perfect, as she retained some control of those muscles. "The taint has to be burned away."

"How could you do it?" The need to keep talking had him speaking his thoughts out loud before he could reconsider. "How could you have that done to you and then turn around and do it to anyone else?"

Stefan slid the crowbar under Andrew's chin and lifted it. Andrew could smell the silver on it and tipped his chin so it wouldn't touch skin. "You think faith is supposed to be easy?" Stefan rolled the muscles on that side and failed to move his arm again. "This taught me what was important. Made me value what I'd gained. Repent and forsake the false Lady and He can save you too."

Andrew spat at him. He'd always thought religion was poison, but this was beyond anything he could even have imagined. Humans had tainted his mind with the worst of the religious evil as well as their silver. This was why Andrew didn't believe. Look what it gave people the excuse to do, encouraged them to do. "There is no human God. There is no Lady. You were tortured in the name of a myth. That's all gods are good for, torturing people."

Stefan brought the crowbar up so it sizzled against Andrew's skin. "There is only one true God. It is the refuge of the weak, to blame Him for their problems. To say that if He does not directly intervene, He does not exist. It is not His place to protect us from every pain of this world. It is ours to have faith."

Stefan sighed, and turned, letting the crowbar fall. "They didn't want to listen to me at home either. Some just aren't willing to allow their souls to be saved. So I had to leave, and find someone else to save. This pack was so kind to me, you know. That's how I knew they deserved purification. They took me in when they saw what I had suffered, because they didn't understand how that suffering had been necessary." He paused as a thought occurred. "It was such a shame about the children."

Andrew closed his eyes for a moment to check how clearheaded he felt. Now was his moment. He had to do this, to make sure Silver stayed safe. His muscles all felt reasonably solid. He opened his eyes and pushed to his feet in one smooth movement, swinging for Stefan's jaw.

He hadn't counted on the silver. Caught by surprise, Stefan's block was clumsy, but the metal sizzled against Andrew's forearm anyway. The agony of phantom heat brought tears to his eyes and slowed him enough for Stefan to take out his knees once more. No, part of Andrew wailed. He couldn't have failed again.

"Enough," Stefan growled, anger backed by the full weight of his insanity coming into his face. He knocked Andrew to his stomach with calculated blows to propping arms and then shoulder.

Then the crowbar fell on Andrew's back. The movement ground Andrew's cheek into the rough concrete. Stefan yanked up Andrew's shirt and rained blows down on the small of his bare back. Over and over on the same spot, burning, burning, until Andrew would have screamed if he'd had the air for it. He could feel the instant the bar broke the blistered skin, like someone poured napalm into the wound. And the bar fell again. And again. Something in his spine crunched.

"There. Now you'll have to listen to me properly." The bloody bar clunked to the ground as Stefan knelt, keeping his hand on it. "It's a trial, the way those of our kind heal. You never have the patience to remain still and listen. But if you don't listen, you won't repent before I kill you. And that would be a shame." He released the bar and took Andrew's chin so he was looking up at him, neck twisted sideways at a painful angle. "But now you won't be walking anywhere, yes?"

Andrew made a noise, trying to make his throat work. Silver. He couldn't fail Silver. The longer he hung on, the longer the pack would have to get her safe. Hanging on seemed the best he could do now.

"You know, I don't think I know your name." Stefan paused, then continued when Andrew couldn't answer. "Ah, well. Perhaps we will be more comfortable inside." He flipped Andrew onto his back, and then took a handful of his shirt collar.

Andrew's sight grayed out with the bumping, jarring drag along the path and over the house's threshold. With one hand, Stefan couldn't have been gentle if he'd wanted to. It was clear he didn't want to.

His back just hurt so much. Andrew tried to concentrate on something else—Silver, hang on to give the others time to find Silver and get her to safety—but the pain dragged at him with every heartbeat and every breath. Maybe it had ebbed, as some healing occurred in the mess of his back even in the wound made by silver, or maybe that was his imagination. His energy had been sapped for so much healing already.

Stefan hauled him up into a chair with one last jerk at his collar. He circled around to the front and adjusted Andrew's legs to make his position more stable, since Andrew couldn't himself. The agony traveled over Andrew in waves in time to his heart. For Silver. Hang on for Silver.

Fire settled over his wrists, and he couldn't move his arms because the muscles were paralyzed. Bound with silver chains. Exactly as Silver's pack had been. Stefan's bare fingers still showed no burns from touching those, either.

"Now." Stefan smoothed lank hair from his eyes, gave a twisted smile, and knelt at Andrew's feet and placed a hand on his knee. Andrew's skin crawled. "Forsake the false Lady.

Allow yourself to be purified in your death so you can see the light of God."

Andrew strained to make his arm muscles work, to snap the chains. So thin. But he couldn't do it. He wasn't strong enough.

Stefan smiled once more. "We have time, don't worry. You'll see." He patted Andrew's knee. "Faith comes more easily when the beast has been burned out of your blood. Selene understands. She just hasn't admitted it to herself yet."

23

"Dare should have returned by now. Something's wrong." Silver didn't need Death to reply, she could see his answer in every movement he made as he paced back and forth across the room. Though it was hard to tell in his ruff's deep blackness, she thought his hackles were up. But more than that, she could feel it herself. They'd brought her back to her mother's pack's den, and they'd locked her up in the closest room before she could run away again.

And Dare didn't return.

Death stopped, going from restless movement into utter stillness so quickly it was like a slap. "What would you do if there was something wrong?"

"Help him." Silver drew her lip between her teeth and bit hard. But where? Where was she going to do her helping? The monster knew how to leave no trail, the same as he knew how to find hers when she tried to hide it.

"You know where they are." Death sounded exasperated. "Stop running from the answer."

Silver pressed her palms to her eyes. The monster would take him somewhere he knew he could work uninterrupted. He didn't work quickly. Somewhere no one would overhear, since he didn't work quietly either. And he knew Silver's former home was both those things, from experience.

Silver threw herself against the blocked entrance, bad shoulder first. Sometimes it was useful the snakes had deadened the pain in that arm. "We have to go!" she shouted at the others in the pack. "We have to go back to my home!" No one answered her, though she could hear them outside. Crazy Silver, babbling again. Always crazy.

Silver stepped away and laced her fingers into her hair, smoothing it flat to her head and trying to hold it there. Holding it as if this time it would stay. But she had no more control over that than anything else about herself. It fluffed right back up. "The others will never take me to him just on my word. There's little I can do without my wild self. I can't run to him quickly enough, can't defend him."

"You still search for her?" Death's words were simple, but so bleak.

Silver swallowed convulsively. She hadn't been ready to admit it to herself, but maybe this was the time. If not for herself, for Dare. "She's not coming back, is she?"

Death yipped in her wild self's voice. Silver found herself

on her knees, tears in her eyes, like someone had torn a hole inside her. But then Death hadn't torn her open, he'd merely made her acknowledge the wound.

"Now you've admitted that, I suppose I have no more reason to be here." Again, there was the bleakness to Death's voice, the voice of the man Silver didn't know. It was the voice Death liked best to use. As Silver watched him walk away, it occurred to her that she would miss him. He had called the fire and watched her burn, but he had never left her. Already, the air near her seemed empty with the lack of anything even shaped like her wild self to fill it.

"Wait."

He tilted his head back over his shoulder. In that moment, she realized what he looked like. A wild self without his tame. She'd told the stories, but she wondered how she could have missed seeing how empty Death was without the Lady.

"Please. Stay with me. Help me. If we are both without our names, denied the Lady, let us at least be alone together?"

Death considered a long moment, eyes inscrutable. Then he walked into the embrace of her good arm. She'd never touched him before, but his fur was soft, tickling against her chin and neck. One would never have guessed it, looking at his harsh silhouette.

"You have what you need to help him, you know," he said at length. "You have another self that can get there quickly enough. You just don't wish to acknowledge her . . . Selene."

Silver choked on hearing the name. "I can't—"

"Even for him? You'd rather I had his voice to speak to you with?"

Silver pressed her face into Death's fur, dampening it with her tears. It wasn't that she couldn't do it, it was that she wouldn't. Somehow, she didn't think Dare would let that stop him.

"You'll help me?" she said into his fur.

She felt more than heard the rumble of his answer. "I'll help you."

Selene rebuilt herself memory by memory, picking them up like hot coals in her bare hands. Her brother's death. The death of her niece and nephew. She tried to pick the memories up faster to avoid pain, like walking across those coals instead. The Bellingham house, her childhood in Seattle. Names: Ares, Lilianne, John.

Stefan.

Knowledge built itself up around her when she wasn't looking, computers and cell phones and cars, all the things she hadn't been able to see without the memories. She knew she was in Seattle, in a house, in a bedroom. It had been Ares's bedroom once. When the last piece fell into place, Selene felt a small flicker of triumph. Why hadn't she done this before?

Then one of the memory coals slipped a tendril of scent into her nose. She remembered what it smelled like when Were flesh burned from silver. She remembered what it sounded like when that Were screamed. Memory linked to memory. She wanted to press hands to her eyes to hold back the tears but her bad arm wouldn't move. That reminded her of the spreading deadness of the silver entering her blood.

She never could escape that linking while her memories were intact, she realized. Not permanently. She could think of only new things, things with no connection to her past, but that wouldn't last forever. She could only hope it would last long enough for Andrew.

She sent her thoughts forward like running on a crumbling slope. No room to pause or you'd fall. She thought about how to sneak out without John or the others knowing. It was lucky they'd put her in her brother's old room. Ares had a half a dozen secret ways out in this house. You could make it to the garage roof from his window, and from there it was only a short jump to the ground. She didn't know who had the room now, but it was another child. She removed several plastic dinosaurs from the top of a bookcase and shoved it under the window. Pulling yourself up onto the sill was all very well when you had two working arms, but she needed the help.

The window had a lock installed to prevent it from opening wide enough to let a teenage Were sneak out at night to go running alone. Selene fished in the gap between the window's bottom edge and the track it ran on and drew out a screwdriver, handle snapped off. Still there. Ares had left the screws so loose it took only a couple turns to remove them and toss the lock away.

Then she had to wait. Pierce was out walking the perimeter. She could see the top of his head below. She needed him to get to the other side of the house, but he was walking so slowly.

Waiting gave her time to think, and she felt the memories

begin again. If only she had someone to talk with to distract herself, but all she'd ever had since the monster injected her was her own mind. Whatever form her hallucinations had taken.

Selene hugged herself as tightly as she could with only one arm. Just wait. Don't think. Concentrate on breathing. Or think of Andrew. He wasn't in any memory except those warped by her insanity. Bringing up his face, his body, his scent, raised a heat that was a good distraction.

In the end, it wasn't so long until Pierce disappeared from sight and had time to reach the other side of the house. It just felt that way. Selene pushed open the window and levered herself out. Moss and dirty roof crud smeared her jeans as she slid down the garage roof. Lowering herself down from there with one arm was more of a controlled fall than anything else.

They still had the old Honda she needed, too. It looked even more broken-down than she remembered, but it was parked alongside the driveway. Bless John, for not buying a new one when the old one still worked, even years after they'd all left for Bellingham. The extra key was still stuck under the drainpipe at the side of the garage, where she and Ares had left it to pass it back and forth when one was grounded and the other wasn't.

The others would probably dismiss the noise of the car door opening and shutting as the neighbors, but Selene took a deep breath before she started the car. She'd have to move fast after they heard an engine so close.

She drove off the grass onto the driveway and floored it,

not bothering to check the mirror to see if Pierce was running after her, or if the others had come to the front door. She realized her speed was a bad idea at the first turn, when her sense of the car's path slid alarmingly. She yanked it back off the shoulder and slowed down. Her muscle memory was adjusted to a car with much better brakes. The more she concentrated on the exact details of what she was doing—which was the accelerator? Which was the brake?—the more things mixed themselves up. Better to trust to instinct.

Navigating was harder. That knowledge was buried inside the dangerous memories, and while she managed to get herself heading north, she wasn't at all sure where to turn off once she was closer to home.

Selene's stomach squeezed and someone honked at her for forgetting to move when the light turned green. Home. Maybe she could find her way home, but did she want to get there?

Andrew. She had to remember Andrew. Selene gritted her teeth and turned on the radio to grating, twangy country. Listen to the radio. Don't think about what waited at home.

This time, the wait was almost too much for her. She drifted onto the freeway shoulder once, the car not feeling quite real under her hand. But she didn't want to die, and the adrenaline burst kept her thinking clearly after that. Mostly.

When she reached the house, she had no time for finesse. She parked in the driveway behind a car with a rental window sticker and slammed the door behind her. Stefan was welcome to know she was here. She had no hope of sneaking up on him, and better he was as distracted as possible until Andrew could deal with him. Selene certainly couldn't.

She looked at the path, rather than the house, so she could make it up to the door without thinking. Everything looked dusty and overgrown, like the house's owners had stopped caring. It made her angry, like it had been vandals, and not just time, that had destroyed their home. Then she reached the bright crimson stain.

She tried to push away the sight, but she couldn't not smell the stench. Stefan's infection and fresh, untainted blood— Andrew's blood—and someone's fear. Silver taint in everything. She smelled like that, she supposed. Never able to escape the poison. The scents bypassed her careful defenses, straight to the memories, and she doubled over with their strength. No. No, keep walking. Andrew's blood, not her pack's. Break the scent into its component parts, its differences. Not the same as in the memories, something new. The stain became a trail of fresh blood dragged over the front step into the house. The door stood open.

Whatever happened, the others would be following her. She'd told them where to go when they first locked her up. She trusted they were smart enough to remember that. She just had to stay alive, or failing that, keep Dare alive until they got here.

Each breath was a struggle. She wanted to run so badly. "Stefan!" she called, unable to make her legs move farther than the first step. "I'm here. I'm the one you want, not him." She leaned on the doorframe so her knees didn't give way.

She couldn't smell him approach over the blood, but she heard his steps. Slow at first, wary of a trick, then jogging. He reached the doorway and smiled at her, smiled with all of the vulnerable charm he'd shown when he first approached their pack. She wanted to scratch it right off his face.

"Selene." He reached for her, hesitated, then gallantly drew back and opened the door wider. "I knew you'd see sense and come back to me. I've missed you so much."

"Stefan." Once Selene said the first word, the next was easier to get out, and the next one after that. "Andrew means nothing to me, you must know that. He just gets off on protecting broken things." She smiled and thought about using the teeth she showed to rip open his throat. She should touch him now. It was like commanding yourself to touch a lit stove. Every muscle held her back.

Once, she might have taunted herself for weakness, using a hallucination as her mouthpiece. Now, she had to set her teeth and find the strength on her own. She stroked Stefan's dead, dangling arm. "I know we're not broken."

He shivered at her touch. She'd never voluntarily touched him before, she realized. She caught a whimper before it made it out of her throat. Andrew needed time, that was all. She'd give him what time she could. Lady grant it would be enough.

24

For several moments, Andrew didn't register that Stefan had stopped talking. His ranting was all the same, anyway. Selene was his, Andrew was going to die for touching her, but he had a chance to repent first. Repent, repent. Over and over.

Andrew had let his head drop, and now he stared at the kitchen floor. A long scratch bisected a piece of the wood laminate. He tried to make pictures with it and the whorls of the grain. A thought gradually trickled past the pain. Stefan was gone. If Stefan was no longer in here with Andrew, where was he? Silver was only completely safe when Stefan was with him. He tried to summon the motivation to do something about it, but when he moved his head the pain just pounded until he was blinded with colored bursts.

"To think you give up so easily," a woman's voice said in Spanish. "Dare." She said it with Spanish vowels.

Andrew's heart no longer had any burst of speed to give, but he lifted his head. Stefan was indeed gone. Instead, a wolf sat before Andrew, up on its haunches. It was blacker than black, like someone had taken a colored-pencil sketch of the room and layered pure ink onto one spot until the paper was sodden with it.

"Isabel never called me Dare." The words came more quickly as he remembered how to use his throat again. "Silver says you speak with their voices, not their words." Andrew drew in a slow breath, floating in a sense of unreality. "Death."

The wolf dipped his head, and spoke in a man's voice. "Silver is an intelligent woman. But does it matter whose words they are, if they are still true?" His voice changed again, Isabel once more. "You need to let me go."

"You're not real. You're a manifestation of her unconscious." Andrew let his head drop again. The boy in him, raised to worship and respect the Lady, was crying out, sure Death had come to take him. His intellect had another worry. Had he been poisoned the way Silver had been? He'd been drifting a lot, in the pain. Had Stefan injected him? One needle-prick would have been lost in the general agony. Was that causing his hallucinations? Maybe it was too late for him now too. Hopelessness dragged at him.

"Let me go." The words carried the familiar snap of Isabel's temper, making her memory so tangible Andrew could nearly smell her.

"I have let you go," Andrew snapped right back, the bright burst of frustration damping down some of his pain. "There have been other women."

"But you clutch your so-called failure so close." Death's ears flattened. "Let go of my *death*. Let go of the deaths you caused. The surest way to continue to repeat that failure for the rest of your life is to never protect anyone again."

"Spare me your preaching. You're not real." But Andrew could imagine Isabel saying just those words, imagine her frown as she advanced on him. Summoning her face rather than pushing it down should have made him flinch, but maybe he had no pain left to spare for it.

"Again, you confuse real for true." The man's voice returned, full of withering scorn. "I wouldn't have thought the mighty enforcer, the man who rained bloody vengeance down upon the Barcelona pack, would prove such a coward in the end."

Andrew twisted and the muscles in his back responded as if they were whole again. He still couldn't feel his legs, though. Paralysis never healed in humans, so how long would it take a werewolf? "I'm biding my time. To heal," he said through gritted teeth.

"Shall I go and tell Silver that? She should just wait for you? I don't think your mutual friend will care to allow her to."

A denial came to Andrew's lips, but he was too busy listening with all his attention to voice it. He couldn't smell a thing over the stink of silver and his own blood. Was Silver here?

"Have you purified him yet?" Silver's voice was unmistakable, though it didn't sound like her usual tone. She spoke like her throat had been scraped raw with sobbing and had never quite healed.

"Why do you care about him? You came back to me." Stefan's pleasure swam over the words, oily.

Andrew couldn't leave Silver alone. Maybe he'd fail this time too, but the need to protect poured back in on him in a rush, blunting anger and pain and fear. He'd fail doing, not fail waiting. That was the best you could ask of anyone in this life.

Breaking through the chains should be like pulling a knife from a wound. The faster you did it, the sooner the pain was done. You had to gather yourself, and—

Do it.

Andrew panted from the agony, but the chains snapped within half a second. With all that momentum, he ended up sprawling forward. He caught himself on his hands, but his legs tangled with the chair in a useless splay beneath him. He froze, gray sparkles obscuring his vision, trying not to pant so hard that he would be heard. Had Stefan heard him?

"But I don't wish him harm," he heard Silver say in the next room, voice raised slightly, to distract from the sound of Andrew's movements. "He helped me get back here to you, didn't he?" Stefan murmured in approval, and didn't come into the kitchen.

Imagining Silver with the man made Andrew's throat clench, but he pushed himself into movement. He couldn't let her bravery go to waste. As he sat up, he realized one chain had snapped under the chair arm, leaving it wrapped around his wrist, dug into the blistered burn. He couldn't bring himself to touch it to pull it out so he left it. He had no strength to shift away, so it didn't matter that touching silver would prevent him.

Silver's voice continued and Andrew sent her silent thanks for her stalling. Then with nothing else to reach for to affect the outcome, he prayed to the Lady. Please, let Stefan be so distracted with his rhetoric that he wouldn't hear Andrew. Please.

"So you call to Her when you have nothing else left. Fitting, I suppose." The black wolf paced beside Andrew, as if mocking him with his four sound limbs. Andrew pushed himself up on his arms, and settled his weight on his hip.

Experimenting, he discovered he could drag himself forward that way. He stopped before going more than a couple inches. All very well to get there, but he had to plan if he was going to save Silver. Some part of him flinched from the effort of planning, but Silver's voice silenced it.

Stefan had dropped his crowbar beside the chair at some point. Andrew pulled his cuff down over his hand to pick the bar up and then dropped it on his legs. Even through the fabric, he could imagine it scorching, but he didn't have much choice of weapons.

Now, he could go. His wrists screamed every time he put weight on his arms, but it was a quiet pain compared to what his back had been at the beginning. Each scuff of fabric against the floor seemed as loud as a shout to him. How could Stefan not hear?

Selene couldn't see Andrew, but she heard someone fall. She closed her fingers around Stefan's wrist and pulled him farther into the house, into the first bedroom. The walls would dampen the sound of Andrew's escape. Probably not enough, but a little. Stefan laughed, too distracted to hear the dragging sounds that followed the fall. The rotting, twisted scent of his attraction increased. She pressed her lips closed and her throat spasmed as she suppressed a gag.

"Why did you run, Selene?" Stefan asked. "You knew we were meant for each other."

He cupped her cheek with his good hand and she couldn't take it any longer. Selene jerked back, but he was too fast and caught her at the side of her neck. He held her that way for a breath, and then kissed her.

She did gag this time. She slammed her arm into his and bit his tongue, but he only tightened his grip and smashed his lips down harder. Part of her mind heard another dragging noise and clung to it, but the rest was nearly too panicked to think. She had to get him off her. Off! He avoided her knee to the crotch, but not the kick to the knee the feint covered.

"Still running," he hissed. He stumbled back a step, favoring the injured side. "Why, Selene?"

If the rhythm continued, another drag would come in a second. She was so stupid. He'd hear it now. Why couldn't she just swallow her disgust and play along? "The human God frightens me. I'm not—" She put an artistic waver into her voice. Keep his attention. She had to keep his attention. Religion was safer than walking the line of teasing without allowing him too close. "I'm not worthy the way you are, Stefan."

"If you repent your sins and beg His forgiveness, He'll welcome you. You proved yourself worthy when you survived."

His voice took on a singsong quality of memorized words. Selene steeled herself and clasped his forearm. He clasped hers back and didn't try to close the distance between them further. Thank the Lady.

It was easier to keep going once Andrew was moving, but stopping would even be easier than that. But he wasn't going to. Isabel was right—Death was right—or some part of his own mind was right. This time, he would protect her. Concentrating hard enough on that thought almost kept the pain at bay. Almost in a way that wasn't even close.

Plant his hands. Drag. Plant his hands. Drag again, wincing at the noise. Stefan should have heard, but Andrew could hear his voice's terrifying cadence, up and down. Smooth and reasonable as he explained something. Distracted. Silver was good at this. He couldn't even imagine what it was costing her. Why didn't she run? She could save herself if she ran back to John and the pack.

The voices came from out of sight in the bedroom, and Andrew aimed for them without allowing himself to stop and consider a plan. He couldn't stop. Besides, what good would a plan do him? What could he do when he got there, half crippled? Distract Stefan from Silver in turn, that was about all. He had a weapon, so after that he could at least go down swinging, by the Lady.

The transition from laminate to carpet caught at Andrew's pants, disturbing the crowbar. He saw it start to fall, knew it would clatter. He knew he had to catch it, he did catch it, but it burned. Andrew's eyes watered as his sight flared white with the agony. Even on top of everything else, he could feel the new burn.

Resettle. Plant his hands. The carpet abraded the newly burned skin, and it felt like he left the top layer behind whenever he moved his hand. He couldn't do this. His strength was draining steadily in the face of all the wounds, and every drag was worse than the last.

He caught sight of them then. They stood beside the bed, Silver edging back and Stefan edging forward. The residual flare in his vision continued as his emotions stoked it. Stefan was touching her. His hand caressed her cheek. Silver looked beyond him to Andrew. Fear had twisted her expression into something older and not herself. She changed her focus so her eyes looked through him and then back to Stefan, but she knew he was there. In that moment of distraction Stefan pressed forward until he pinned her legs to the side of the bed with his.

"Stefan, no. No. Stefan!" Silver struggled to get out from under him, but he just ground his hips against hers. She shrieked, and her eyes caught Andrew's. He could read her message as clearly as if she had spoken. She'd distracted all she could. From here, she would fight, and Andrew would be on his own.

Good. She should have fought all along, fought and run. Leave Andrew here with what he'd earned by being stupid enough to be caught. Rage burned his skin from the inside, eclipsing the silver burns on the outside, but it consumed his energy too. He'd kill Stefan. Torture him until he wept and then kill him, and tear out his throat, like the others. But he couldn't move. He didn't even have the breath to snarl.

"Silver knows you can, Dare," the black wolf said, threading though the door, past Andrew. He came to stand beside Stefan's legs. The thought of Silver's faith freed Andrew from the locked paralysis of his need to annihilate Stefan.

Silver wrenched herself away, dragging half the blankets with her. She tossed them to tangle Stefan's feet as she scrabbled back to a safe distance, screaming curses. "Lady set your voice to screaming for eternity until it shreds apart!" Stefan laughed, still even and pleasant, and stepped over the fabric without hurry.

It took three more drags to reach Stefan. At the second Stefan stilled, attention caught by something, who knew whether it was smell or sound. Andrew closed his hand around the crowbar, and pulled himself the last few feet one-handed as Stefan turned. He ignored the burn of silver against his skin and swung the weapon with all his remaining strength at Stefan's knee.

Something cracked, and Andrew's pleasure flared at Stefan's grunt of pain. Yes. The bastard should suffer. Stefan tumbled backward. Andrew tried to roll aside, but when his legs didn't respond the other man ended up sprawled half across him. Silver followed a moment later, driving her knuckles into Stefan's throat.

That stunned him for a moment, but Andrew was still

pulling himself out from under the other man when Stefan regained use of his arm. Stefan yanked at Silver, writhing to throw her off.

Silver pinned his one good arm with hers and sat on his chest. Andrew finally dragged himself out of reach, panting. "Satan's whore!" Stefan screamed, his voice coming back raggedly after the throat strike. "You belong in Hell! All of you! You and every one of your spawn, until the world is cleansed of your beastly stink—"

It started just as an impulse to shut the man up, but Andrew leaned over to hook outstretched fingers into a pillow among the tumbled covers hanging from the bed. He tossed the pillow over Stefan's face, following it with all the body weight he could bring to bear from his position.

Andrew met Silver's eyes over Stefan, watching as each jerk of his body came closer to dislodging her. Maybe it was Andrew's lack of strength, maybe it was uneven coverage from the pillow, but the man's struggles did not abate with the lack of air. Andrew's mind screamed at him to tear with teeth he didn't have and couldn't shift to get, or punch with strength that was long gone. And all he could do in the end was hold on, pressing down. Hold on for Silver.

The black wolf looked on impassively. Andrew locked gazes with Silver. "Can't you tell Death to— Just ask him—"

Silver bit her lip, shaking her head. Her eyes drifted right over the wolf. "I can't see him—" She gasped as Stefan bucked again.

"Right there—" Andrew indicated Death with his chin. Why couldn't she see him now, of all times, when they needed him the most? He caught the wolf's eyes himself. He just wanted this to end. "Please—"

"I thought you'd never ask." Death pounced on Stefan. His jaws reached through Andrew's hands and the pillow and plucked up something from within Stefan. Death tossed it into the air, caught it, and swallowed. Stefan went limp. Andrew drew in the first breath that actually felt like it gave him air since he'd first seen the man. It was over.

Death stepped back, regarding them both. "Remember me, Dare," Stefan's voice said, but robbed of the glinting sharpness of its earlier insanity. Andrew's heart thrashed back to its greatest panicked speed at hearing that voice. It took him a moment to register the actual words. The next moment Death was gone, as completely as a hallucination would disappear.

Silver's head dropped, a sob working its way free. Tears began to patter down a moment later. The weeping wracked her entire body.

"Silver. Silver, puppy. It's over." Andrew could only run his fingers along her cheek without overbalancing himself. The moisture trickled down to the burns, and the salt stung so badly he had to drop his hand again. Her pain stole his breath away again. It was all right. He wanted it to be all right for her.

"No." The woman before him caught his eyes, and forged a connection so tight he knew even before she said it. "Not Silver." She shivered, a helpless movement that looked like it might shake her apart, but she still reached out to gently remove the chain twisted around his wrist. He'd forgotten it was there.

She slid it into her pocket. "John and the others should be here soon. Andrew. I want to stay, but I can't—"

Andrew managed one more drag over to catch her as she collapsed, shivers walking the line of a seizure, and then pulling back again. "The snakes . . . left their skins behind. Are they coming back? Where is the Lady? Death? Come back, please."

Tears of his own stung in his eyes. "Oh, puppy." He wanted to make it all right, but maybe there wasn't an all right in this world for Silver. He held her as close as he could with his injuries, and listened as her madness returned.

25

Andrew wanted to pass out. It seemed only fair. He deserved that relief by now. Silver slipped unconscious quickly enough. Andrew pulled them half the length of the room away from the dead man before he gave up and just lay with his arm around Silver. He closed his eyes, but his mind kept running in quiet misery.

After a while, he tried to think what to do if the others didn't come. His phone was destroyed and the landline in this house would have been disconnected. He tried to think beyond that, but the best he could do was repeat those facts over and over.

Footsteps. His sense of smell was so dulled by the stink of death and silver and blood he couldn't tell who it was. Please, not humans. Please, Lady, please. Dark laughter bubbled up painfully from somewhere inside him. Praying to the Lady twice in an hour after a decade of atheism. He was seriously slipping.

"Dare? Silver? Thank the Lady." John entered first, followed by Pierce, Laurence, and the woman whose name Andrew still couldn't remember.

After that, it was easy to slip away and ignore the questions. He didn't think he passed out, but time did jump a little. John carried Silver while the others took Andrew between them, probably so they wouldn't have to touch the mess of his back. They were gentle, but he had so many burns, it wasn't much more comfortable leaving the house than entering it had been.

The car lulled him as he lay half on the floor of the trunk, half on the folded-down backseat. He could keep his arm around Silver. He thought he remembered arriving at the Seattle pack house, but it might have been a false memory to link being in the car with being in bed and eating. He had the most wonderful steak he'd ever eaten in his life, just picking it up and gnawing. Then sleep.

His next sharp impression was of an empty spot beside him where Silver should have been. That brought him fully awake, heart pounding, but the Seattle pack's scent was everywhere around him, nothing of Stefan.

He was back in John's room—his room. John's scent was even more pervasive now Andrew was actually in the bed. Andrew rolled his shoulders in discomfort. At the moment, the scent of another alpha male just served to remind him of how weak he was. Maybe he could ask to change rooms.

He had more important concerns at the moment, though. Andrew took quick stock of his injuries. He couldn't feel his legs. He felt along his back and his fingers met bandages over what felt like unbroken skin, but when he pulled up the fabric of borrowed pajama pants and pinched skin on his thigh, only his fingertips conveyed sensation. Like he was pinching someone else.

The transition from form to form often aided healing, so Andrew reached out for a shift. He'd rested, eaten, and it was still not far off full. It should have been easy. He should have felt it right there as he reached, the snap into a new configuration his for just a moment of concentration.

But nothing happened. He could feel it there, just beyond his reach, but no amount of concentration made it happen. Andrew held his breath for a moment, trying to keep his heart from racing out of control.

He'd never tried to shift this heavily wounded before. Maybe he just needed time to heal. He figured he'd be able to walk soon enough even without help. Wounds made by silver always took longer to heal, and a werewolf could heal in a couple minutes what would take a human weeks. Why shouldn't it take days for him to heal something that a human never could? He just needed a little patience.

His other injuries seemed minor in comparison to his back. The burn on his palm screamed when he pressed it. The other burns on wrists and jaw were dull aches. It was strange to find the swath of burned skin without stubble amongst the growth along the rest of his jaw. He must have been out for a day or so.

Everything else aside, his need to use the bathroom was getting too desperate to be ignored. He concentrated, trying to make his leg muscles move by sheer force of will. Nothing happened. Well, the bathroom wasn't that far away. He had dragging down by now.

He hadn't counted on the getting up and down part. The sink helped him in the bathroom, but getting back on the bed was impossible. The rest and food had helped, but he still didn't have the strength in his arms to lever himself straight up.

He leaned his head against the bed and stared into middle distance, feeling the quicksand of self-pity dragging him under. No matter how much he pushed it down, the thought kept coming back. He'd seen Death, like Silver. What if he could never shift again, like her?

Andrew couldn't remember everything from when Stefan had pulled him into the house to when Silver had drawn him away, but he would remember something like an injection. Wouldn't he? A residual hallucination or two didn't mean he'd been permanently poisoned like Silver. Andrew pressed a hand to his back, feeling the scar tissue ridges through the bandages. Did they radiate toward his heart as Silver's did?

"Poor baby," a male voice said. Andrew closed his eyes, but when he opened them, the wolf-shaped hole cut into deep-space blackness remained. "Crying to himself. It's so sad."

"You're not real," Andrew spat at him. "You're a hallucination. From the silver." His heart surged too fast again. He reached for the shift with every fiber of his being and nothing happened. But of course nothing happened. By now his own panic was just screwing him up. This didn't mean anything. He was like the teen girl, trying too hard in the wrong direction. He needed to heal, calm down, and then try again. Have a little patience.

He balled up his fists in his lap, and pain flared in the burn on his hand. He ignored it. Lady, please. Let all of that be true. Let him not be crippled, stuck in human forever.

"For one who claims to not believe, you call out to Her often enough."

Andrew blinked at Death through a film of tears. "A handful of times is hardly often." And much good the prayers did him, as ever.

Death came to sniff right up in Andrew's face. Andrew flinched back, but he didn't have far to go with the bed right there. Death sat back on his haunches. "So you delight in telling yourself." Death let his tongue loll out in a canine grin. "A little faith won't kill you. I would know."

Andrew flexed his hand again to make the pain flare. "Where was She, then? When all but one of the Bellingham pack was killed? Didn't they pray to Her?"

Death's manner drained of all animation. "You know why I brought mortality to Her Children. It is the way of the world. We are none of us outside of the world. She cannot change that."

Andrew looked away. He would think about that truth later. Not now. He looked back at the sound of Death shaking himself all over, the earlier smug humor returned. "The only constant of the world is change. I'd wait to see what change brings before I fell into despair, if I were you."

A knock sounded on the door, and Andrew found himself alone and light-headed. Lady, what a realistic hallucination.

John entered after a pause. "Oh, good. You're awake. Silver's downstairs eating. You should have called earlier." John's tone held no hint of how much he'd heard of Andrew's conversation with Death. The household would have heard Andrew moving around from the start, though, so something must have prompted John to stop waiting politely to be called.

He crossed to Andrew as if he planned to boost him up onto the bed, but checked when he saw Andrew's expression. Andrew wasn't going to let another alpha pick him up like a child.

John considered him in silence for a moment. "You planning to keep your pride and sleep on the floor all day?"

Andrew let himself acknowledge the weakness that permeated his entire body. He hurt. All over. And the floor was hard. "All right," he said, and didn't struggle when John gave him the boost. He dragged himself back to lean against the headboard without any help.

"I'll get breakfast." John returned a few minutes later with a tray bearing a heart-attack special. The plate was piled high with bacon, ham, eggs, and toast slathered with butter. Andrew didn't waste any time before digging in, though he did use the fork this time.

John hovered. Andrew eventually paused between bites to eye him. The food made it easier to pull up a confident mask and the mask reminded him of something he needed to do. "You should consider yourself alpha again. I'm in no shape to hold the position, and I was planning to give it back anyway. I don't need to be in your room."

"You can transfer power officially when you're up again. I don't want it said I stole it back while you were too injured to resist. Besides, Silver wouldn't settle until she was right next to you. My room has the biggest bed. And the shortest path to the bathroom." John looked over his shoulder at that door. The drag marks on the carpet stood out clearly.

He seemed to realize he was looming, so he dumped a jacket off the chair and nudged it to face the bed more directly. He flopped down, confident body language proclaiming his resumption of authority, even if he didn't acknowledge it directly. There wasn't much difference between being beta to an invalid alpha and an alpha yourself, after all. "You up to telling us what happened? We lost you in the crowd and then bumped into Silver coming back the other direction. No trace of you."

Andrew picked up a bacon strip and snapped it in half. "He caught me off guard. Threatened me with silver bullets. They weren't, as it turns out, but I couldn't risk letting him shoot me and then snatch Silver unopposed."

John hissed between his teeth in sympathy. "It doesn't make sense, though. We saw his dead arm when we—dealt with him. It looked like Silver's wound. Why would he be using silver at all?"

"He was injected by humans in Europe at the turn of the

last century. I found out about him just before everything blew up, never remembered to tell you. He took his torturer's words to heart. He thought he was saving us for the human God." Stefan's voice came back to Andrew in memory, and his stomach flipped, threatening to reject his breakfast. Saved, purified, killed. Was Stefan to blame, or were the humans who had begun this all, over a century ago? Did it matter now?

Andrew pushed the tray away, about a quarter of the food left. His memories were stronger than his remaining hunger. He leaned back into the pillows. "I wonder how Silver knew where to find us."

"She said Death told her." John looked at his hands, and Andrew closed his eyes to shut out the tone. Did John believe Silver talked to religious abstracts? It sounded like he was at least considering the possibility.

Did Andrew believe it?

"She's used him as a mouthpiece before for things she could have figured out by simple logic," Andrew said. It sounded halfhearted compared to his usual protests.

John didn't argue. "What I still don't understand is how Silver got there. I mean, we know how—she climbed out a window and took the beater we keep around for when someone's car is in the shop—but I had no idea she even remembered how to drive."

Andrew focused on the opposite wall rather than see her expression again in memory. Older, more aware, but twisted with such pain. "It wasn't Silver. It was Selene."

Silence. John jerked to his feet. "You mean she—? But this morning she seemed less lucid, not more."

Andrew swallowed, remembering Selene's words. *Andrew. I want to stay, but I can't—* The only words she'd ever spoken to him as herself, he supposed. "I think the effort cost her more than she had. Not only facing up to the knowledge about her pack, but having to do it in the house with their blood on the walls . . ." He clenched his hands. "No wonder she took refuge in deeper madness."

John opened his mouth as if to ask another question, but he seemed to think better of it and took away the tray instead. "She'll be back up here soon, I expect. I think she feels safer with her rescuer." He still sounded a little annoyed that Silver wouldn't accept the protection of family over a stranger, but the emotion was mellower than before.

"Funny, considering she was the one who rescued me." Andrew rubbed a hand over his back. It would heal in time, and then he'd be able to shift. He had to keep telling himself that.

John switched the tray to one hand to open the door onto a waiting Laurence. He growled at the other man. "I told you. He's still healing. Out." He pointed down the hall.

"Just five minutes." Laurence wiggled past, his slight frame an advantage for once. "Dare, please. I just want to talk to you."

Andrew sighed and beckoned Laurence forward. He might as well get this over with. He assumed Laurence was going to whine about Rory again, but while Andrew agreed that

Roanoke should never have treated his beta that way, Andrew couldn't do anything about it.

Instead of speaking, Laurence knelt beside the bed, head bowed. Andrew stared at him in shock. No. Not that. "I can't," he said, gesturing desperately for Laurence to stand.

The man refused, though he did raise his head. "We need you as Roanoke, Dare." When Andrew just shook his head, he drew out his phone, chose an address book entry, punched the speaker phone on, and held it out as it rang. "Boston agrees. You'll listen to him, won't you?"

John placed the tray outside in the hall and returned to place a warning hand on Laurence's shoulder, grip tight. "I told you, he has to heal."

"Is that Seattle I hear?" Boston's voice came from the phone. "I couldn't agree more. Is Dare there?"

"Not from lack of trying on some people's parts." Andrew was grateful Boston wasn't present to smell or see his false bravado.

Benjamin's chuckle was rendered only a little less rich by the phone speakers. "Excellent. Well, much as I disagree with Laurence's timing, I do agree with his basic thesis. We need you here, when you're healed. Rory has stabilized things for the moment, and I suspect he'll be anxious enough to get his beta back to ask no questions, but things will only last until the next crisis. We need someone with true strength at the helm."

Andrew pressed a hand to his face. "I can't." Not when he might never be able to shift again.

"Dare." The word had a snap Andrew remembered from the dark, suicidal days when he'd first returned home from

Spain. "Remember a decade ago, when I told you to take the time you needed to pull yourself together? I didn't mean forever. I'm not going to let you go back to running now you've proved to yourself you can do better. Trust me, I'm not the only one who's not planning to let you wiggle out of this, Roanoke."

John exhaled in amusement, possibly in agreement. Well, of course Seattle would agree, he'd much rather have Andrew on the other side of the continent and out of his business. Andrew pressed the heels of his hands to his eyes. Flattering, certainly. But Benjamin didn't understand. It would be literally impossible for him to be an alpha if he couldn't shift. "If I heal—" He growled to stop Boston objecting to the "if." "If I heal, I'll come back and see about dealing with Rory. My word." He pressed a thumb to his forehead to mark the oath. It was true enough. If he healed enough to shift.

A thought occurred to Andrew, shaken loose by hearing Boston's voice. "Your woman, that you sent after that lone— Stefan must have been up there casting about for Silver's trail, before finding it at the pack house—is she all right?"

Benjamin's strained silence gave Andrew all the answer he needed. The older man sighed after a moment. "If that falls on any head, it's mine. Don't be taking that on too."

John must have smelled a hint of Andrew's stomach-churning guilt because he jerked Laurence to his feet and stole his phone. "There. Five minutes. Out." He shut off the speaker phone and put the phone up to his ear. "I'm afraid visiting hours are over." John said "mm" a couple times dryly and ended the call.

"You should probably sleep," John told Andrew after Laurence had left looking pleased with the promise he had secured. A suggestion, not an order. It was respectful of him. And however little Andrew liked the idea of finding Death again in his dreams, speaking with a nameless Boston woman's voice, exhaustion sucked him down the moment he closed his eyes.

26

It was pleasant to drift in the mist. Silver ate sometimes, and kept the warrior's presence near her, but didn't otherwise think about anything. It was restful. Just her and Death and the soft Lady's glow of the mist.

It didn't last, of course. The mist cleared, the Lady's light changed to indicate the passage of days and weeks, and memories slid in like sparkles at the edge of her vision. A name, most of all. Dare. Silver drew her nail along the diamond-backed skins the snakes had left on her arm and remembered him killing them.

"Have you decided to rejoin us, then?" Death curled against her side. She sank her hand into the inky blackness of his fur to scratch, and he pretended he was in no way enjoying it. "Your mate will start harming himself soon if you don't do something about it."

"What?" Silver looked down at Death. "Harm himself how—" She stuttered to a stop as she realized that her moment to contest the mate part had come and gone. But it didn't matter what she called the two of them if Dare didn't agree.

"He is trapped, unable to walk, in another alpha's room. You think he won't reopen the injuries pushing himself too hard? He needs someone to channel his effort."

Silver pushed herself to her feet. "I should have realized myself how trapped he'd feel."

Death rose with her. "What, and make the same mistake yourself? Walk before you run, girl. You're only lately come back to awareness." He laughed when Silver glared. "Go help him find his wild self. Tell him you can see it."

Silver frowned. "Why? He knows it's there."

Death bumped the back of her legs, and didn't answer. She allowed him to channel her in the right direction.

She found Dare just placing his feet on the floor, wiggling his toes. His wild self pressed close to his legs as if frightened. He looked hurt, coarser white fur coming in as a stark bar across his back, but it was clear he had no thought of leaving Dare.

Silver let another memory in, Dare dragging himself to her using only his arms. Her heart squeezed. "You're not supposed to be walking yet," she said, crossing to playfully shove him back onto the bed. Dare yielded under the push but sat right back up again.

"I can almost walk. Even if I can't shift." He said it like he wasn't paying attention to her, too caught up in his need to push himself until he proved he was strong enough.

"I think you need to wait to walk." Silver knelt so she pressed against his lower legs, holding them against the bed. "And I don't know why you feel your wild self doesn't come when you call, but I think it's most likely you're so afraid of failing you call too softly."

Dare's face twisted and he put a hand to her hair. "I know you want to give me hope—but I can't feel it. It's been weeks. I'm nearly fully healed. And I should be able to feel the shift right there now we've gotten so close to the full again, and I can't."

"My wild self is dead," Silver said, needing to hear it out loud as much as he did. It hurt, but not as much as yesterday. And she knew tomorrow would be better still. "And I know that because she's gone. Your wild self is right here." She ruffled the wild self's ears and Dare shivered like maybe he felt it. "Don't worry so hard. He's waiting for you."

Silver scooted away and turned her back as he pulled off his pants, to give him a little privacy for the moments of transition from tame to wild self. She shrugged off her jacket and then slung her arm over Death's flank and scritched along his side, burying her nose in his fur.

Dare was silent for a long time. His next grunt of effort still came from a tame throat. Silver growled. "Don't try so hard! Just fall," she said without turning.

Her next breath, she smelled the change in scent from bare skin to musky tang of fur and she sighed in relief. The wild self sprawled on the bed like his back legs didn't work right in that form either, but he panted open-mouthed in satisfaction.

The bandages no longer fit, so Silver ran her fingers along Dare's belly and back to pull them away. The white fur stuck up awkwardly as she brushed her fingers along it. Dare growled. His tame form's smooth skin took gradual shape under her fingers.

"You should leave those on," he said, twisting to frown at her. His joy at finding his wild self robbed the expression of any heat, but that joy quickly flickered out. "Oh. Silver. I'm so sorry. Here I am celebrating, when you . . ."

She tossed away the bandages. "You're healed enough," she said. The rest of his worries she just ignored. Later, she could better explain to him why she was finally at peace with Death to walk in the place of her wild self.

His tame self's skin wasn't so smooth after all, there along his back. It had the same white ridges as her snake skins, only his were a landscape of mountains and valleys where hers were barely raised. She explored them with her fingers until he shivered, and then she kissed them instead.

She heard his enjoyment in the deep, warm quality of his huff of surprise. She saw it in the way his wild self opened his mouth in a panting grin. But then he twisted over and away from her, covering his lap as he sat up. "We shouldn't—"

Silver's heart squeezed. Lady. Had she been wrong? But she'd heard his attraction in his voice, seen it in his body. She could smell it. He wanted her. Death laughed, and his words popped into her memory without him having to repeat them. *So hold him down.* Well, then. She'd try that. She brushed her hair from her face and climbed to kneel over him, straddling him. "Why not?"

He looked up into her face. Resistance slipped away from his expression and she could smell his attraction come ascendant once more. Then he smiled, and Silver's heart soared.

He cupped the back of her neck in his hand, tilted her head to the side, and nipped the skin he exposed. She made a small noise and ground herself against him. She planted her hand on his shoulder and shoved him back. She laughed at his mock exclamation of surprise and leaned over him. She started a kiss but broke it off soon enough to nip hard at his earlobes and the side of his neck.

Balancing on one arm grew harder, and Silver finally fell against his chest. She tried to hold in her growl, so frustrated with herself. Why couldn't she do this one thing without showing how crippled she was? Rather than let her get up, he curved his arm around her tight and reassuring and rolled them.

Silver put a hand on his chest, and grinned up at him. This would work as well. She rather liked it in fact, though not for always, of course. Mustn't let him think he would always be on top, or in control. "Don't start taking this position for granted."

Dare chuckled. "Never."

Afterward, Andrew watched Silver as she fell into a doze. Since she was on her stomach, Andrew caressed her back's smooth expanse with his gaze. Wounds made with silver scarred like they would on normal humans, so his back would never be smooth again. Neither would the ridges on wrists and jaw ever entirely fade.

He drew his fingers along the dip over Silver's spine. Her back was flawless and beautiful. He still wasn't sure why he'd believed her when she assured him his other shape was still with him, but he had, and that had made all the difference somehow. Tipped it over.

Footsteps thumped up the stairs. Andrew registered them only peripherally until they stopped at the door. "What the hell?" John said as he yanked open the door. He was still in business slacks and shirt, ID badge from a company Andrew vaguely recognized as a software firm hooked at his belt. He must have just arrived home from work.

Andrew rolled to raise an eyebrow at him. "A little privacy?" No one had true privacy in a pack house, not when everyone could hear and smell what everyone else was doing, but society functioned based on everyone pretending they couldn't.

"You're disgusting." John crossed to the bed in two strides, hands fisted at his sides. "Get up."

Andrew sat up properly and frowned at him, realization coming slowly. "She's a grown woman—" He dug into the covers to find his pajama pants.

John loomed over him. "Get up," he said between gritted teeth. Looking into his eyes, Andrew had no doubt that John thought Andrew couldn't.

Damned if he was going to give the man the satisfaction. Andrew took a deep breath after pulling on his pants and pushed off the bed. His shift back and forth must have done something, because his legs held. He leaned most of his weight against the bed and they started shaking almost immediately, but they held.

Silver brushed past him as she slid off the bed. "Aren't you going to ask me? Because there are only two people whose consent matters here, and you're not one of them."

John ignored her. "You—you!—were the one telling me that after killing Stefan she lost what lucidity she'd gained. And now you turn around and—"

"Stop it," Silver said. She tried to interpose herself between them but John strong-armed her away without even looking at her.

"This isn't your business." Andrew tried to say it with conviction, but the shaking in his legs was getting worse and worse. "Don't make this into something it isn't."

Silver growled and stomped, smelling like rage, to rummage in her leather jacket dumped beside the bed. Andrew could only watch her in his peripheral vision. He wasn't going to show weakness by taking his eyes off John.

"You were the one talking about thinking with your dick." John brought up his hand as if to grab Andrew's shirt to choke him, but was foiled by his bare chest. "How could you—?"

"Seattle." Silver's voice was peremptory.

John paid no more attention than before, but Andrew knew Silver and names, and he'd never heard her use that one before. He broke the stare with John to look at her. She had a thin chain bunched up in her hand with a section held taut across her fingers like an imitation of brass knuckles. The metal rested on her skin without burning. Andrew's first sickened thought was of Stefan, the madman practically caressing his weapons. But no, he'd seen Silver touch it before too, at the house. He rubbed his wrist. It wasn't what the injection had made either of them that mattered, it was what they had chosen to be. Silver had touched it to save him from pain.

This was the same chain, he realized—she must have cleaned his blood from it—but John didn't seem as sensitized to the metal's smell and ignored her. "Seattle," she said again. "Look at me when you're pretending to defend me."

John started to turn, and she punched him in the stomach. He folded over it, taking it like he would in a play fight. Then he felt the sting of silver through his shirt's fabric and his eyes grew wide. Andrew's muscles clenched in memory of the metal's touch, but he just fisted his hands. The big baby. He had no idea what a real burn felt like.

Silver drew her arm back, threatening another blow. "Are you listening to me now?"

"You're touching it. Bare skin. How are you touching—?" John's question came out breathless.

Silver brought up her fist so the length of chain was millimeters from the underside of his chin, forcing his head up. "Do not challenge one who walks with Death. She has stood before more power than you could ever hope to wield."

She paused a beat, waiting for an answer, but John's attention was too tangled up in fear of the metal. She looked so beautiful in that moment. Her scarred arm hung dead, her white hair stood out stark, but none of it mattered when her inner strength and power shone from every movement and confidence filled her scent.

Silver smiled, expression sharp enough to cut. "Now. Do we need to have the conversation again about how I am an adult and entitled to make my own decisions? I may no longer be able to see all of your world, but neither can you see mine, and that does not mean that I have no mind." She dropped her hand a little so he had room to nod. "Right?"

"Right." John swallowed, and backed away from her. "Lady above, Dare. You sure you have any idea what you're getting into?"

Andrew collapsed into a sitting position on the bed as his legs gave out. "Yes," he said. Oh, yes. He could hardly believe that John could see that strength and not want to strive to be with it, strive to match it himself. John gave Andrew a hunted look and then escaped, shutting the bedroom door behind him.

Silver let out a long breath when he was gone. She opened her hand to let the chain dangle. "Sorry. I didn't mean to break in on your fight. He just pissed me off so much." She pooled the chain in her jacket's open pocket and then came back to climb onto his lap.

"I thought I'd misremembered you touching that chain bare-fingered after the fight. You're immune to silver burns?" Andrew said, resting his cheek against hers.

"He was. I suppose I am too." Silver shivered at the mention of her attacker, but otherwise passed through the moment fairly easily. "It's not really worth it, I assure you." She laughed, a sickly sound at first, but getting stronger. "You're coming in white." She smoothed back the hair at his temple, fingers lingering along the roots. "Not all over, though, I don't think."

"I think my self-image can survive it," Andrew said, and pressed her tight against him.

27

It felt good to stand tall again. Andrew had made short trips around the house for several days, but today was the first time he'd dressed properly and collected his things. Time to leave. He could feel the quivering tension every time he was in the room with John, and he was sure it was grating on his nerves just as much as on Andrew's.

He relished the accomplishment of walking confidently across the house even if he did have to rely on a cane. The length of smooth, dark wood had been a gift from one of the pack. His pride stung each time he had to reach for it, but all he had to do was look at Silver and the sting faded. She bore her injuries with a grace he could only hope to achieve someday.

Perhaps he looked like an aging statesman, more wise in the ways of the world than most of his colleagues. As Silver had predicted, his hair was growing in white in two streaks over his temples. He'd considered dyeing it, but Silver had made her white hair part of herself. He wasn't going to do anything less.

Besides, it suited him to wear the mark of his ordeal so prominently. To remind the others of what could happen if packs looked only to themselves.

He picked a spot in the entranceway and stood braced, both hands resting on his cane. "Call the pack together, would you, John?" He raised his voice to carry throughout the house, and people trickled in on their own. They could undoubtedly guess what was happening, but no one spoke as the whole pack pressed into the hall and the stairs and rooms beyond. Andrew felt the heavy weight of their attention like humidity. He might have been able to distinguish the different flavors to their relief—were they thinking good riddance to him, or just grateful to get back to the familiar?—but he chose not to.

He searched among them for Silver, but though he could smell her somewhere in the house, she didn't join the pack. A message to them that her allegiance was with Andrew and she wouldn't be rejoining her former pack, he suspected. That and her own dominance might confuse the situation. Silver was good with such subtle communication.

John nudged people aside to stand in front of Andrew. He stood with his hands clasped at his back with a martial sort of stillness. "This pack is yours," Andrew said, bowing his head to John. "I only borrowed it. I regret that circumstances made it necessary, and I'm grateful to all of you"—he lifted his head to look at the others—"for the obedience you gifted me with."

Now was the hard part. His legs were sound enough to walk, but ease of getting up and down still eluded him. Humiliation buzzed at the back of Andrew's mind, but he squashed it. He was returning power to John. Only right he should look a little vulnerable. He leaned all his weight on his cane and bent his knees to go down to one.

"Stop that." John stuck out a hand and hauled Andrew back up straight. "We owe you for saving Selene and stopping that madman."

Relief and gratitude softened Andrew's feeling, however suppressed, of resentment toward John. He was a good alpha in his way. The two men shook and then Andrew stepped aside to let John wade into his pack, accepting touches and smiles from everyone. The bright noise of the aggregate of voices grew louder.

Andrew felt suddenly sharply alone standing there, but as people dispersed into the house, he could see through the doorway into the kitchen to a head of white hair. He made his careful way over.

Silver sat at the table, her back to the entryway and transition of power. Andrew joined her, leaning the cane against the table. Silver laid her injured hand on the table, palm up. Andrew sat and put his on top to let her exercise her returning control. The press of her fingers against his skin, one by one, was light but there. She'd plateaued at that much movement in the last few days, but it was better than nothing even if she never went any farther.

"And now we figure out where to go," she said, voicing his thoughts.

"I had some thoughts about that." John surprised Andrew by appearing in the doorway, a road map in his hands. He strode to the table and smoothed the map flat over the wood. "We do have pack property down in Vancouver—Vancouver, Washington," he clarified, seeing Andrew's frown. "It's right on Washington's southern border. I know you mostly got along with her, but Portland would still probably be giving you the hairy eyeball from right across the river. And I don't think you'd want to be in Bellingham."

Andrew smiled wryly. "No."

"Mm. I'd recommend you head east to Ellensburg, personally. We go up to Snoqualmie a lot, but we don't actually go all the way over the pass. There's not much there, forest-wise, since it's in the rainshadow of the Cascades, but it would do temporarily. Billings doesn't come right up to the border much. It's a college town, so there'll be a lot of cheap housing if you want to get a place to rest up for a while."

Andrew bent his head over the map, examining the city and its surroundings in the flat false colors of elevation. This offer was unexpected. It would solve so many problems, though. "You could just kick me out of your territory entirely. I wouldn't think less of you."

"I could do worse than being allies with Roanoke and having him owe me a favor or two."

Andrew looked up at the gravity in John's voice. He wouldn't be challenging Rory for a good few months yet, but he'd given his word he would if he healed, and he was healing. It still sounded strange to hear John say it. "You sure?" he asked Seattle.

John extended a hand instead of answering. The two men shook on it. Then John extended the hand to Silver. She blinked in surprise, but took it a moment later. "And Roanoke's mate," John clarified. "Something tells me you two will make a formidable team."

"Took him long enough to realize it," Death said, voice sardonic. Andrew turned his head quickly, trying to pin down the lump of blackness at the edge of his peripheral vision, but he found nothing. It was just the power of suggestion taking a long time to fade. And the laugh he thought he heard at his reaction was pure imagination.

He turned his eyes to Silver instead, and shared a smile with her.